No-List Alex

Alex Campbell Real Estate Mystery Novel

Volume One

By Charles Chaplin
(no kidding)

**Binx
Publishing**

Seattle, WA

The Legal Disclaimer

This is a work of fiction. Clinton is not a real city. Names, characters, places, incidents and events portrayed in this novel and the excerpt from the forth-coming novel are the product of the author's imagination and entirely fictional. Any resemblance to actual persons or animals, living or deceased, business establishments, places, locals or events is entirely coincidental. No legal advice is given or implied in this work of fiction. Real estate laws vary from state to state in the United States. If you have legal questions concerning real estate, you should always check with a licensed, board approved, attorney within your state/city that specializes in real estate law.

Published by Binx Publishing Seattle, WA

ISBN: 978-0-98521-030-4

Books by Charles Chaplin

Fiction

The Alex Campbell Real Estate Mystery Novel Series

No-List Alex (1)

No Serenity (2)

No Rest (3)

<u>Note</u>: these titles can be read in any order.

Nonfiction

The Smarties Books: The Consumer's Insider Guides

Home Buying For Smarties

Home Selling For Smarties

WARNING: This is not *the* great American novel, what a surprise! For the cost of an overpriced movie ticket, this dip into pulp fiction will hopefully make you chuckle. May it provide you with a diversion from the airplane's turbulence and distract you from the screaming baby in the seat behind you. Hopefully it will give you refuge from the unwashed blob with Doritos breath and flaking dandruff who is hanging over into your narrow seat. This novel is not politically correct. It is meant to entertain. If something contained herein gets your undies (you are wearing underwear right?) all bunched up, kindly stop reading; there's plenty of unwatched television out there waiting for you.

1

You know what the problem with most real estate agents is? They make a few sales and begin to think their shit smells good. To start with, most agents suffer from narcissistic personality disorder. Who else would buy their own bill board with their face blown up the size of a grand piano? Or plaster their mug shots on rotting bus-stop benches, and send out post cards with a halo-over-the-head, mug shot and their new "favorite" cookie recipe? I guess I can humbly say that I don't fall into that narcissistic abyss. The last time I checked, I hadn't paid for any bill boards around town touting my professional services, or paid to plaster my face at bus-stops. And the only client prospecting recipe post cards I could send out would be for some tasty dog kibble.

My name is Alex Campbell. I just turned forty, although some people peg me for younger. I got carded until I was thirty-eight. That may sound good but in real estate, a creased face can mean more dollars. The whole older is more trustworthy and experienced line of thinking. When I started real estate, over three years ago, my broker encouraged me to wear business suits and ties, have my teeth whitened, lease a Mercedes, blah, blah. I eighty-sixed those cosmetic approaches. Talk about feeling like a phony, much less like a local news anchor clone. I prefer to do things the unconventional way; just be me and be honest. I've often thought my advertising tagline should be, *"Alex Campbell…No Bullshit."* I can only imagine my broker's face if my monthly mailer and promotional copy sported that spiffy tagline. But it would be the truth. I tend to horrify people by being what some might say is bluntly honest. Just yesterday, I told a first time buyer she was better off continuing to rent rather than buy. That was indeed the truth. What seems obvious to me is usually a novel idea for most of the real estate agents in my office. I've always been the odd duck out and at my age I no longer really care. In fact, I now see it as an asset, something to be proud of. Too bad the fifteen year old version of me couldn't have seen it that way.

It's a long story, how I ended up in this biz of schlepping houses. It's a nerve racking business. One month flush with cash from a few sales, then maybe a few months of no sales. But it keeps my dog in kibble and gives me a new adventure to tackle. A corporate, carpeted cubicle with florescent lighting and casual Friday pizza parties (i.e. they buy you cheap pizza and expect you to work overtime for no pay) just isn't my pond to swim in. Every time I take on a new client, it's like tuning into another soap opera. The drama and issues people create in their lives never ceases to amaze me. Never mind that I am not one to watch or enjoy soap operas.

Anyhow, real estate is always a challenge regardless if you are selling in a big city, a rural area, or somewhere in between. Somewhere in between is what I chose and settled into. Big city living proved to be too much for me and living way out in the sticks? Well maybe I'll graduate to that once I've completely had it with the human species. For now, my real estate agent shingle is hanging here in Clinton, a mid-size city of around three hundred thousand. Like Goldilocks, this one fit just right. Flipping off another driver or slow moving person at a crosswalk is *verboten*. Clinton is big enough to keep things somewhat impersonal but small enough to keep people minding their manners and acting civil as they peruse the grocery aisles or try and park their SUV tanks. I say "acting civil" because we all know (or at least any veteran real estate agent can tell you) beneath that smiling public veneer can lie some nasty demons.

Today I am on the road heading to the Bluffs to take on a new listing. The Bluffs is one of Clinton's chi-chi neighborhoods. It sits high up on the north end of town, with old oak trees and views that look out over Warner Sound. This is the kind of listing appointment that would have most real estate agents' panties in a tight knot with dollar signs flashing in their pupils. In fact, if any of the other real estate agents at the Viper Pit (a.k.a. my office) knew I was heading out to the Bluffs to take a listing, they would—well let's just say the vibes wouldn't be nice. Having grown up in a household with money I am not one who is easily charmed by money. Not to say a listing in the Bluffs wouldn't be nice, but I suppose I'm somewhat detached. I've experienced firsthand how an abundance of money does not equal happiness. Easy some might say, you grew up with money and you've got a trust fund. That doesn't apply in my case. I declined my trust fund and I've held just about every job imaginable since I stumbled out of college. I wouldn't be heading to this listing appointment at all if I hadn't liked the potential client when I met her at my office a couple of days ago.

That's another thing I do differently in this business that is considered stupid by most of my colleagues. I pre-screen every buyer (or now seller) that I work with. If I don't like their attitude or feel we aren't going to get along well, I decline to work with them and refer them to someone else. This really annoys my broker but I adhere to (after much experience) the sagely bumper sticker philosophy, *Life is too Short for Assholes; I Already Have One and I Don't Need Another One.* I speak from experience when I say turning down a potential client is rough, especially when you are down to your last $1,000. This theme of only working with clients I like goes along with my belief in trusting in the good or not surrounding yourself with bad energy. Sometimes that is no easy feat.

A week ago, Catherine Tilberts called me and asked about listing her house. I explained to her that I'd need to meet with her first at my office to learn more about her, her expectations, etc.… I told her if we both got along, then I'd make an appointment to visit her home and provide her with a comparative market analysis. From there, we would both agree on a viable list price and I'd get to work. She was a bit taken aback. Most prospective agents would have been on her door step, with a for sale sign in hand before she ended the phone call. However, Catherine had seen my promotional postcards and someone she knew told her I'd done a terrific job helping a friend find a great condo.

We met at my office on Monday and hit it off. I explained how I only take a listing if it is priced right and she was agreeable. One of my pet peeves in this business are agents who "buy" listings. Meaning they provide the seller with an unrealistic and inflated list price in order to get the listing. Then, as the months drag by, they whittle the seller down to the reasonable list price while the house sits unsold. Usually, it sells for less than the going market rate because now it has the taint of being listed for so long and *something must be wrong with it if it hasn't sold*

4

yet. What a waste of time and I think that's slimy but it is par for the course. Of course, sometimes it is the owners and their egos that dictate the inflated price and in those cases I've walked. Once again, the *Life is too Short for Assholes…* motto applies. I can tell you it's hard to walk away from a listing, especially when you've never had one. But working with people who are hard headed to begin with, who won't listen to reason, (i.e. the comparable house sales) you are just setting yourself up for a long battle. It's true, you will probably eventually sell the damn house. But the tantrums and crap you'll put up with from the sellers, it's just not worth it to me. I prefer well behaved children.

Catherine was impressed with the fact that I would only take her listing if it were priced right. She is probably somewhere in her seventies and is ready to sell the house she raised her children in and move on to a new life. Her husband passed away a few years ago and she wants to pack it up and head for the beach. I could sense she is a no bullshit kind of person as well. Just the seller/listing I've been waiting for. Three years in this business and I have not had a single listing. I've walked away from one and lost out on two others. They don't call me "No-List Alex" for nothing at the office. My luck has been with first time home buyers, the category most agents turn down or put at the bottom of their client priority list. First time home buyers are more nervous, take a lot more time, and usually don't have much money to spend. But for me, the pluses are they do spend some money, which is better than nothing, they are usually excited about buying a house, and most are very respectful and polite.

I digress. Catherine Tilberts asked me to stop by at 11:00 on Thursday, walk through the house with her and then discuss the list

5

price. She had already told me that she wanted to list with me. She said she liked my honesty. So, I'm off to my first real listing appointment and in the Bluffs, no less. I had just finished with a client I had been working with for over a year. She was a real head case from the word go. A triple, non-fat, latte, cell phone implanted in her ear, voice like the sound of a shrieking parrot, nut-job. However, I did like her enthusiasm and she liked my bluntness. She had this whole fantasy about relocating to Clinton, it was going to be her own nirvana after her divorce went through. It turns out, after one year and sixty-four houses toured later, she and hubby decided to give the marriage another whirl. The nirvana relocation to Clinton was dead; hubby's career in Boston was a no compromise. Yep, I was pretty bummed. My patience with her was already fraying, but I'm still holding out for the divorce, so maybe in another six months she'll be back.

Driving around the Bluffs can be a challenge. The roads are steep and they meander all over the place. In fact, I think a better name for the Bluffs would be the Maze. The streets wind every which way and abruptly end. It's strictly intuition that gets you to a specific address in the Bluffs, Mapquest and GPS be damned. I managed to hone in on my psychic real estate agent radar and after a few missed turns, I found the opened iron gates and driveway for Mrs. Tilberts' abode.

The Bluffs was designed and built by a famous architect between 1905 through 1930 and it is the neighborhood where only Clinton's old guard dare reside. The open driveway gates of some houses are just pretentious left-overs from the new money that built the Bluffs over one hundred years ago. None of today's new money in Clinton would be welcome in the Bluffs, nor would the Bluffs appeal to them. While the views in the Bluffs are killer, the houses themselves are not the desired mega mansions/zero lot lines so in vogue with today's latest "made its." Tearing down an existing house in the Bluffs and building a new house on steroids is nigh on impossible thanks to the existing Bluffs land-use regulations and its preservation committee review board. Catherine Tilberts' house is a 1922 red brick Federal style affair. It is a 5,500 square foot, three story, house with five bedrooms, four and a half baths, and a view of Warner Sound. I noted the enormous boxwoods must be original and the huge magnolia tree in the center of the circular drive could actually pre-date the house.

I was about fifteen minutes early, which is no surprise because I am always compulsively early or on time. Even when I try to be late somewhere it doesn't work, go figure. The house looked pretty well maintained. The windows could stand to be cleaned before listing, but otherwise the "curb appeal" in real estate agent slang was right up there. Catherine told me to come around to the side entrance off of the kitchen as that is where she spends most of her days and the main doorbell wasn't reliable (another item to fix before listing). I noticed a cut-out in the boxwood hedge to the left of the main entrance and followed the moss covered flagstone pavers to the back of the house. At the end of the mossy path were stone steps which led down to a nice sized flagstone terrace and medium sized rectangular swimming pool. All perched on the bluff overlooking the sound. I could already feel the real estate agent ad writing wheels churning, *"Prestigious north end estate with stately pool and sound views..."* Damn if this biz doesn't start to affect you.

To my right, were stone steps leading up to what I presumed to be the kitchen. I was correct. The light blue bullet shaped door was ajar and I knocked loudly, calling out hello. While I waited, I noted that the kitchen and the whole back of the first floor appeared to be one huge glassed-in sun porch---talk about selling points! Still no response, so I pushed the door open a bit more, popped my head in and started using my real estate agent yell, "Hello, Mrs. Tilberts it is Alex from Winterfrost Real Estate...." This went on for a while and then I decided perhaps she was upstairs and couldn't hear me. So I let myself in, leaving my business card on the kitchen counter as required by law. The view from the kitchen was incredible—small twinkling waves from the sound far below with a few sail boats bopping up and down. The well maintained kitchen's décor was straight out of 1975 *House Beautiful* decorators-on-acid. Lime green custom cabinetry, hot pink and electric blue striped wall paper, custom drapery, gorgeous wide plank hardwood floors, white Formica counter tops, and Sub Zero stainless appliances from the mid 1970s---long before *nouveau* yuppies even knew what stainless appliances were. This was going to be one great listing. Even the dated kitchen reeked of quality and craftsmanship. Now I just had to find the owner.

2

I walked out of the kitchen into a narrow hall which opened up into the foyer. A traditional black and white marble floor with a geometric pattern gleamed underneath an old brass chandelier. I gave a few more loud hellos and decided to take the grand curving staircase. Upstairs, were four bedrooms, three with a view of the water. Each bedroom was a time capsule of youth when Catherine's children had left home. One bedroom was painted peacock blue. It sported an Eagles *On the Border* concert poster, a *Ski Vail* poster circa 1975, what appeared to be a red glass bong, and an old wooden tennis racket. Obviously, a male spawn had flown from the nest somewhere in the mid 1970s. Another bedroom was a fading hot pink number that had lime green carpeting, also fading, a wicker desk set in citrus yellow complete with an orange wicker shaded lamp. Multicolored, silk horseback riding ribbons shimmered along the roof of the white, four poster canopy bed. A huge stuffed Panda, missing one eye, completed the bed tableau. I noticed a set of Nancy Drew books next to what appeared to be old purple and green cheerleader pom-poms. An ancient, white digital alarm clock let me know that it was 11:15. I left the pink bedroom, still calling out hello in case Mrs. Tilberts heard me. I entered a mint green and black tiled Jack and Jill style bathroom which connected to an adjoining school bus yellow bedroom. This room was clearly another daughter's room. The fading Jefferson Airplane poster, old guitar with flower embroidered strap, home-made ceramic pots, tie-dye bed spread, macramé glop, various anti-war stickers, led me to conclude this was the "radical/artsy" daughter and she left the coop circa 1972. This was all interesting and my mind was quickly trying to figure out if we should clear some of these items out before listing or leave them there for their nostalgic charm; still, no Mrs. Tilberts. I reached the master bedroom, knocked loudly on the open door and entered a peach colored, more up-to-date, decorator done, *boudoir*. Framed pictures of the various three children adorned almost every flat surface in the large suite. French doors opened up onto a small but usable balcony overlooking Warner Sound. The accompanying master bath was done in white marble and it had pretty much remained the same since the house was built. In today's world, the master bath would not be considered big enough. Today, most people think it's not a master bath unless it sports a unique porcelain appliance to clean each of your body parts and enough square footage to house a family of four from Ecuador. It was a nice master suite but where was the master? My, "Hello, Mrs. Tilberts…" were starting to get a bit old. I went up to the third level where a great room and office were located along with a storage room and small galley style kitchen. The great room and office had large dormer windows with views of the sound on one side and the front circular drive on the other—still no Mrs. Tilberts. I tromped back down to the first floor. I glanced in the formal living room, the dining room, the study, the guestroom, and the enormous glassed-in sun porch (which spanned the entire back side of the house) nothing. I peeked out the windows which surrounded the front door and saw my old blue Volvo sedan and the two-door white BMW Mrs. Tilberts had driven to my office on Monday. Back in the kitchen, I was about to leave a note but glancing up I noticed the door leading to the basement and thought I'd give it a whirl.

The light in the basement landing was on and the basement stairs were carpeted. Down I went. It was a fairly large basement, all lit up with fluorescent ceiling panel lights. I did not detect mold or notice any obvious cracks in the foundation, always a good sign for a listing. A series of small rooms were in the basement. One room was a small bedroom with a twin bed and half size window along its ceiling. This room connected to a three quarter style bath, possibly the maid's quarters at one time? Next, was a room with a large work table, wrapping paper rolls, professional tape dispenser, along with other various unused items such as an ancient sewing machine. The final room must have been a pantry at one time, a few old bottles of pickled something or another remained on the built-in shelves. At the end of the hall was a small open room with painted grey cement flooring. In it was an ancient, zinc laundry sink, an ironing board that folded out from the wall complete with a professional iron that was mounted above from the low ceiling. A clothes drying rack with a red sweater on it sat in the corner. In the very back, down two narrow cement steps was a narrow door. Light was shining out of the small gap between the cement floor and the bottom of the door. I knocked loudly on the narrow door, again calling out but no response. As I opened the door my nose was immediately assaulted by the strong smell of natural gas. A glaring light bulb hanging from the ceiling revealed the worst—a stack washer and dryer and in a house this size! However, before I could get too upset about the problem these mini-appliances would cause with potential buyers, I noticed an ancient, blue, hot water tank making a hissing sound in the crammed corner. To the side of the tank was a fold out metal chair and I found Mrs. Tilberts—sprawled on the floor in front of it. I reached down and checked for a pulse or breathing, nothing. She clearly wasn't going to be doing the wash anymore.

I quickly stepped out of the little room and pulled the door shut behind me. I began to cough and realized there was a major gas leak happening. Any little spark and my listing was going up in smoke. Of course that really didn't matter, because the owner appeared to have moved out already. I stumbled up the basement stairs and out the kitchen door while fumbling in my pocket for my cell phone, all the while hacking away. Remembering all those warning signs posted at gas stations, warning not to use your cell phone because they could potentially spark and cause a fire, I put my cell back in my coat pocket. I ran out to the front drive, my feet stumbling on the loose white driveway pebbles. I leaned onto my car hood, dropped my clipboard and then fished out my *raison d'etre,* my cell phone. For once, I could make a call on the little fucker and not be charged. However, I can think of better things to do than dial 9-1-1 on my cell phone for free.

Naturally, the first two attempts at dialing 9-1-1 resulted in dropped calls. I finally coaxed it into connecting by standing on a low brick wall on the far side of the driveway next to an ancient oak tree. Once I had the emergency person on the line, I couldn't recall the damn address. So I put the phone down and ran down to the entry gate where the numbers were mounted in ancient black iron, 2467. I told the emergency operator that in addition to a body, there was

12

clearly a gas leak and the gas company would need to come out pronto. To which I was informed that was not their concern and I should contact the gas company directly, emergency personnel would be there shortly. Shortly turned out to be more like twenty-three minutes, but who's counting? No one was doing much of anything except verifying what I already knew. Finally, the gas company arrived and shut off the gas line. The house's front door became a beehive of firemen, police, and other assorted uniforms all swarming inside. I was told to wait outside with Detective Davies.

Boy did my day go to hell, an 11:00 a.m. appointment turned into an all afternoon affair. I had no real information about the deceased except for her name and that it appeared she had three children. On and on the police wanted to know what I was doing there and on and on I explained I was there for a listing appointment. Finally, a maid from one of the houses nearby appeared and she knew the woman who worked part time for Catherine Tilberts and called her. So, it was the maid who was able to get in touch with the one of the daughters. The daughter, Mary Beth, roared up in a bright red Range Rover, simultaneously screaming and crying as she ran up to the next door neighbor's maid. Mary Beth became even more distraught as the policemen filled her in on her mother's death. She grabbed her purse and popped open a pill box, placing a couple of peach colored tablets on her tongue (Xanax the anti anxiety wonder drug no doubt) and wiped her raccoon rimmed eyes. She started to speak with Detective Davies, but then she spied me. Her pale pink lips went downward into a Grinch-like scowl. She lashed out at me, "You! You must be that slime ball real estate agent that my mother was foolishly talking about.

13

What did YOU have to do with all of this? Why is he here officer? I DEMAND to know why!"

With that, she tried to lunge towards me but another officer grabbed her flailing arm and restrained her. Before I could say a peep, the officer suggested to Mary Beth that they go sit inside. Detective Davies asked me if I knew Mary Beth and once satisfied that I had never met her, he gave me his card and said he would be in touch for further questioning. He also asked me to let him know if I had to travel out of town for any reason.

3

Well so much for my grand, first listing. Winding my way out of the Bluffs, I decided having seen a not-so-fresh Mrs. Tilberts on her laundry room floor and testing my lungs' capacity to ward off noxious gas fumes was too intense. It was time to pay my friend Lexi a call. Lexi is an artist by trade and free spirit by heart. She is somewhere in her sixties and stopped counting her divorces at four in 1985, when she decided marriage was just an illusion. That all sounds nice but what she really means is her last husband was an oil executive for one of the major global cartels. When she took him to the cleaners for infidelity, she got half of everything he had, which even in 1985 was no small sum. She's worked since then as an art rehab counselor for teens. This from the woman who thinks coffee doesn't taste right unless there's a bit of whiskey in it. Lexi is the kind of woman you wish you had as a mother and on another more grown up level are damn glad you didn't. Her "little farm" as she calls it lies off the interstate access road that skirts the south side of Clinton. I turned down her unpaved and dusty driveway, and drove past her latest sculptural creations. The creations currently consist of what appears to be old metal bed frames spray painted with various hues of puke. She likes installation sculpture or some such, but lately her main focus is that her pieces be organic. Organic, meaning she coats her sculptures in honey and other sticky food substances. The food coating is in an attempt to attract birds and mostly ants and rodents, to "interact" with her art forms. I'd say she was a bowl past her hit point but Lexi is a reformed pothead who now hates pot, so who knows.

15

"You haven't stopped by in over three weeks Alex Campbell and you better not be stopping by to ask if I have heard anymore news about the potential development that's going in next door."

"It's nice to see you too Lexi, and bullshit. When have I ever asked you about the development you say is going in next door to your little art farm? Also, I was here two weeks ago. Remember, for Wanda's birthday? And by the way, Wanda wants her hair piece back." Wanda is the mortgage person I work with and her hair piece is another story.

"Too bad for Wanda. Her hair is now part of my latest work. Take a look, and since you are up, stop in my kitchen and pour us a little tea."

Tea, in Lexi's world is whiskey with a scoop of instant Lipton Tea powder stirred in. Normally, I'd politely decline but it's not every day that you encounter a dead client when you go on a listing appointment. I poured a small cup of Wild Turkey for me, sloshed out a glass full for Lexi, topping hers off with a heaping teaspoon of Lipton's finest. As usual, her kitchen was a complete mess. I tried not to knock over the towering stack of newspapers and magazines located next to her old harvest gold refrigerator. Walking through her living room, I noticed the cake plates with chocolate cake remains from Wanda's recent foray past forty-five. Lexi's "little farm" might as well just be called the roach motel of Clinton. Oh, to be an *artiste*!

Lexi's art studio is the sagging front porch of her house. She had all the railings removed and an open carport like attachment added. Part of it is enclosed with clear, construction wrap plastic to keep the cold out. She has florescent light fixtures haphazardly attached to the metal ceiling and next to what once was the brick front walk, she had concrete poured. She is fond of saying she is inspired by working out in the open. Truth be told, she burned down ex hubby number two's house while using her blow torch on one of her creations. That's why she hates pot. Seems hubby two and she were quite the stoners circa 1977 and she claims it was his pot that made her accidentally burn down his ancestral 1880 Georgian revival homestead. However, anyone who has seen Lexi wield her blow torch knows that pot had nothing to do with that fire.

"Ahh, thank you kind sir." Lexi muttered while removing her welder's mask and setting her weapon of destruction, the blow torch, down. Yep, Wanda's hair piece was indeed part of her new creation. There it was perched on top of some crooked pole like a bird's nest gone bad. I learned years ago, never ask the *artiste* what exactly any of it was. The work is supposed to speak to me, language merely clutters the senses. "So Alex what brings you out to the farm this afternoon?"

"You don't even want to hear it." With that I proceeded to fill Lexi in on my morning and afternoon's "fun" exploits and she proceeded to fully quiz me as to the angle of the body, where the gas leak was coming from, and exactly what the daughter named Mary Beth said word for word. Wacky as she may be, Lexi can be very analytical and linear when she chooses to be.

"Are you telling me the damn gas powered hot water tank in the laundry room was the source of the gas leak Alex? How did it start leaking? That's too bizarre and more to the point what in the hell was

17

that old lady doing down there in her little laundry room with the door shut, while the hot water tank's gas line leaked?"

"Good questions. I'm not so sure myself. But you know, that little door into the laundry room, I think it was such that it had to be closed in order to access the stupid stack washer and dryer. When I first saw that stacked unit, I was way disappointed. Do you know how picky buyers are about appliances these days and especially a stacked unit for such a big house? However Lexi, the more I think about it, I bet Catherine had the stack unit installed after the full size ones died. With just one person living in that big house, what did she need with a full size washer and dryer? Still, it's very odd, huh?" This I asked while taking another swig of my pure Wild Turkey, imagining it was mixed with some 7-Up to wash it down.

"Well here, draw me the layout of this room in my little art notebook." Lexi said, while tossing over her purple blank page *artiste* notebook that she is never without. Inspiration calls, even when you are sitting on the toilet or so Lexi says. I dutifully sketched out what I could recall. Once on paper, it did seem to verify that in order to use the washer and dryer you had to shut yourself up in that room. I pondered aloud, "Why there is a door to that little room, it is anyone's guess."

"Well duh, honey! You said there were two tiny steps down to that room, so at some point it must have led outdoors or to another unheated part of that old house. The door was probably a left over and you know how people just leave well enough alone. The door stayed there and all these years the big butted maid probably cursed it every time she did the Tilberts family laundry. Now that Catherine was doing her own laundry, well why bother. Leave the damn door, even if you have to shut it behind you." Lexi took a big pull on her Wild Turkey instant Lipton Tea concoction and sighed.

"That's all true perhaps, but still Lexi, how fast can a gas leak cause you to pass out and then kill you?" I too took a pull on my Wild Turkey and promptly coughed it out my nose.

"Ohhh, my favorite--whiskey buggers, how attractive. You know a gas leak can knock you out in no time flat Alex, especially in a small enclosed space. It will eighty-six you just as good as putting a running Eldorado in the garage and shutting the slider. Alex you don't have to use your shirt sleeve to wipe your nose. There's a rag somewhere over here in my metal scraps."

"Thanks, I prefer starched broadcloth to Aunt Lexi's art snot rags."

"And I prefer real estate agents who don't wipe their noses on their shirt sleeves—*touché!*"

We gabbed some more, I felt a bit soothed from the Wild Turkey and just before Lexi was going to invite me for one of her *impromptu* dinners, I cleverly recalled I had to rush home so I could take Clyde out for his walk.

4

Taking Clyde for a walk, now there's an experience. My mutt Clyde looks like Benji (the late 1970s movie dog) except on a really bad hair day. My little mutt has grown up and what was once cute and wild at thirty pounds is no longer so charming at sixty-five pounds. I have been told numerous times by all sorts of dog experts that around age five is when your wild dog will begin to mellow. Well let's just say Clyde defies the experts in spades. At age seven, Clyde is still as wild and hard headed as ever. He literally flunked out of three dog training schools and in my opinion, he is the sole reason the *Clinton School For Better Dogs* promptly shut down a week after Clyde terrorized the owner into kicking him out of class. The owner, a prize winning dog trainer of thirty years from Germany, promptly relocated back to the fatherland less than a month after her Clyde experience.

Anyway, Clyde and I have come to a mutual understanding. The morning walk is mine and the evening walk is his. This means I am currently being pulled helter-skelter all over my neighborhood. In fact, I just assisted Clyde (unwillingly) in flattening Mrs. Burton's clump of purple foxglove planted next to her mailbox. Not that she will really care too much. You see if Clyde were a human, he would be the major movie star, gigolo type—able to charm and weasel his way out of any unfortunate event. Clyde manages to win over all humans who have damn good reason to be angry with him. Just last week, he escaped my clutches and took off after a roller blader. He knocked the poor guy over, and proceeded to lick him. The man was startled but instantly he was saying it was okay and asking me what kind of dog Clyde is, his age, etc.... I once made the mistake of taking Clyde with me on a buyer's tour. The buyer was a dog lover and she insisted on meeting my dog. Three houses into our tour, it became evident Clyde was running the show and the client wasn't paying a bit of attention to any of the houses we saw. So much for making Clyde work for his kibble.

My neighborhood is an interesting dog walking area. It is situated on the southwest end of Clinton, skirting the edge of the Clinton's downtown. The area consists of 1920s bungalow houses (in various stages of decay and repair), a couple of red brick apartment buildings, and a number of old factory/wharf buildings, some of which have been converted into offices. From a real estate agent's perspective, my neighborhood is a no-man's land. There is no official neighborhood name. It literally falls between two city council seat districts, so it is quite often overlooked when it comes to civic upgrades and funding. To the north lies the downtown. To the south is a greenbelt and west is Warner Sound and the waterfront rail road tracks. Many years ago, there was a major waterfront beautification project in Clinton. Rail road tracks were redirected away from the waterfront; parks and retail were put in. The beautification project stopped abruptly where my neighborhood starts. The waterfront near me consists of old rotting piers, some factory buildings (mostly vacant), rail road tracks along the water's edge, and a few off-the-radar cafes and bars. There is another line of rail road tracks to the east of my neighborhood that goes through the downtown area. So my hood is literally on the wrong side of the tracks time two. We have a mixture of older retired couples who used to work in the factories many years ago, young just-marrieds, and assorted artists, free spirits. As elsewhere in the nation, the home values in Clinton have sky rocketed over the past few years; even my little area has seen values shoot up. Fortunately, there are enough over-marketed and glitzed-up neighborhoods with official names, to keep my corner of Clinton under the radar.

I still couldn't get the image of Mrs. Tilberts choking to death on natural gas fumes out of my head. What puzzled me is how she could have been in that small room with the door closed and not been aware the gas was leaking. Did it start to leak once she was shut in there waiting for her whites to finish the rinse cycle? It didn't make sense to me, but then again little in this nutty world ever makes sense to me. I felt pretty sure Detective Davies would be calling me soon to ask the same questions again. I was a little concerned he may consider me a suspect, if they were considering foul play. I did have an alibi as to where I had been prior to my listing appointment.

My current buyer-from-hell could certainly attest to the fact that I had been showing him one of the new downtown lofts from 9:30 to 10:40. This buyer-from-hell is a recently relocated lawyer whose sole purpose for living is to make partner in two years. Besides being an overly educated, know-it-all bore, he recently has begun to think he is a shrewd real estate agent as well. At 10:20 he was lecturing me on the importance of always bidding at least $15,000 below the asking price and the importance of knowing what the seller paid for a property.

Nothing like those two hot buttons to set me off. First, underbidding is usually a horrible idea in an increasing market. In a relatively small market like Clinton, word travels fast and he'd be seen as a cheap skate and a lawyer to boot! Unless we can prove, with comparable listings, that the place is indeed overpriced, underbidding is always a huge mistake. In short, it pisses the seller off. In this case, the loft is priced correctly. Next, knowing what the seller paid for his/her property is pretty much useless information in a seller's market. The only thing that matters is what the current market will bear, period. So what if the seller is making a handsome $70,000 profit on the sale? It doesn't concern the buyer. The place is going to sell for what the market dictates and knowing the seller is making an enormous profit will only torture the buyer and or make him/her feel jealous and ripped off. I always say, "Don't ask, don't torture."

Clearly, my current buyer-from-hell lawyer had missed out on my "don't ask" lecture. By 10:40, when I left to take off for Catherine's house, Mr. Lawyer was still whining about how unfair the list price seemed. He also had his boxers in a knot wanting to know exactly what the seller had paid for the loft five years ago.

Clyde and I finished our evening walk without further incident, except for the stray squirrel or two he wanted to chomp. Safely back in my little house, I put Clyde outside in the fenced in back yard with a big bowl of water and a new soup bone. My house is a one bedroom, 800 square foot arts and crafts bungalow built in 1919. It is situated at the end of a small dead-end street and was probably originally built for one of Clinton's many factory workers. It has a small garage which is too narrow for today's cars so I converted it into a studio/workout space. When I purchased this house three years ago, it was literally falling down. Long abandoned, it was just about to the demolition stage. I saved the original windows, discovered hard wood floors under a layer of red, 1940s linoleum and had the hand carved mantel piece restored. Besides that, no original charm, as we say in the biz, remained. It was almost a complete redo/rebuild. I had skylights put in and opened the space up so it is a two room loft now. It has a small open kitchen with polished concrete counters and hand blown glass tile backsplashes in shades of blue, green, and magenta. I installed lighting behind the glass tiles so they look like colored gem stones at night. Now, the whole back of the house is one huge glass wall. Glass and steel trimmed garage doors in the living/kitchen area so I can open it up during the warmer times of the year. In my bedroom area I installed french doors. It's been a labor of love and a lot of sweat equity, but I am approaching the finish point. My next major project is to work on the small stream that flows through my back yard and install a fish pond area with a man-made water fall. The sound of water is my Valium. Fortunately, my property backs onto a greenbelt, so nature is never far away.

Having settled Clyde in the back yard, I attacked my emails which consisted of two queries from prospective buyers and ten spams. I suddenly wondered why the cell phone had been silent all day and discovered I had set it on mute prior to my listing appointment with Catherine. I had five voice mails. They varied from an escrow agent calling me about a client's signing appointment, two calls from Wanda wondering how my day was going, a call from my broker letting me know I had a commission check waiting, and the final message was from Detective Davies. He called to let me know that Catherine Tilberts' cause of death was still officially undetermined. He would be in touch if he had any questions, but for now my statements checked out. Checked out? Did that mean they were thinking Catherine's death wasn't an accident and that I was a suspect? Oh the joys of an over-active mind. I decided to forget it all, popped a few natural sleep aid supplements, climbed into my bed, and was snoring by 9:30.

5

The next few days were a typical real estate jumble. With three active buyers I was busy previewing various properties, taking clients out on tours, and dealing with cranky sellers and pompous listing agents. I was on my way to meet Wanda, the mortgage person I usually work with, for a business lunch. Of course, a business lunch with Wanda usually means liquor and hours of catching up. Wanda Billings is one of the top loan officers with Safety Mortgage. She's an independent representative, which means she can shop for and provide her clients with a wide array of loan programs. Unlike the banks, which typically can only offer their own loan and mortgage products. Wanda has been in the mortgage business for ten years and is known around town as quite a feisty character. Before becoming a loan officer, Wanda was a beautician and her sense for shall we say over the top hair styles has never left. In the staid world of numbers people, Wanda stands out like a Manhattan hooker in an Amish meeting house. Wanda came up the hard way and by twenty she had started her own hair salon, appropriately named Salon Wanda. Salon Wanda still exists but Wanda no longer does hair. She is now a silent (sometimes) owner/partner. Miss Liz ,Clinton's most infamous or famous (depending who you ask) drag queen, now runs the salon and Wanda still makes a nice monthly stack of green off her hair salon. Somewhere around her mid thirties, Wanda realized there was more money to be made in the mortgage business and with her natural ability with numbers she was a hit. At first, it was hard because Wanda had to tone down her look and be somewhat docile to fit in with the numbers people. However, once Wanda proved herself to be a popular loan officer with a large and growing following, her managers and brokers kept their collective mouths shut as the more flamboyant Wanda began to surface. Today, no one would dare give Wanda any grief on her somewhat wild appearance or her in-your-face attitude. Wanda may be a bit on the colorful side (literally) but she is the definition of integrity. The number of buyers she has saved from predatory lenders is legendary.

"Now I know what you are gonna say, so just keep it zipped Alex! I know we were supposed to meet at 1:00, but I had a real problem locking in some rates this morning and then Miss Liz called bitching to me about the damn stationary dryers again and then---oh yeah baby give me one of those orange rum drinks that woman over there is having---," said Wanda interrupting herself to order a drink from a passing waiter before continuing on with her typical long winded hello.

I of course, knew Wanda would never make it to lunch at 1:00. I showed up and 1:30 and only had to wait fifteen minutes for Wanda to arrive. Naturally, I chose not to let Wanda know this and allowed her to go into her *mea culpa* for the forty-five minute wait. I had already ordered a virgin Pina Colada. For some reason, Wanda and I always end up drinking retro frozen drinks. Wanda took one look at my white frozen drink, slurped up some of it, "OH no! Not gonna do at all today. Hey, baby—yes you with that tray— bring him one of these here Coladas with some rum in it and get steppin' on my frozen orange and rum drink. Jeesh Alex, you think that fool would know his jingle is gonna be in getting us spiked—don't he realize where the tips are at?

27

Must be new. So baby, how are you doing? And what is going on with that woman you found dead? I didn't see nothing on the TV about it."

"Well, it didn't make the media and as of this morning I was informed by the police that it has been officially ruled an accidental death. Seems she was waiting on her wash and the gas leak filled the little laundry room up in no time. They say a gas leak makes you fall asleep and then it kills. They figure that is what happened. She dozed off, fell out of the chair, and then died. The funeral is tomorrow at St. Thomas Episcopal Church up in the Bluffs. I've got the obituary right here. It ran in the *Clinton Observer* on Sunday."

"Oh lord, you mean I gotta read something? Well you might as well go ahead and see them." What a relief! Wanda has needed reading glasses ever since she passed forty and has stubbornly refused to get them, something about only old people use glasses to read. Wanda pulled out a bright red pair of reading glasses from her five hundred pound fuchsia pocket book. Perching them on the end of her broad nose, she took the obit clipping from me, glancing up as if daring me to make a comment about her new reading glasses. Good thing they are only reading glasses too, because with normal glasses she'd have to push them up closer to her eyes and her stick-on eye lashes would never allow for that. Wanda proceeded to read the obituary out loud. Wanda does most everything out loud.

"Mummmph, *Catherine Anne Tilberts, seventy-four, long time Clinton resident, died in an accident this past Thursday at her home. Wife of the deceased Harrison Roberts Tilberts, Jr., Catherine is survived by her children Sally Anne Tilberts, Timothy Pierson Tilberts and Mary Beth Hilson. Catherine was an active member of the Friends of the Clinton Public Library and a supporter of the Clinton Art Museum. Contributions in lieu of flowers, to the Harrison Roberts Tilberts, Jr. State School Scholarship Program. Service to be held at St. Thomas Episcopal Church on Friday at 11:00 a.m.* Huhh, well it sure don't tell you too much about the lady now does it? Oh, put mine down right here baby and take away his kid's drink. Now let me see, bring us one of those cheese and fish appetizer things.

So that's the breaks baby, your first listing, and one in the Bluffs no doubt, and here the owner has to up and die on you. Too bad you didn't get her to sign that listing form when you met her at the office. But you know, that probably wouldn't stand anyhow what with the Will and kids. Speaking of which, are you gonna go to the funeral? You can meet the kids and maybe you can get them to list the place with you Alex. They know their mama wanted to list with you, so they'll probably choose you."

I hadn't really thought about attending Catherine Tilberts' funeral. Wanda did have a point; maybe this wasn't a lost listing after all. "You know Wanda, perhaps I will attend her service tomorrow. Make an appearance so to speak. But that daughter I ran into, Mary Beth, you know she was really hostile towards me. She acted as if I'd pestered her mother into listing the house and as if I had something to do with her mother's death. It was a relief to get a message from Detective Davies today, letting me know it's all been ruled an accidental death. He had me thinking they were trying to find a murderer and I was a suspect. But his message said they ruled out foul play. You know, I always tell my clients that hot water tanks can go bad anytime after ten to twelve years. They start to leak water or the

29

gas line can spring a leak. The tank at the Tilberts' house was a dinosaur. I wouldn't be surprised if it was thirty years old." The non-virgin Pina Colada did taste better and I intended to cut the sweet taste with the cheese and fish appetizer, if Wanda ever let my hands near the plate.

"Damn these little things is spicy! You know that daughter was probably just acting that way because her mama was dead. So you had a Detective Davies call you, huh? Is he cute, does he wear one of them tight trooper uniforms or is he municipal and in those blue duds?" Wanda has a thing for men in uniform or more truthfully Wanda has a thing for men period.

"God, listen to you Wanda. I don't even remember him that much. He has darkish hair and he was very calm, polite. He doesn't wear a uniform; he's a detective so he's plain clothes."

"Listen to you! He got darkish hair. What the hell does that tell me? I wanna know how tall he is, did he have on a wedding band, is he muscular, how old he is, did he have a big snake hiding in his pants, was he a romantic type or a rough and tumble kind of guy? Details, Alex!"

"Wanda I don't know where you learned the insti-scan process, but you do have the eye for detail."

"Yes and detail is what makes the man or woman, or whatever it is you are trying to find this year. You are so out there in the clouds sometimes Alex. I swear, I don't think your feet would touch the ground if your balls weren't so heavy."

30

"My, what?" I said choking on a tiny cheese and fish thing. How did Wanda--never mind! "Look, I wasn't checking him out and F.Y.I. Wanda, I don't switch hit on an annual basis. We've been over this and you know where I stand on relationships. Being bisexual and being monogamous with myself is suiting me just fine for now."

"Fine? Ain't that just short for fucked up, insecure, neurotic and evasive? I didn't say you had to check him out, but at least keep your eyes open baby! You know I don't give a rip about which sex you are getting some from. I just think you should be getting some that's all. Mumph and if you ask me, this whole fudge royal approach to sex is just too confusing. I say, pick a team and go to bat."

Wanda loves to refer to my bisexuality as an ice cream flavor, the whole vanilla and chocolate metaphor I suppose. "Look Wanda, I don't want to discuss this again right now. I know you think I should be dating, but for now I am perfectly happy being alone. Is that so hard to understand?"

"Yeah, ahh-hum, okay baby, whatever you say. Oh, look they got ribs as their special today! Hey you—yes baby—bring that order pad over here, I want the ribs and I'd like some extra sauce with them. Also, we need a basket of your breads over here and take this plate baby, we're done with these cheese and fish do-dahs!"

Lunch continued past 4:00, until they informed us we had to leave so they could prepare for the dinner crowd. Wanda left feeling a bit peeved that they'd rushed her. I left feeling a bit slushy from the frozen drink. I hurried off to an appointment with Mr. Lawyer to show him a new downtown condo listing. He'd lost out on the loft because he bid so low the seller practically spit sparks. True to my prediction, the seller did not counter Mr. Lawyer's ridiculous low ball offer and promptly sold the unit for full price to another buyer. Hopefully this will be a case of "Lose and Learn" but with this guy's ego who knows.

6

The funeral at St. Thomas was brief and to the point. I noticed Mary Beth, dressed in a black designer dress and expensive looking spiky shoes; her dyed blonde hair was perfectly coiffed. She was on the verge of hysteria. Her raccoon eyes were leaking, as she glared at me while walking behind the casket down the aisle. The older daughter, Sally Anne, who I already nick-named artsy was true to form. She had long brown hair which was turning grey and was decked out in an ankle sweeping, maroon and black jumper dress thing. She held her sister's hand as they walked down the aisle. After one of Mary Beth's louder wailing outbursts, I noticed Sally Anne rolling her eyes at their brother Tim. Tim seemed fairly detached from the whole process. He was in a standard black suit and sported longish brown hair, which like Sally Anne's was starting to turn grey in spots. He remained a few steps behind his sisters throughout the whole process. Wanda is incorrect. I do notice details. At the reception in the church hall, I noticed several of the city elites buzzing all about. I was just about to leave when Sally Anne came up to me and introduced herself.

"Hi, I am Sally Anne Tilberts, thank you for coming. I understand you are Alex Campbell and you discovered our mother's body."

"Yes, I had an appointment to meet your mother to list her house. I am sorry for your loss."

"Thank you. You know I am still in shock. As I told the police, mother and I usually met at her place for a morning walk, it had become our ritual. I would drive over to the Bluffs Espresso Café, park

33

there, and get some fresh scones for us. Then, I would walk over to mother's house and she would have fresh squeezed orange juice and coffee waiting. After that, we would go for our early morning walk. The morning you found her, she was just fine. Mother mentioned to me that she had met you and really liked you a lot. She said you were a real straight shooter and she had never encountered that in a sales person of any sort, much less a real estate agent. Mother said you had an appointment later that morning with her to list the house. She was so ready to move on with her life, start a new one. She wanted to live at the beach. I just don't understand how she could be all fine when we went for our walk and then die from a gas leak. It's all so surreal. The police say that the hot water tank was very old, well past its use date. But with mother it was always, 'if it ain't broke don't fix it.' Mother could really pinch a penny when she set her mind to it. May I have one of your business cards Alex? I'm named as the executor of mother's Will and we are still going to need to list her house. I'm sure if mother liked you, then we will like working with you as well."

Sometimes the universe is strange in a good way. "Here's my card and thank you. Please give me call when you are ready to discuss listing your mother's house."

As I turned to leave, I noticed raccoon eyes had paused in another one of her loud crying squalls, to look over at me and glare again. She also appeared to be shooting daggers at her sister as well and she was popping more peach colored tablets in her mouth. Oh well, so much for sibling love and a sober funeral.

The St. Thomas parking lot looked like a Mercedes, Jaguar, BMW dealership lot. I took special care to ease my aging Volvo out without scratching any of the expensive cars. Not that I wasn't used to this panoply of overpriced cars. The lot at my office is filled with the latest SUV creations and black is the real estate agent choice of color, at least for the past few years. Before that, it was champagne and red is always a close second. Lately though, I have noticed they are gravitating towards white and silver. Sometimes I think I should sell these luxury cars. To each their own, but I vastly prefer to own my car rather than spend almost an entire year's salary on a hunk of metal just to impress myself and clients. A few agents in my office probably do outright own their $80,000 wheels, but most are just a lease payment away from the car repo, boogey man. True to form, when I pulled in the Winterfrost Real Estate parking lot, there were five Mercedes SUVs, a sprinkling of BMWs, and some high end Audis thrown in for good measure. I suppose every real estate office is a viper pit in its own way. My office is the number one office in Clinton, with over seventy agents and the egos and turf battles never cease. I usually try to run in, get what I need and split.

Today, that was not to be the case. I passed by the usual flock of vultures smoking in the parking lot and was entering the rear entrance when who should I run into but one of Winterfrost's top agents, Share Shelton. Share is pronounced "Sharee" and ironically Share certainly does not "share" much less remotely know of the concept. Share is somewhere around sixty, but claims she's forty-five. What hasn't been nipped, tucked, injected or inflated, is covered in tight shiny fabrics or hidden beneath a pound of special order Tammy

Faye Bakker make-up. Her taunt, leathered, epidermis is a surreal orange hue which comes from her frequent spray tan applications, either that or she is an alien. Share is known in real estate agent circles as the *Winterfrost Madam*. I'm quite sure had Share been around in the mid 1800s, she would have run a very profitable Wild West bordello.

"Well, Alex what are *you* doing here? We hardly ever see you. Are you still in the business?" Share emphasized her last word by loudly tapping her blood red stick-on talons against the door frame. Today Share's reddish-orange dyed hair was spiked up extra high. She wore enormous purple tinted glasses with tiny sparkles in the frame and some kind of designer gold logo on the frame's sides. She was in a sedate ensemble today. Tight black spandex pants (black is thinning), a purple sport coat with one large gold button near her naval, and a bright red, stretch top underneath, which barely covered her recently re-inflated cleavage. Nestling in her age-spotted tit valley, was ramble of chunky gold and colored beads. Share was almost clearing six feet today, her red and purple stiletto heels adding at least foot to her height. Her shoes must be custom ordered from a drag queen web site or else she gets Tina Turner's cast-offs when her tours are over. Out of her hooker heals, Share probably barely clears five foot two and that's allowing for half foot of hair.

"Oh, hello Share. Of course I am still in the business. I just submitted an offer for a client on your downtown condo listing, remember?

Share immediately huffed up her purple clad shoulders, her lips (painted in at least three different shades of red) turning downward, revealing her capped white teeth, a couple with lipstick smudges on them. "Well! Of course I know you submitted an offer on MY downtown condo listing. We'll just have to see if your buyer is qualified enough for it to close or not! I've got a listing appointment in the Beaumont to attend." With that, the *Winterfrost Madam* shot out the door; her spiky bitch shoes making loud clacking sounds against the concrete, various gold bracelets and whatever else jangling. She left her usual vapor trail of extremely strong perfume. Stinky's signature odor, (a blend of freesia, rose and musk with some kind of spice) which would linger for at least another fifteen minutes. I nicknamed Share "Stinky" when I first smelled/met her. I don't gossip with anyone at the office, so "Stinky" is my private nickname for her. In Share's defense, she is the top agent in the office and she does have a loyal following. I give her credit for that, but as a person, well let's just say the reptilian world might suit her better.

I followed Stinky's vapor trail to the office mail room. The viper pit was fairly empty save for the usual coffee pot klatch of real estate agents. These types come and go month by month. I call them the ghosts. They linger around the coffee machine and mail room day in/day out, gossiping and fretting about their lack of business. I don't know who they think is going to buy a house from them in the office, but they sure do seem to enjoy spending their entire day there. Occasionally, they might venture out into the field and preview a new listing. Then promptly rip it and the listing agent to shreds, while bemoaning their lack of business. Most of these types come from corporate jobs where they were paid to wander the carpeted cubicles and gossip and bitch all day (corporate jobs, where they not so incidentally, received a monthly paycheck for their efforts).

Today's little buzz *de jour* was about Share's listing appointment in the Beaumont. The Beaumont is the *nouveau* version of the Bluffs. The Beaumont sports houses on steroids galore, in assorted flavors. Faux French Provincials, mock Tudors with eclectic touches, Greek Revivals that shouldn't have been revived, and the latest *Gone with the Wind* Tara with fiberglass columns. Most boast updated touches such as five car garages tacked onto the front of the house. In short, the Beaumont offers anyone with deep pockets and no architectural sense or taste, the tacky mcmansion of their choice. A perfect match for Share, in my humble estimation. I managed to retrieve my commission check from my mail file without any vipers spying it and then trying to discover the amount. I grabbed some forms I needed and slipped out the door without being cornered.

Back in my metal cocoon, I headed off to meet a potential buyer. My monthly postcards actually do bring in clients sometimes. Sure enough, this guy had received my postcard and wanted to meet to see if he could stop renting and buy something. Normally I would have met him at the office first, but since he also needed a mortgage person I set this appointment up for both myself and Wanda. Safety is always an issue in this business and no agent, male or female, should meet a new client alone, no matter how vanilla/safe they may seem.

7

Vanilla certainly is not the adjective that comes to mind when one meets Fred Carlton. Even Wanda appeared a bit bug-eyed when Fred opened the door to his second floor work loft apartment and ushered us in. "Nice of you two to stop by. I've been receiving your monthly postcards for a long while Alex, glad to know there's a real person behind the mug shot photo on them. Have a seat on the sofa there beside the sling." Fred was somewhere past fifty and was stuffed into very tight black leather pants. Handcuffs were attached to the waistband, which was somewhat obstructed by his very hairy gut. He had what appeared to be fishing weights hanging off his pierced nipples and sported a leather collar with metal spikes that looked sharp enough to cut glass. When he stepped back to let us in, his black boots with spurs creaked. Or no, maybe it was his too-tight glistening leather pants, which unfortunately appeared to contain a pair of tube socks stuffed in the crotch.

Wanda gave me a quick peek and then walked in the door. "Well, Fred it's nice to meet you, hope we ain't interrupting nothing," she said while walking over to the sofa where she picked up a black leather flogger so she could sit down. "Say Fred, what kind of duster is this? My mama never had no feather duster this industrial! But hey, I don't dust so I wouldn't know what they are putting out these days." Wanda plopped down on the brown sofa, her bright orange flamingo top splaying out behind her.

"Ahh, yes Mr. Carlton it's ah, great to meet you, glad to know my postcards are actually looked at." I let out a ridiculous, self conscious titter and immediately sat down next to Wanda.

Wanda let out a whistle and said, "My, that is one interesting swinging chair you got there Fred!" Hanging from the ceiling rafter was what appeared to be a sling of sorts and over on the far wall of exposed brick were neatly arranged metal and leather hooks, clasps, and god knows what else. "So," Wanda resumed, "as you know I am a mortgage person and before Alex can take you out to look for your new home, I have to get some information from you and pre-approve you for a loan. First question I gotta have answered is, what is your occupation, Fred?"

Fred slowly lowered himself down into a blue easy chair, his leather pants creaking as he sat. He smiled at us, clearly enjoying the moment. I suddenly thought, if he'd lose the red bandana tied around his head, shave the handle bar mustache off, and put on a shirt to cover up his hairy gut, he might pass as one of those wholesome, gay, middle aged, male models they hire for father's day ads. "Well Wanda—Alex, I'm in what you might call the personal needs line of work. I'm a certified S and M and bondage coach. I've been doing this work for seven years now, ever since I resigned as the choir master for a major Baptist Church. It's really fulfilling work, helping clients discover and surpass their own limitations and boundaries."

I'm thinking, certified? Did the man say, certified S and M coach? When did that world become institutionalized and start issuing certifications? Wanda didn't miss a beat with her pen and clipboard

40

and replied, "Hey spanking Bob and Betty to pay the electric, ain't nothing wrong with that! Why don't I just fill in under occupation that you are a counselor, sound good? You know lenders can be a bit stuffy Fred. Although I got quite a few people in my money world that I would like to see you take this here feather duster thing upside their pimply asses!"

"Well Wanda, I am a professional. They would need to hire me to provide my flogging service, in order to achieve their personal fulfillment goals. I don't just beat people that would be far too simple Wanda. No S and M and bondage is a very complex world onto itself."

Part of me was thinking, yeah I bet it is and the other part was thinking, good for Fred for putting his kinky side to work for him. Fred then jumped up, well squeaked up is more like it, "Ohh! Where are my manners? Would you two like some lemonade? It's fresh and I've got some nice snicker doodles that I just made this morning. Here let me get them, I'll be right back."

While Fred was getting the snicker doodles and lemonade, I got out my client in-take form and took a gander around the living room. There was the hanging sling, the wall of instruments. and on the coffee table was the *de rigor* Robert Mapleforth book. The building was an apartment house that had once been a warehouse. Mostly artists and an assortment of work/live spaces such as Fred's now occupied the building. There was one large, wood framed window which overlooked what appeared to be a used tire lot. In my real estate agent frame of mind, I began to wonder what someone who rented in this building could really afford to buy.

I should not have spent too much time pondering Fred's ability to purchase. Turns out, Fred's business is thriving and the work/live apartment he planned to convert into a full time work space. He wanted a nice salt box house in the 'burbs. With his thriving business consisting of regulars who paid top dollar and his on-going training seminars, the salt box in the 'burbs was not going to be a stretch at all. It could be an all cash deal if Fred so desired.

After setting up a time to take Fred on a house tour, Wanda and I left. We went to my house, so she could visit with Clyde and I could make a pitcher of frozen Margaritas. "Damn Alex, you are almost finished with this little place and those glowing tiles look even better after some of this drink." Clyde was sitting on Wanda's feet, literally, and every now and then she'd toss him a corn chip. "You know in this world, we can laugh a bit about Fred, Alex but I tell you it's them normal acting ones you best steer clear of."

"No dispute from me! Remember that PTA president, soccer mom, Junior League, woman I helped last spring?"

"Oh, the one who was gonna buy that house in the Lee District off Marvin, who had three ex husbands because of the pet tarantulas?"

"Yep, that's the one. She looked all June Cleaver perfect, but there's a reason why she lives alone with those pet spiders. Augghhh, gives me the creeps just thinking about her."

"I know baby, life is just too damn strange, ain't that right Clyde? Hey is that your cell ringing, you gonna get that?"

It was Sally Anne Tilberts calling. She wanted to meet the day after tomorrow at her mother's place and asked me to bring all the listing paper work with me. They were ready to list. This was a good enough excuse for Wanda to demand I go out with her. So, off to Wanda's bar haunts we went but not before Clyde peed on her leg at the front door. I'm sure it was a completely purposeful and spiteful move on his part. He knew Wanda was taking me out somewhere to have fun and he was jealous. However, in true Clyde fashion, Wanda found it funny and blamed me for not taking Clyde out on enough walks. Enough walks my ass! The dog had three walks that day AND he lives in a fenced in yard, so he can pee almost in any time he wants.

8

The next day was a blur of showings and placating Stinky's (Share) fragile ego. Seems she needed reassurance that my lawyer client (the buyer-from-hell) was actually good enough to purchase her client's listing. Mr. Lawyer had lost and learned and was now agreeing with reality and offering a very reasonable amount for Share's listing. Now that my client's ego was tamed, it was time for the listing agent's ego to go haywire. In short, Share was doing everything in her power to make this deal as impossible as she could. Never mind, that it was her job to represent her seller and sell the damn place. No, like many agents, Share had her own egotistical agenda and it came before her client's best interest. She tried her best to convince her seller that my buyer's offer was not enough, we came in $2,000 less than the list price and the list price was indeed $2,000 over according to the most recent comps. It was just another day in real estate. I'd made a touring appointment to take Fred (a.k.a. Mr. Leather) out for a tour of suburban salt boxes, but he had to cancel at the last minute. Big client flogging appointment I suppose. As a real estate agent, the first thing you have to master is the never ending last minute cancellations, changes of mind, etc... that clients pull. I always tell myself to not take it personally, but some days are easier than others. Sometimes I want to hand a out a general manners guide to everyone I see and preach to them the merits of living up to our commitments, to saying thank you, to thinking of others, etc....

However, Thursday rolled around and I was still in the real estate game so off again I went to the Bluffs. I had pulled the tax records for Catherine Tilberts' house, ordered a listing packet from the title company, making sure they noted the court order which is necessary to transfer title from the deceased to the estate. I had my listing forms in order. I was a man on mission. This time I wasn't leaving until I had the listing and I didn't care who I found dead on the laundry room floor. I knew the stars weren't aligned right when I pulled into Catherine's white pebble drive and among the parked cars there was a gleaming black SUV Mercedes with the vanity plate *SOLD*. "SOLD" is Stinky's trademark. Sure enough, when I got out and approached the front door, I could smell her vapor trail of freesia, rose, musk and god knows what else. What in the fuck was Stinky doing here? Before I could complete that thought, the front door popped open and out came Stinky, followed by Mary Beth. What a sight they made. Share was wearing a puke-green, cheetah spotted top. Her life preserver tits were practically falling out. Thankfully, they were held in place by a big, chunky, gold cross hanging from a thick glittering chain wedged in between her inflatable friends. She wore black sun glasses with huge gold C's on the frame ends. Her plumped up lips were only two shades of magenta today, her stick-on talons in a matching shade. Share's hair was its usual orange hue and spiked a bit higher than the norm. She wore black, skintight, leather pants (camel toes over age twenty-five, really?). Maybe Share and Fred should meet? She was teetering on her usual ten foot tall, bitch heels, which naturally matched her puke-green cheetah spotted top.

Mary Beth was wearing what appeared to be a Ralph Lauren, pseudo horseback riding get up. Her raccoon rimmed eyes were shooting daggers at me again. "Oh it's that horrible real estate agent that tricked mother Share! I don't know why Sally and Tim insisted on having *him* stop by."

Share let out a little gasp looking straight at me, turned to Mary Beth and said, "Okay my dear, it's been such a treat to see your beautiful childhood home and feel the love and joy inside. I can just sense your mother's presence looking over you and your siblings, guiding you three through your time of pain. Here's my card, and I want you to call me when you are ready to list. I think your sister and brother will realize the importance of listing with someone like me." With that she clasped Mary Beth's hand, her thick gold bracelets clacking while pressing her business card into Mary Beth's hand. She walked down the steps holding Mary Beth's arm, "And if any of you need to talk, to process your immense grief, you know I am only a phone call away. Any time, you call me, and I'll be there to listen, to honor your pain, to facilitate your healing."

I wanted to throw-up (projectile, a-la Linda Blair preferred) but I could only manage a quick, "Hello Share"— which she pretended not to hear. Before I could beam my clipboard at the back of her orange hair, Sally Anne appeared and put her hand on my arm, "Hey Alex it's great to see you. Mary Beth is going to join us. I guess she's going to see Share to her car first. Come in, Tim is in the sun room." I followed Sally Anne into the house. Sally Anne looked back at me and said in a lower voice, "Don't be put off by that other real estate agent Alex. Mary Beth insisted on bringing her by. Tim and I only want to list with you, we know you are the person mother wanted to work with and spoke so highly of. Mary Beth, well, she's just being Mary Beth.

She knows that real estate agent and insisted that Tim and I meet her before we sign with you. Ahh, here's Tim."

Tim was busy opening the french doors in the sun room and making fanning motions with a magazine. "My god, that woman smells like a walking whore house or like the perfume girl at Macy's spraying all that crap out in the air all day long. Alex, good to meet you, do you know that woman?"

I had to bite my tongue hard to keep from replying, *oh you mean Stinky?* Instead I overcame my penchant for bluntness and replied, "Hello Tim, nice to meet you as well. Sure, I know Share. She's a real estate agent in my office. Sally Anne tells me Mary Beth wanted you all to meet her."

Tim rolled his eyes and plopped down on a yellow chintz covered wicker sofa, "Oh yes. That whore on parade is one of Mary Beth's *friends*," he said greatly exaggerating the word friends, "seems she is helping Mary Beth list her house, what with her divorce and all. Mary Beth thinks Share should list mom's house too. Spoiled brat, always telling us what we should do. Always getting what she wants. Little miss perfect, Cindy fucking Brady—hah, now she's getting a divorce."

Well, there was the first open sign of sibling squabbles. From the sound of it, the youngest sibling, Mary Beth, and the middle one, Tim, were not on the best of terms. This animosity obviously went way back. Odd though, because the reading I've done on birth order, the middle child is usually the go-between or diplomat between the oldest and youngest child. So much for shrink theories with this bunch of siblings.

Sally Anne sat down in a white wicker rocker and turned toward a small table set up with a tray of assorted sodas and mineral water. "Oh, Alex please sit down and don't mind Tim. Would you like something to drink?" I replied no thank you and she continued, "Tim and Mary Beth are a bit at odds but underneath we all get along I suppose. As I mentioned to you, Tim and I definitely want to list mother's house with you but Mary Beth isn't real crazy about listing the house and she just wanted us to meet---"

Tim interrupted, "Oh, cut the crap Sally Anne. If Alex is gonna list the place he needs to know the whole story." Tim turned towards me, I'd found a wicker easy chair to sit in and had propped my clipboard and files up on the arm rest. "You see Alex, Mary Beth is getting unhitched from her husband and I know he's elated, but trying to keep her from running him into bankruptcy. Anyway, Mary Beth wanted mom's house. She approached mom and tried to buy her out. Pulled all this shit about how she was getting divorced and her children needed a good home to live in, even though the kids are away at boarding schools, summer camps, and are almost never home. She thought mom should understand and allow her to buy the house at a below market rate."

Ahh, here we go with the real family politics now. Sally Anne cut in, "Well that is true Alex. Mary Beth is going through a difficult divorce and is being forced to move out of her home as part of the settlement and---"

Tim looking more annoyed, "Settlement? Little Mary Beth Gold Digger is getting her just rewards, finally! Seems her hubby has been able to somehow pull off not letting her have their mega mansion, he's got half-time custody of the kids, and the alimony is only going to cover the kids expenses. Miss Mary Beth is being forced to get a j-o-b for the first time in her life. She thought she could weasel mom into giving her this house and when that failed, she tried to make mom sell it to her for less than half its true value. So, Mary Beth was way pissed when she found out Mom was listing the house."

Sally Anne quickly interjected, "Which I'm sure Alex, you can now understand why Mary Beth has been so, well, less than polite to you."

Less than polite, how about nail spitting bitch? Before I could respond, Mary Beth entered the room, making a loud clamor as she poured herself a diet soda. She glared at Tim who was sitting in the middle of the wicker sofa. He was mock smiling at her, while indicating she should have a seat next to him by patting the yellow cushion. Mary Beth turned away from him and leaned against the door frame, "So you are Alex Campbell? Well, tell us why we should list this gracious house with someone like you?"

With that, Sally Anne started to admonish her sister but I waved her off and replied, "Why yes, I am Alex Campbell and this is indeed a gracious house as was your mother. As you may know, your mother intended to list this house with me. I am here today because your sister and brother invited me." From there, I proceeded to show my marketing comparisons for the house. I suggested a list price and explained the commission and excise tax fees they would have to pay, and I outlined my marketing plan for the property. Mary Beth snorted, gave little laughs or sighs as I made my pitch, but I ignored her. I finished and looked around the room and asked if there were any questions.

Sally Anne thanked me and Tim said it sounded good to him. Mary Beth walked over to the drink table and banged her glass down and began refilling it with more diet soda, "Well, aren't you impressive with all these recent sales comparisons! Funny, Share doesn't think this house should list for such a high price."

That was no surprise to me. Share has quite the reputation among real estate agents for taking listings at prices that she knows her own buyers can afford. She then sells the listing to her buyers about three minutes after the listing officially posts. She doesn't want to be accused of keeping pocket listings, so she circumvents it by officially listing the property. In reality, the property is sold before it lists. Her reason for doing this is greed. She gets to keep the whole commission this way, both sides the seller and the buyer, it's all hers. So if she can convince a seller to list their house at a lower price that one of her buyer's can afford, she still comes out ahead. Screws the seller over, but hey, this is real estate, so much for integrity or karma. Of course, Share has also been known to do the reverse of this and overprice a listing at a price that she knows one of her buyers will pay. It was no surprise to me that Share had not presented any comps and was suggesting listing the property for about $50,000 less than what the market currently showed was correct.

I again chose (forced myself) to be diplomatic and not blunt, "Well Mary Beth, I base my list price on what the current market will handle. I like to show my clients what the current state of the market is and let them decide what they want to do. As you may know, I have a policy of not taking a listing if it is not priced right. If you all decide you would prefer to go with Share's suggested list price then you are more than welcome to have her list your mother's house. I can't guarantee my list price is exactly what you will get, but I can say that based on the statistics available, I am comfortable taking the listing at this price point."

Mary Beth let out a little snicker, "You know Alex, Share Shelton is a big player in Clinton real estate. I'm sure what she says is a viable list price is accurate. After all, she's had more than her share of big time listings. How many listings have you had Alex?"

Here we go; she's going for the jugular. "Yes, Mary Beth, Share is a very successful real estate agent and she has had quite a number of listings in her career. I can understand why you would be impressed with her experience. However, I think statistics and the recent comparable sales are also crucial in determining the right list price. I have provided you with that. As far as experience, Share has more listing experience than I do and she has been in the business longer than I have. There is really nothing more I can say. I have provided you with recent sales data which I think adequately justifies my suggested list price and I have provided you with a comprehensive marketing plan. I know your mother liked me and was comfortable working with me. I think you three now have to decide who you are most comfortable working with." With that, I stood up and shook Sally Anne and Tim's hands. Mary Beth rolled her eyes and scoffed when I attempted to shake her hand.

Before I could turn to leave, Tim grabbed the listing packet I had placed on the wicker coffee table and said, "Where do we sign Alex? We want to list with you. It doesn't matter if Mary Beth agrees and signs off or not. Sally Anne is the executor and according to the Will, if two of us agree on an issue, such as who to list the house with, then it's a done deal."

Mary Beth promptly smashed her glass onto the slate floor, "Well I guess once again you two rule and decide everything, fucking typical!" With that she began to cry and ran off for the front door, slamming the door behind her like an out of control sixteen year old.

I mentioned I would be happy to come back and meet with them another time, but Sally Anne and Tim insisted on completing the listing paperwork. "Don't let Mary Beth's theatrics upset you Alex. We are used to them. Mother never knew what to do with Mary Beth. I guess the saying about the youngest child being the most spoiled is true." said Sally Anne giving me a weak smile as she signed the papers.

Tim laughed while signing his name, "Spoiled is far too polite a term for that miserable bitch. Here you go Alex I've finished. Are we legally listed now?"

I explained the listing would go live tomorrow and that I'd return then to have some pictures taken for the online and brochure marketing. I didn't want to touch the sibling and family resentment issues that I had just witnessed and made a bee line for my car. Sally Anne and Tim waved goodbye and it wasn't until I was half way down the drive that I noticed my rear passenger side window was broken. Someone had thrown a small caste iron door weight through it. The black little horse door weight lay on my back seat, surrounded by window glass crumbs. I thought about going back and asking Sally Anne and Tim about it, but decided they'd had enough family feuding for one day. I'd return the door weight to them later. It was clear who the horse back rider was in that family, such a unique calling card.

9

The next day, I rushed off to an 8:00 a.m. client signing appointment which fortunately was on the outskirts of town at Equity Escrow, near Lexi's. I had explained to my buyers (for the third time) that they were merely signing today. They were signing the loan paperwork, handing over the money due. they would not be the legal owners of their new townhouse until the end of the week; i.e. the closing date specified on the first page of the purchase and sale contract. I try to be patient, but sometimes! There are so many clients and some real estate agents too, who always confuse the signing date at escrow with the closing date. Assuming you live in a traditional closing state, you sign a few days before your closing date. You are not the legal owner until the county has recorded the deed in your name on the closing date.

Once my buyers were again apprised of this fact, I raced off to pick up Lexi. Lexi is now the official photographer for my listings. She's got quite the eye for lighting and can work a film and digital camera like nobody's business. Since the real estate business went online, the photographs of a property are now more important than ever. With my first listing, especially one in the Bluffs, I figured it would be wise to pay someone like Lexi to make sure the pictures were top notch. Lexi was sitting on her camera travel case by the entry to her property, along with her light tripod and deflectors. It was quite the site. This woman dressed in paint splattered overalls, yellow sneakers, and wearing a droopy green hat, sitting with her camera supplies next to a beat up mail box that has some kind of rusted metal junk welded to its top (Lexi's sculpting strikes again). "Hey there Mr. Shark, I see you are the real estate agent about town today. What's up with the broken window?" I explained the broken car window to Lexi, while helping her put the camera supplies in the trunk. "That's pretty damn creepy Alex. This woman sounds like a total psycho. Oh, this little horsey door stop is kind of cute. If I were you, I'd keep it as payment for replacing your window."

"Yes, well a horse door stop is not really my cup of tea Lexi. I'd prefer Mary Beth keep her damn door stop to herself. You know, she and her brother Tim are like oil and water. They could barely stay in the same room together for more than ten minutes."

Lexi chuckled while changing the batteries in her light meter, "You know who Tim Tilberts is don't you Alex?" I shook my head no. "He's the owner of that skank bar down on Dock Street. You know the one, near that mafia run chop shop where I go to get the scrap metal for my art pieces? It's called the Wharf Rat."

Lexi has a way of knowing all sorts of odd ball facts and characters around Clinton. I'd warned her before, about getting scrap metal from the mob characters down near the abandoned wharf. How she ever met up with those people and started buying scrap metal from them is anyone's guess. "You think Tim Tilberts runs a bar down near the wharf? That's a long way from the Bluffs don't you think? I just assumed he lived off of some trust and pretty much puttered around like the rest of them. Investing in a sail boat, tinkering with classic cars or becoming a golf junkie."

"Alex, you know firsthand that life isn't that simple. No, I'm pretty sure Tim is the owner of that dive bar and if I remember all my gossip correctly, he squandered his trust money. You should look up where he lives in the tax records Alex, just for curiosity sake." Lexi finally had her batteries installed and the meter flashed, causing me to almost drive off the road.

"Hey! Watch the meter Lexi. I'm driving. I'd like to get us to my first listing photo shoot alive. So that's interesting, Tim runs a dive bar. What about artsy, the older sister? Her name is Sally Anne. Does she weave baskets all week long or what?"

"This is good Alex. You are developing an ear for gossip. Although I suppose this is just good business sense, to know as much about your clients as possible. Well, I know that Sally Anne Tilberts is a long time volunteer with the Clinton Women's Shelter and she is a potter. She attends many of the local art openings, events, and she throws some interesting pots. They are a bit too conventional and pedantic for my taste, but she had a couple of small vessels in the art fair last year. She's been around a long time. Very nice person, keeps out of all the art politics."

"Well, speak of the devil Lexi, there's Sally Anne now waiting for us." I said while driving up the white pebble drive. Sally Anne was letting us in for the photo shoot. She had two sets of keys waiting for me. Which I compulsively tested before putting one set in the key box and the other in my pocket, to keep in case there was a problem with the key box. Per my request she had made sure the door locks worked properly. Nothing annoys me more than to take a buyer to a listing, only to discover the key sticks in the lock or you have to jiggle the key for ten minutes to get the door open. Talk about frustrating! How hard is it for the listing agent to make sure the key and locks are working properly before putting the house on the market? Not to mention, the number of phone calls the listing agent must receive from real estate agents trying to show the house, who can't get the lock to work.

I introduced Sally Anne and Lexi. Sally Anne recalled seeing some of Lexi's sculptural installations. She was very polite and apologized for her sister's outburst. I didn't really want to bring up the broken window/horse door stop but Lexi cut in, "Well, you could say your sister left her calling card in Alex's car yesterday." With that, I suggested Lexi get set up to photograph the foyer. Sally Anne persisted, so I took her out to the car and handed her the cast iron horse door stop. Sally Anne looked shocked, "Oh, god! I am so sorry Alex. I don't know what got into Mary Beth. Maybe it's the divorce stress? I mean, she's always been a bit, well, undisciplined. Mother never could really say no to her. But this, this is really uncalled for. You let me know how much that window costs Alex. This is the door stop mother used for the front door." Sally Anne said she'd be back in a few hours, to see if I needed anything else. I gave her a copy of the marketing verbiage to review and went back inside to help Lexi.

The shoot was going really well. We managed to get the perfect mid-morning light for the pool, sound view, back of the house shots. We decided not to shoot the basement at all, but Lexi still wanted to see the "death scene." So down we went. In the little laundry room, the ancient blue, hot water tank was gone. The Tilberts children had the tank replaced shortly after their mother's demise and now a brand new Bradford White hot water tank was holding court.

There was no gas odor or any indication that anything had gone wrong. Maybe the new hot water tank would detract potential buyers from obsessing on the stack washer and dryer? Lexi pulled out her small format film camera and started shooting the room. I was a bit alarmed. "Relax Alex! These are just some art shots for my own personal use. I'm not gonna publish them, just morbid artist curiosity is all. I'm sure the police photos are better than mine. Too bad they erased the chalk outline of the body. So where was it? How was she lying?"

I really didn't want to go into it and in fact, that little laundry room was really starting to creep me out. I pointed to where Catherine's body had been and Lexi promptly shut the small door. Shutting herself up in the room. "Don't freak Alex. I'm just getting some shots from her point of view. Kind of stretching that whole victim metaphor if you know what I mean."

Sometimes Lexi could be such an annoying *artiste*. I told her to hurry it up and was turning to leave, when Lexi let out a gleeful cry. "Wow! Alex, one of the cops left their handcuffs under the washer in here."

Handcuffs under the washer? This was going to be another strange day. Lexi wasn't kidding. Underneath the washer were a pair of handcuffs. Lexi was already wondering aloud why the cops would leave their cuffs, while I pulled out Detective Davies' card and went outside to stand in the special spot where the cell phone works. When I reached him, he too was surprised by the handcuffs and said he doubted any of the cops had left their handcuffs behind. He said he'd be out and not to touch anything. About a half an hour later,

Detective Davies and another cop showed up, just as Sally Anne rolled back in. They fished the handcuffs out from under the washer. They were indeed, not police department issue handcuffs. Detective Davies said they were professional grade handcuffs and there was an engraved name on them, "Mistress Xtc." Everyone drew a blank stare, looking at each other, Lexi arching her eyebrows. Detective Davies asked Sally Anne if it would be okay to bag them and take them into the station for further study. Sally Anne agreed, "But what are those handcuffs doing under the washer? You don't think they were mother's? Do you think they had something to do with her death?"

"I can't say ma'am. Could be they have been down there for some time, but we didn't find a layer of dust on top of them. I would guess they have not been under there very long. Since they were in the room where your mother's body was found, it would seem wise to check them out. Make sure they didn't play a part in her death."

"But mother's death was ruled accidental. You don't think someone hand cuffed her do you? I mean, how would that work? She died from the gas leak right?" Sally Anne appeared to be getting upset.

"Ma'am I can't say what role if any these handcuffs played in your mother's death. I will call you as soon as the lab checks them out and we can go from there. For now, I wouldn't worry." With that, Detective Davies and the other cop left.

It was a bit awkward, but Sally Anne thanked us for finding the handcuffs and said she liked the marketing verbiage. Starting tomorrow, the listing would be completely up and the broker's open would be the day after. I set the key box up, attaching it to the steel pipe that fed into the gas meter located on the side of the house. Last week I'd shown a house where the listing agent had "secured" the key box to a branch on a shrub. With a small saw the branch and the key box could easily have been removed. I promised to call Sally Anne after the broker's open and let her know how things went. She said she'd call when she heard something from Detective Davies. Off Lexi and I went, to format the pictures so I could post them online.

10

The broker's open was off to a fairly good start. Wanda showed up and set up shop with me in the kitchen. She'd gone in fifty/fifty (as per the law) with me on some pastries and coffee. Broker's opens are open houses that are held just for real estate agents. The idea is to get other agents excited about your listing and then they'll show it. I am on the fence about broker's opens. Most real estate agents don't bother attending them anymore. They do most of their previewing online, hence the importance of having Lexi take nice photographs. Today's broker's open wasn't too bad. About eight agents had come through. All oohh-ing and ahh-ing over the views, the majority stuffing their faces with pastries and not bothering to go upstairs. The stairs were too much exercise for them I suppose. All was okay until Wanda nudged my ribs and gave me one of her bug eyed looks, "Alex, what is that smell? You smellin' it? Smell like someone broke a bottle of perfume, and it's a nasty perfume. Whew!"

Oh shit. That smell could only mean one thing. Stinky had arrived. Sure enough, who came clacking into the kitchen wearing a crimson red pant suit with a small matching red beret perched atop her orange hair. "Well, well, well. If it isn't Alex and his first listing! Looks nice. So what did you do to get them to list with you Alex?" Share said while sauntering over to the kitchen work island, drumming her red stick-on talons against the butcher block counter top. "What did I do Share? I presented them with the facts and they made their decision."

Share put her acrylic nails up to her black, rhinestone encrusted shades and lowered them dramatically, peering over the rims, "Ohhh, do tell Alex! And what facts might those have been? Huh? You tell them bad things about me Alex, was that your angle? You tell them that trust fund babies should only list with trust fund babies, was that your hook Alex?"

Now my blood was starting to boil a bit, "No Share, I told you I merely presented them with the---,"

"The facts. Yeah right Alex. You told me that already. Ohhh, what do we have here? Nice four-color, marketing sheets about the house. My, you are good Alex! And these must be the mortgage propaganda sheets. Pity, they are not as nice as your sheets Alex." Share said while fingering Wanda's brochures. She gave Wanda a sly wink. I noticed Wanda looked as if she was about to let go with a response, so I quickly interjected, "Ahhh, Share wont you have some coffee and there are some pastries here from the French bakery."

Share gave a wry smile in my direction, picked up a chocolate covered croissant then put it back down. "Ohh, these *are* French aren't they Alex? Not very patriotic on your part, but I'm not surprised. You know they do look good, but unlike some people I watch my weight," Share said while staring directly at Wanda, "and you know Alex, I'd rather leave these for *someone* else to eat. I wouldn't want to deprive anyone around here of a chocolate binge." With that said, Share's cell phone began to ring, her custom *Yellow Rose of Texas* jingle piercing the silence. She flipped open her cell phone and said in her syrupy, chirpy voice, "Share Shelton your personal real estate agent, how can I help you?" She sent a Grinch-like smile in my direction and then click clacked out of the kitchen in her spiky, crimson red, bitch boots. Wanda had completely crushed her coffee cup, the dregs spilling out on the countertop. She was muttering as her fists clinched open and shut, "I *know* that cunt, pardon my language, didn't just dis me like that to my face Alex! Gonna go flatten that red bitch Alex. Gonna wipe her Tammy Faye face all in this here chocolate pastry." I had to grab Wanda's arm and use all my strength to keep her from charging after Share. Fortunately, Wanda's cell phone began to ring; hers with an Aretha Franklin *Respect* jingle. I was able to trick her into answering it, thus leaving Share alone. Thank god Wanda follows her mantra of "business first." I suppose in this case, it is business first and cat fight, ass kicking later.

That was the climax of the broker's open. We had a few more agents come through and Wanda and I were shutting up shop, when my own cell phone gave a ring. Mine doesn't have any special jingle or theme song. Just a tin can sounding, ring--ring. "Hi Alex, this is Marc Hilson, Mary Beth Hilson's soon to be ex-husband." I had to sit down on the front steps, this was too bizarre. I sat there listening while Wanda paced around the front muttering about Stinky. "So great," Marc concluded, "I'll see you tonight around 7p.m. Alex. Please bring all the paperwork I'll need to sign, with you." I hung up and watched Wanda pace and mutter. Finally, Wanda stopped and looked over at me, "What you staring off into space for Alex? Who was that on the phone?"

"Well Wanda, that was Mary Beth's soon to be ex-husband and he is listing their house for sale. Each of them is picking a real estate agent and then they will co-list it. He wants me to be his agent. He says he's heard Mary Beth non-stop bitch about me and he figures if she hates me so much, then I must be the real estate agent for him."

"Sweet Jesus! If that ain't some fine way of getting business Alex. Damn, that's good. Hey you know what? I think her husband is *the* Marc Hilson."

"The who?" I replied. Wanda looked at me getting annoyed, "Damn, how out of the loop are you Alex? I said he's *the* Marc Hilson. You know, the man who developed the Clinton downtown mall? The one who put together the whole redevelopment--bring whitey back downtown to shop--thing? The man is a major investor/developer in Clinton Alex. Every butt kisser in the city lines up to shine his pucker and you don't know of him?" Wanda was now shaking her head and hoisting her fifty pound, citrus yellow, purse up onto her shoulder.

"Well excuse me for not reading *Butt Kissers Weekly* Wanda!" I replied, a bit pissed off with her tone.

Wanda shrugged, "Okay 'nuff said. So you now know who he is and you better get yourself ready to list his place tonight. Baby, I know it's gonna be a top notch listing. Shit, it'll probably put this Bluff place to shame! So who's the other agent gonna be that you will be co-listing with Alex?"

"Ohhh, fuck. If it's who I think it is Wanda, you definitely do not want to know." Wanda looked a bit perplexed, then her eyes went bug eyed, "Oh no, you mean, that smelly, red---? Okay, you just call me after your appointment tonight. I want to hear all about it. Here, take that Hilson man one of my brochures, you never know when he might need himself a good mortgage person."

11

Aco-listing with Share? Oh this was going to be just ducky, but at least it was another listing. Maybe the "No-List Alex" slogan could be retired? I scrambled to look up the Hilson's house in the tax records and get as much information as I could about the available listings in the area, recent sales, etc.... I pulled up to the Disney-esque looking main gate which keeps everyone in the Beaumont safe from the big bad world outside. The rent-a-cop at the gate looked as if he had barely passed puberty. He did have a list with my name on it. So once I showed him my driver's license, the gate partition magically flipped up and I was free to move about the Beaumont. The Hilson's mcmansion is located on Turnkey Drive. It sits on top of a sloping lot and sports a huge five car garage right out in front of the house. If the house were a dog, it would be a mutt and not in the cute way either. It was a cross between an English Tudor father and a 1980s faux French Provincial mother, with a couple of odd relative's genes thrown in for good measure (i.e. arts and crafts touches, federal style windows). I suppose architecture books might politely describe the house as eclectic *nouveau-riche*, circa early 2000s.

Marc Hilson is somewhere in his fifties and looks the part of a successful businessman. Fat gut in a blue and gold golf shirt, gold watch, black chinos. While giving me a tour of the five bedroom, six and a half bath house, Marc told me that the two kids were away at boarding school and Mary Beth was temporarily living in an apartment. They avoided each other as much as possible. We went over my comparable data and he showed me the price Share had told Mary Beth

66

to list the house for. It seemed a bit high. Which probably meant Share had a buyer who could afford to pay more than the market value waiting in the wings to snap this place up. He told me that Share was aware that she would be co-listing with another agent. Marc had let her know that he wanted two public open houses a month and each agent needed to be there. Public open houses in the Beaumont were a bit odd, but if the seller wants it, I'm there. I told him I could do an open house for the upcoming Sunday and would make sure the ad was in the *Clinton Observer* real estate section and work out the details with Share. Marc would have to make sure the rent-a-cop at the gate would let the public in. He said that would not be a problem, as he was the president of the Beaumont Homeowners Committee.

I had Marc sign his half of the co-listing paperwork and told him I'd turn it into my broker the next morning. And that was it. Listing number two was taken care of. Marc didn't say a word about Mary Beth and I certainly didn't ask. I did ask him where he was planning to move once he sold his house. Marc's face looked off in the distance with a small smile, "Well Alex, you may not know much about me but I have political plans. I hope to run for the Clinton City Council in the next election. I plan to find a more suitable home in the inner city. Maybe you can help me find that once I unload this place? Of course, running for office might be a bit more difficult with the divorce but I'm hopeful. I'd like to help play a bigger part in making the city of Clinton a more vibrant and industry friendly place." Great, this developer/investor now wanted to unleash his version of Gotham on our city by influencing the city council. Not exactly my kind of guy, but business is business and I have a listing to sell.

12

C o-listing a house with Share Shelton. I could think of many other diversions which might prove more fun, such as hammering my thumb or getting a root canal. However, another listing is another listing and it certainly was confirming that my "No-List Alex" streak was ending. Writing the ad for the *Clinton Observer* Sunday open house section was a real charm. Share's original draft went something like this, *"Live in lush Baronial splendor in a true Beaumont palace! Stunning architectural detail make this 5 bedroom, 6.5 bath, executive mansion the exclusive place your heart wants to call home. Tuscan tiles, faux marble columns, a 4-tier crystal chandelier and Gone With the Wind stairway complete this exciting entry tableau! Brazilian hardwood and plush designer carpeting throughout, gourmet chef's kitchen with Miele, sub Zero, Viking, hand milled cabinetry—too many classy features to list! Luxuriate in the master suite's rose marbled spa, entertain in your formal dining room which seats 12. Watch your children playing by the pool while safe and secure in a monitored gated community! Your friends will love your formal media room which seats 12. A must see for any discriminating home owner! Let everyone know that you have arrived when your luxury automobiles sport the coveted burgundy Beaumont residential owner stickers! Open Sunday from 1-3. Listed and hosted by Share Shelton & associate; Winterfrost Real Estate."*

Besides the fact that Share had blatantly broken several fair housing laws in the ad; i.e. calling it an "executive" mansion, mentioning children, using hot legal no-no, words like "safe" and "secure", her missive was nauseatingly long. She conveniently failed to put my name in the ad, also a rule violation for a co-listing. Oh details, something that never troubles Share. I red inked the ad, taking out the obvious law violations, adding my name and shortening up her prose. When she saw the revised ad, Share had a meltdown. A long shrill screech filled the Winterfrost back office, "What have you done to my masterpiece? I worked on this ad all last night. I've been listing mansions forever and I KNOW what sells and this ad SELLS! How dare you disrespect my ad, you novice little runt! You'd never have this co-listing if it weren't for me. I KNOW what kind of ad a Beaumont listing deserves!" On and on her shrieking went. Along with the clanking sounds from her jewelry *de jour* which from the looks of it, the jewelry shopping channel held another gold plated, cubic zirconium jamboree.

It took the intervention of the office's designated broker, Todd Blund, to assuage Share's shattered ego and get her to agree to remove the fair housing violation verbiage and add my name. Todd said, while giving me a somewhat pleading look, "You two need to reach a common ground and act like true professionals on this listing. The ad cannot have fair housing law violations Share and it must have Alex's name. But your description is of course wonderful Share and why don't we just leave that part alone Alex?" I nodded and bit my cheeks to keep from laughing out loud. Share huffed and sniffed; ahh, just another fun day in real estate. I headed out of the Viper Pit and wondered about the state of humanity. I thought pre-school was bad enough when kids threw their tantrums. In the sand box kicking over sand castles, fighting over sand pails, biting and screaming over who got which swing, or turn on the slide first. No one ever informed me that pre-school was merely a preview of coming "adult" attractions.

13

I was pondering the meaning of the handcuffs under Catherine's stack washer and dryer when I pulled up to pick up Fred. We had a few suburban salt boxes to go tromp through and it appeared Fred was dressed for the part. He had on baggy khaki pants (no roll of socks bulging through the crotch this time, thankfully), penny loafers, a madras button down shirt, and a light blue wind breaker. I wondered if the fishing weights were still sprouting from his nipples but quickly shuddered that thought away. My reaction to his suburban ensemble must have been apparent. Fred smiled while fastening his seat belt and said, "Howdy Alex, don't be too alarmed. I usually only wear my work clothes in my loft. Out here, I'm just the ex- Baptist Choir Master going to find the perfect little cottage. Looks like we have a few to look over, eh?" I tried to act un-phased as I pulled away and headed off for Rosedale, a neighborhood developed next to the Lee District with houses from the late 1930s through the late 1960s. Rosedale is a young family type of neighborhood, Clinton's version of *Leave it to Beaver*. I could only imagine the splash Fred was going to make when he served up his scrumptious snicker doodles at the neighborhood dessert party, while sporting his "work" clothes! Maybe it is best not to imagine that. He'd probably get a lot of inquiries from the bored housewives and their corporate climbing husbands looking for some kind of kinky diversion. We were touring the first house, a mid - century rambler with nice hardwood floors, but also with original leaky aluminum windows that definitely needed to be replaced. I asked Fred if he knew anything about handcuffs. Instantly, Fred's eyes lit up,

"Ohhh, Alex! Are *you* interested in attending some of my training workshops? I've got a group workshop next Saturday and we'll explore the many sides of handcuffs and other forms of bondage."

Oh my god, the man couldn't seriously--, "Oh no, that's not it Fred. No a handcuff workshop is not what I'm interested in. I---," Fred beamed a huge smile back at me, "Now Alex, there is no need to be ashamed. Why bondage fantasy and handcuff role play are absolutely normal and you must free yourself from your repressions. You know a series of private training sessions with me might be the best route for you. I have a special beginner packet of five, one hour long sessions with one free session included for only $1,500." Did that man just say $1,500 for a session packet to teach me about handcuffs? Damn, he has the yoga world beat in spades. I thought a yoga packet of five classes for $200 was pretty steep. "Ahh, no Fred that's not what I had in mind at all. I know you have special knowledge of these kinds of things and well there's an incident the police are looking into regarding a listing of mine. Some handcuffs were found in a room where the owner died. The police thought the woman died from accidental causes, but now the handcuff discovery has thrown a kink, ahh,—so to speak—into her cause of death."

Fred's brows crumpled a bit and then he replied, "What kind of cuffs were they Alex?"

"I didn't know there were special brands, but I suppose that makes sense. The police said they were professional grade cuffs and there was a unique engraving on them, *Mistress Xtc.*"

Fred's eyes widened for a quick second, "Well, professional cuffs with a unique engraving that does sound a bit odd. You wouldn't happen to know what the police intend to do with those cuffs would you? I mean are they trying to track down the owner? Do they think the owner of the cuffs might be involved in that woman's death? Who was this woman who died Alex?"

Instantly, I knew that Fred knew something; too many questions. "The woman who died was Catherine Tilberts. I listed her house in the Bluffs. She died from a gas leak in her laundry room. My photographer Lexi found the handcuffs and they are trying to figure out what a seventy-four year old woman was doing with handcuffs under her washer and dryer."

"So the police are involved and are they treating this like a murder? I can tell you many older people are very active in the S and M, bondage community Alex, age has nothing to do with it. Are you certain that the cuffs had *Mistress Xtc.* engraved on them?"

"As certain as I am that you have no interest in this 1955 rambler we are standing in Fred. Do you know this Mistress Xtc.? Is there any help you can provide the police?"

Fred gave a quick smile, "Alex in my line of work, discretion and client confidentiality are the hallmarks of the trade. If I knew anything about this supposed Mistress Xtc., I couldn't tell you. My profession is very strict about keeping what happens in the room, in the room. There's no grey area. Just like a shrink and a client, or a priest and their confessional. It stays between the parties involved and no one else."

"Even if the owner of those cuffs may have had something to do with Catherine Tilberts' death, you still can't give the police a tip Fred?"

Fred, sighed and shrugged, "Never have I come across this situation Alex. Unless the police are officially calling this a murder and unless someone's life is directly in danger, I can't comment. I will tell you though, those handcuffs are definitely unique sounding and certainly the name engraved on them would lead one to think that perhaps the owner had something in common with my industry."

"Well, that's diplomatic Fred. I really doubt Catherine Tilberts was a part of your profession and community, so I'm curious as to who left those cuffs in her house and why they were found in the same room she died in. Guess I'll just have to continue pondering that alone. Are you ready to see the next house? It's the 1948, Cape Cod on Dexter Avenue. It has "original charm" as we say in the industry. Built-in pull down ironing board, built-in flour and sugar sifters, and vintage steel topped counters." A typical snicker doodle making, hard working S and M instructor's, suburban delight.

14

The next couple of days were full of the usual real estate agent ups and downs. The buyer-from-hell lawyer finally put in an offer on a Lee District townhouse and was reviewing his inspection report. He decided lofts were over-rated, which actually meant he lost out on the one great loft that was available because he refused to offer the right price. Now, in order to puff himself back up, he decided lofts were not the place for a young lawyer on-the-rise to live. I didn't give a damn what he thought or if he purchased a cardboard box under a bridge for his royal abode. I just wanted him sold and off my client list. Ruthless, but true. I have a new client, a couple with a baby on the way. They had placed an offer on the third house they saw. Unfortunately, the inspection did not go so well, the foundation was severely damaged. So I got them out of that deal and I was out trying to find the right house for them.

Sunday rolled around soon enough and I was up at dawn doing the week's laundry and trying to get a set of yoga in before Clyde insisted on his morning walk. Clyde won of course; yoga would have to wait. We walked over to the rotting piers; he sniffed every last timber, barked at the sea gulls and then pulled me up the street to Sasser's Bakery. Sasser's is an old family bakery that has been around since the late 1930s. Its once red sign is so faded, it is now pink. The large plate glass windows are always steamed over. They specialize in breads and pastries for the regional restaurants and some of the upscale yuppie coffee houses and green grocers in Clinton. Most people do not even know Sasser's has an actual store front where the public is welcome. Yet another advantage of my between-the-tracks neighborhood, only locals and delivery people in the know stop by Sasser's. It's not easy to find either. The actual bakery part of the building takes up a half of block of a rundown warehouse and the store front entrance is off a small, unofficial side street. The unnamed street consists of old, cobbled stones with an embedded track where the crates of freight used to be run when off-loading the ships, back in the day.

Naturally, Clyde is more than welcome at Sasser's and Daynia, who runs the store front, always has a treat for him. "You and this dog are late for Sunday. You don't have work to do today Alex?" This was Daynia's greeting as she popped a treat in Clyde's mouth and promptly set a strong cup of Sasser's special coffee down on the faded blue linoleum table for me. I gave Daynia a weak smile and she proceeded to explain to me which pastries were worth eating that morning. She always has a new preference, based on what has not sold. I settled for a blueberry concoction and picked up a pawed through copy of the *Clinton Observer*. The real estate section listed our open house ad. I cringed, thinking about how much Share's excessive verbiage was going to cost us. I noted the other ads for open houses and then realized I had to get back and get ready. The walk back was fairly brisk. A few times Clyde pulled one of his stubborn stop and sniffs, saw a squirrel and tried to insist we go in the opposite direction to chase it. But, I finally got him home and situated out in the back yard. I put on my real estate open house drag. Meaning, I made sure my hair was not sticking up straight and the parts of my shirt which accented my sweater were ironed. It's not as if I am a slob, but sometimes the details of dressing bore me. I put on my spring green cashmere sweater and brown wide well corduroys. Biff and Muffy would be so happy to know me.

Driving over to the Beaumont, I wondered what kind of turn out we would have for this open house. Sometimes the first public open house for a property is deluged with people, mostly looky-loo neighbors. This can be especially true if it is an upper end listing. In addition to the neighbors, you then get the curious critters who want to see exactly what they are missing out on by being cursed with the fate of the working stiff. However, a listing in a gated community can keep the open house traffic down; people are intimidated by the gate. Regardless, I had my stack of A-board signs to place and that took over thirty minutes of setting up. The A-board is the bane of a real estate agent's existence. The A-board states the company's name, the agent's name and number, reads "Open House" and has a directional arrow. They cost a fortune because the real estate company usually dictates that you must use their sign vendor and only purchase their pre-approved signs, which naturally are marked up a ridiculous amount. My ten Winterfrost A-boards that I set out on various corners, cost me close to a grand. Fortunately today it was sunny. It's always a charm to set the A-boards up in the rain and then better yet, dry them off before loading them back in your real estate mobile. I arrived at the Hilson's abode at 12:45. I hate to arrive at an open house too early and chase people out of their house on a Sunday. I noted that the yard sign had been installed in the front lawn (another agent expense) and was a bit peeved to note that Share's name rider was above mine and the sign had been placed such that my name was mostly concealed by a boxwood shrub. I'm sure Share had nothing to do with the sign installation and my name being obscured. About as sure as I know that Clyde isn't in the back yard scheming new ways to catch the squirrels that live in the big oak tree.

I parked my car in front of one of the five garage doors, grabbed my brief case, and headed to the front door. Marc was at the door, polishing the brass knocker, "Hello Alex. Good to see you are here on time and ready to sell this place. I haven't seen Mary Beth's agent yet." No surprise there. Marc then showed me how he had programmed the house stereo speaker system. I had him switch the music selection from Kenny G to classical and asked him to turn the volume down. No sense in the house sounding like a dentist's office and two hours of Kenny G would definitely put me over the edge. I would be hallucinating drill noises and dental assistants in masks. I noted that Share installed a self promotion booth of sorts on the "entry tableau." She had placed a large color photo of herself along with her business cards and personal brochures on the main entry table. There was a color flyer for the property, which I helped create. However, Share made a font size change since I had last seen it. Now her name and number appeared three font sizes larger than mine.

Marc showed me how the electric pool cover worked and generally babbled on about the house like an overprotective mother. I gently guided him to the door and told him to enjoy his afternoon. His house was in great shape and I would make sure it was still standing when he returned at 3:00. True to form, right at 1:00, the first of the curious neighbors arrived. All with the pretext that they might know someone who is just perfect for the house, which technically could be true but more than likely they were there to snoop.

Around 1:30 Wanda showed up. She had a couple of coffees and a box of donuts along with her mortgage flyers for the property. Wanda is old school when it comes to open houses. She loves doing them and always shows up with something to keep us awake. By law she can't be there unless she has her own brochures and a flyer specifically detailing mortgage options for the property. "Oh here baby, take these donuts for me. Sorry I'm late, but Reverend Stiles got himself in a knot with his sermon this morning. And that damn choir of his, didn't stop the halleluiah's until nearly 12:30. I thought I was gonna leave a puddle on the pew if they didn't finish up and let me get to the ladies! It was a good one though. I got next to that new couple that moved here from Cleveland and gave them my card. You know I'll send them along to you, Alex, if I can get their fat black butts in my office and pre-approved. Don't know what the hell they are waiting for. Rates ain't gonna do no special dance just 'cause they from Cleveland. I told them they best just get on it and buy. Quit paying some landlord their nut, unless of course I'm the landlord!" Wanda thrust the box of donuts at me while pulling off her large salmon colored church hat. All while balancing the coffee tray and mortgage flyers, and sniffing loudly. I took the donut box and led the way to the kitchen, "Why are you sniffing Wanda? Do you have a cold or allergies?"

"I'm sniffing to see if that smelly bitch is here. She don't have her fake boobs here yet does she? Thought she was supposed to hold the open house too? Ain't that what the owners said when they co-listed the place? They want the both of you here for open houses?"

"You are correct, but so far no Stinky." I then proceeded to give Wanda a tour of the house and when we reached the master suite Wanda let loose.

"Alex, what the hell do two people, or now one since she's not living here, do in a bathroom that is big enough for a family to live in? Hell, they got stuff in here I don't even know what part of your body you supposed to clean with it."

"You are preaching to the choir on that one with me Wanda. Anyway, I suppose some people must enjoy these bathrooms, because they keep building them." We went back down stairs, drank our coffee and greeted another gaggle of neighbors who oooh'd and ahh'd and smirked their way through the house.

At 2:00, Stinky arrived. Today's ensemble consisted of acid green spike bitch boots and matching slacks. A shiny gold suit coat, with a fake magenta flower pinned on the coat's lapel, accented her magenta top with its low scooped neck, designed to show off her inflatable friends. Today in her freckled tit valley, Share sported a chunky turquoise and acid green necklace. It was odd; she wore only one bracelet; a large charm bracelet, which consisted of a gold cross and a gold dollar symbol. Her fingers however made up for her lack of bracelets. Today on Share's fingers, it was the cable TV ring collection gone wild. There was a large acid green ring to match her clothes (I'll give Stinky credit when it comes to matching her clothes and add-on items), a huge turquoise number, and assorted cubic zirconium specials. All displayed above her gleaming magenta stick-on talons. The woman must have a third world manicure slave, chained in her bathroom who every night color coordinates her nail color with her carefully planned wardrobe.

"Well Alex, I see you have things set up here. I just got finished with a client so of course I couldn't be here at 1:00. Oh, and I see you brought your *little* mortgage person with you today. How old fashioned of you. I didn't know *successful* mortgage people still did open houses anymore. Business must be slow for you Wendy, so you are more than welcome to attend my listing's open house. My, and you brought donuts to keep yourself fortified! Did you bring a ham to eat for a late lunch as well Wendy?"

Wanda's eyes bugged out and she almost choked on the chocolate glazed donut she was eating. Before she could jump into the fray with Stinky, I intercepted. "Nice to see you Share. The open house started at 1:00. I got here at 12:45 and Marc showed me around. Wanda will be sitting with us for the open house today. She was nice enough to make some mortgage flyers and bring donuts."

"Yes, that's good you got here at 1:00 Alex. As I said, I was with a client so I couldn't be here."

"Client my ass…" Wanda muttered through a mouth full of donut.

"What? You say something sweetie? I know it must be hard for you to talk with all those donuts. Well Wendy, don't let me interrupt you. It looks like you still have half a box left to finish."

Before Wanda could respond I interjected, "Oh, Wanda was just going to give herself a tour of the house, weren't you Wanda?

80

While she does that we can discuss where you put your A-boards and why the yard sign is installed next to the boxwood shrub so that my name rider doesn't show."

"I saw all your A-boards out Alex, so I just put one of mine down by the drive's entry. No sense in putting out too many A-boards. I don't know what you mean about the yard sign, is there a problem?"

"Yes Share, let's go outside and I'll show you. Wanda can look around and keep her eye on things if anyone pops in."

Once outside, I showed Stinky the yard sign and she feigned surprise as to how the sign installation company could have possibly installed it such that my name was hidden. Before she could continue, *Yellow Rose of Texas* began to chirp from her cell phone. She picked up, and schmoozed away, clicked off, and then informed me, "Gee, that was another client Alex. I hate to do this but I'm going to have to rush off and show them that other listing here in the Beaumont on Fordham Drive. I'll be back as soon as I can. I just hate to leave you here to do the open house solo, but business calls!" She then hopped in her Darth Vader SUV and took off. Stinky has a lot of nerve and I didn't believe she had a client to show a house to. Even if she did, she should have shown them after the open house. Anyway, at least with her gone I wouldn't have to worry about Wanda beating her to death.

I turned to walk up the drive and spied Stinky's one A-board. She had placed it right next to the drive's entry and it sported a big color photo of her. She had also doctored it up and attached a rider that read, "Another Exclusive Share Listing!" I took the rider off, while muttering at her gleaming mug shot. Those kind of riders are supposedly against Winterfrost's A-board policy. However, if you are a big agent like Stinky, Winterfrost pretty much rolls over and plays your bitch any way you like it. While I was putting Stinky's rider in my car's trunk, a middle aged couple pulled up in the drive in a white sedan to see the house. They weren't neighbors. As we walked up to the front door, out popped Wanda. She smiled at the people and then said to me in a low voice, "I found something you should see in there Alex." Then she shook hands with the couple, told them she could answer any mortgage questions they may have. I went through the house with the couple, trying to keep a respectful distance and not do the usual agent rant, "And this is the master bath, and this is the laundry room"—no shit they have eyes and can hopefully see too.

Downstairs Wanda was standing by the front door. We both politely waved goodbye to the couple while I muttered, "Don't get too excited, they are wish-they-lived-here's and there's no chance they are going to purchase anything in Clinton. They are from Houston and are here visiting their sick aunt. They go back home on Tuesday."

Wanda retorted while smiling big and waving, "Who cares. When you see the surprise I found, you gonna get just the laugh you need!"

The surprise, Wanda was so excited about, was upstairs in one of the master bedroom closets. One of Mary Beth's closets I would guess, since it held a few articles of women's clothing. In the back of this walk-in closet, Wanda discovered a hidden door in the paneling which opened by tapping it, thus releasing the magnetic latch that kept it closed. Wanda has a special sense for snooping and discovering people's quirks. Each open house I've done with her, she has always

82

found something odd. I think it is her version of Nancy Drew combined with show and tell. Someday, we will have to discuss her childhood and see what events led to her snooping addiction. Inside the panel were a few built-in shelves. The top three were empty, but on the floor was a cardboard box. It held a flogger, like Fred's, and what appeared to be a whip, a leather face mask thing, and a few other assorted S and M accessory items.

"Guess we know what gets the freak on round this house, now don't we, Alex? I suppose the spanking got old, 'cause they sure 'nuff have split up." Wanda pulled the bull whip thing out of the box while smiling, "Damn, I could sure go upside that smelly Share's white ass with this here switch. I'd knock that glued-on smile off her nasty little face, show her just who WENDY really is! Here hold this thing and give it whirl Alex. It might be good for you. Give you some new ideas. Get you out there lookin' for some new Fudge Royal. Or no, maybe with this here added, we can start calling you Rocky Road!"

Wanda thrust the whip into my hand. I have to say, I thought it was stupid but the idea of chasing Share with it made me grin. "Go on," Wanda interrupted, "give it a crack Alex. Damn, you think maybe we should hook this Mary Beth woman up with Fred? Wonder if she used to chase her husband around this big ass master suite with this thing? This whip would leave your behind wailing something fierce! You be standin' up all day, after mama done crack yo butt with this here. Makes my mama's switch look like a walk in the park! This is some crazy shit Alex. No offense, but what the hell is it with all these white folks and money? Got a whole pile of green to go and lie in and spend and they wanna go spank each others' butts and run around with leather feather dusters and what not, makes no sense to me."

I tuned Wanda out and was focused on the whip's handle. On the very tip of the handle was a small imprint. Defying all aging experts, I still have twenty-twenty vision and I don't have to hold items three feet away from my face in order to read them. Imprinted on the whip's handle it read, *"Mistress Xtc."* I didn't know whether to laugh, run, call Detective Davies, or continue to fantasize about chasing Stinky around the house with the whip.

15

What do you do when you discover something illegally and feel in good conscious that you have to let someone know about it? Since Wanda found the whip by snooping (thus illegally) there was no way we could haul it out and call the cops or take it with us. Wanda decided she would take pictures of the assorted "merchandise" and its location with her cell phone. Then we would meet with Detective Davies and let him know about this off the record. She clicked some shots and we carefully put everything back where it belonged. I wanted to ponder it all, but Wanda had me call Detective Davies immediately and I left him a voice mail asking if we could meet with him.

Marc returned to the house at 3:00 and I gave him a report of who had been through. Wanda let him know Stinky that had not actively been there for the open house. We chit-chatted, smiled, waved, and rolled out of the Beaumont. Wanda wanted to check on things at Salon Wanda, as late Sunday afternoon is one of the busiest times at the shop. Also, she wanted to show off her new hair thing. I tailed her custom green, late 1980s, Lincoln Towncar to the shop. Wanda loves her car and refuses to even consider looking at any new cars. She could probably pay cash for just about any car she wanted, but her "green baby" is it. She even had the engine replaced once. Salon Wanda is loctated in a wooden 1930s house, converted to commercial use probably in the 1950s. Long ago, the front yard turned into a gravel parking lot and today it was full. So, Wanda and I parked out on the street. Before Wanda acquired the building, it had been Ace's Pawn Shop and many other small business incarnations prior to

that. Wanda fixed it up; there were six chairs as they say in her biz and
they were always booked. You can always smell the peroxide, relaxer,
and all the other assorted deadly hair chemicals, when you step onto
the somewhat tilted front porch. Wanda had the building painted a
lively lime green with a fuchsia front door. Supposedly, she is having
one of Lexi's neon artist friends make a big sign to go out by the street.
But that project has been delayed, because Wanda and Miz Liz can not
come to an agreement as to what exactly the neon sign's image should
be. Inside, the chemical odors were stronger. It was a beehive of
activity, with six stylists and at least ten customers all in various stages
of some kind of hair production. The various sounds of blow dryers,
water running, a Diana Ross CD playing, and a whole lot of gossiping,
laughing, and bickering going down. A typical day at Salon Wanda.
Wanda said some hello's to various customers, walked over to the
stereo, and promptly hit the eject button. "Damn Miz Liz. If I have to
come in this here place and hear that woman singing one more of her
tunes, you and me is gonna go at it! Aint it enough that you *are* Miss
Ross most evenings? Don't give me no shit about how you just
learning more lyrics. You could out Ross the Boss any day, when it
comes to remembering the lyrics to all her songs. Let's get some slow
groove going on here for the ladies, huh?" With that, Wanda smiled
mischievously as she popped in a Barry White CD. Sure as shit, most
of the "mature" women started to ooohh and ahh, as Barry's deep
voice blended in with the dryers and assorted noises. Miz Liz shot
Wanda a drop dead look, but she was too engrossed with the pile of
hair she was weaving into a young woman's head to get into it with

86

Wanda. When Wanda and Miz Liz go at it, it is lethal. So lethal, customers will literally head out to the front porch and back courtyard area in their plastic capes, with assorted hair glop on, to wait out the fracas. Miz Liz was a quasi Mister Liz today. With her natural, closely cropped, afro died a sun gold color, no makeup and earrings, or eye brows for that matter. However, the fire engine red, stick-on finger nails did perhaps give away that something was afoot in the traditional gender role department. She grunted in Wanda's direction, gave me a warm smile and said, "My, look what Miss Wanda brought to us today ladies! I've been trying to get my hands on that man's head of hair for years now. Think what all I could do with that thick brown hair. When you gonna let me at it Alex?"

I gave my standard sheepish smile and followed Wanda to the back. Wanda said she wanted to stop by the salon to show me her new hair piece, but I knew that was a pretext. What Wanda really wanted to do was check out the till and take a look at the day's receipts thus far. Sunday afternoon is one of the salon's busiest days. I don't think there has been a day yet that Wanda has missed stopping by to check the salon's daily tally. By Wanda's smile, I could deduce a lot of hair do-ing had gone on that day. She popped the fridge open, took out two wine coolers (which I hate) and led us out to the rear courtyard. When she first bought the building, the courtyard contained a huge pile of rotting tires and assorted rusting metal (a goldmine in Lexi's world). Wanda had turned it into a proper courtyard complete with ivy trellis, assorted flowering plants, and a large custom made fountain in the corner. There were nice patio chairs and benches to finish it off. The fountain was Salon Wanda's moniker. She had Lexi alter a life size, fiberglass copy of Michelangelo's *David* into a fountain. However, Wanda (via Lexi) had David's penis altered to the size of a horse's penis. From that porn-star sized organ, spewed enough water to put out a house fire. The fountain had been the talk of Clinton when it was first installed and some people actually stopped by the Salon just to see it. There were two women sitting out in the courtyard reading magazines. One presumably waiting for her appointment, the other had foil and glop in her hair. Wanda plopped into a chair, kicked off her salmon colored church dress shoes, and popped open her wine cooler. "So Alex, we got Mary Beth pegged as the likely Mistress Xtc., what do you think this Davies cop is going to do with that?"

I shook my head, gagging as I sipped at the sickeningly sweet wine cooler. "I'm not sure what he'll do with it Wanda. We didn't find it in a legal way and who is to say it means anything. Maybe Mary Beth fancies S and M and for some strange reason, her set of handcuffs ended up under her mother's washing machine. It could be a coincidence and nothing more."

"Yep, it sure could be but it also sounds very strange to me. I'm not sure Detective Davies is gonna be able to do anything with it."

My cell phone rang and I picked up. Speak of the devil, it was Detective Davies returning my call. I told him Wanda and I had found something which might have some bearing on the handcuffs found in Catherine Tilberts' laundry room. He asked where we were. When I mentioned Salon Wanda, he said he didn't need the address, "It's that bright green building on Fulton, the one with the big dick water fountain out back, right? I can be there in about ten minutes. Okay to stop by and chat with you guys?"

Detective Davies' blunt take on the water fountain caught me a bit off guard and I struggled not to choke on the wine, "Ahh, yes that's the building and we'll be here." Once Wanda learned he was coming over, she hopped up and dashed inside to put on her new Beyonce hair thing. Nothing like a man with a badge or uniform to get Wanda purring.

When Detective Davies arrived, Wanda met him at the door and brought him out back to the courtyard. Wanda's new wig thing was blonde and while I couldn't quite understand why she wanted to change her hair, the blonde did look nice on her. Wanda was on high purr, while seating Detective Davies in a cushioned patio chair, offering him a Coke or a wine cooler. "No ma'am, I can't drink while on duty but thank you anyway. A Coke might be nice though." Wanda smiled big and wide and took off to get him a Coke. Detective Davies smiled at me, looked at the fountain and said, "Some fountain, huh? I suppose she had it made special for the Salon ladies. Sound of that flow is enough to put any man with prostate troubles or dick envy to shame. So what have you two discovered that might pertain to the Tilberts' death?"

I proceeded to fill him in on exactly what we found and how we found it. Wanda returned and interjected, "Here's your Coke honey, with extra ice. I wouldn't want you to get over-heated or nothing." He thanked her and asked some questions about the door panel, how we discovered it. Wanda explained she had an unusual predisposition for snooping and then she showed him the pictures she had taken on her cell phone.

Detective Davies finished his Coke and smiled, "Well you two are a couple of junior detectives in training. But what you found is not exactly enough to open an investigation on Mrs. Tilberts' death. We can infer that the handcuffs and items you discovered belong to Mrs. Tilberts' daughter, Mary Beth, but that in itself is not enough to open an investigation. As you know, her death was ruled accidental. Now off the record, I think there may be more to this but until we have the proverbial smoking gun, we will have to sit back and keep our eyes and ears open. I certainly want to hear from you two if you find out anything else. I will do some unofficial questioning and see if I get any news. Could all be perfectly innocent, but asking around shouldn't hurt. Naturally, as an officer of the law, I do have to tell you to watch your snooping Wanda. But as Pete Davies, off-duty guy, I want to commend you two on being so alert." We all made small talk and then Detective Davies hit the road.

Wanda walked him out and came back all aflutter, "Alex, you didn't tell me about that man. Where are your eyes? They don't make them no hotter than that! He gave us his first name too, did you notice that Alex? He sure smiled a lot and I know I saw me some big man nipples underneath that uniform shirt."

"Oh, Wanda please. Okay, so we know we can't officially do anything with this information and Officer—Pete—wants us to stay alert and find out more if we can." I filled her in on what Fred told me the other day regarding the handcuffs and we agreed that perhaps we

90

should try and have a little chat with Fred and see if he would tell us what he knew.

16

Tracking down Fred Carlton turned out to be a snap. Fred called me early the next day and said he wanted to put in an offer on the 1948 Cape Cod. If all went well, Dexter Avenue was going to have its very own official certified S&M and bondage instructor. Oh, the possibilities at the Tupperware parties could get very interesting. I pulled comparison sales data for the area and typed up the purchase and sale agreement. Nothing pisses me off more, than an agent who hand writes their purchase and sale forms. There is no excuse for that these days. All the forms are available online and there's a backspace button if you make a typo. A far cry from the days when they used carbon copies and hand wrote the offers, which many idiot agents still do even today. Talk about sloppy. Turns out Wanda wanted to review some loan options with Fred so I picked her up on my way over to Fred's flat. "I don't want to bring up the Mistress Xtc. and whip thing Wanda, until we get Fred through the paper work. I want to make sure he is focused on his offer. If the opportunity arises, we can ask him more but if it doesn't, we need to stay focused on the task at hand, his offer."

"Agreed, and can you slow this car down a bit? I gotta get this lash back on and I don't want to poke my eye out." Wanda's eye lashes sometimes come unglued and it always creeps me out when she re-glues them. I keep envisioning her long nails stabbing her eye. Plus, glue, yes real horse by-product, voluntarily swabbed on your friggin' eye lid?

Fred met us at the door, his leather pants squeaking as he led us in to the "living room" area. Wanda gave me a sly smile, "My you get up pretty early to spank people, don't cha' Fred?"

"Now Wanda, I've told you before I don't just spank anyone. This morning I had an early training session with a client and I've got someone coming at noon. Lucky for you two, I did have time this morning to make some lemon wedge bars. Would you like coffee with them?"

I told Fred coffee would be great and gave Wanda the evil eye. Once Fred had his hostess spread set up and we were munching on his confections and slurping coffee, I spread out the paper work for his offer and led him through it page by page. While we were making our way through the pile of forms, Wanda got up and started perusing Fred's assorted torture devices or as he would call them, his training equipment. "Fred, who the hell puts this damn thing on? That's enough to mess up your hair for weeks. Not to mention you best make sure you ain't got no makeup on." Wanda said while holding up a leather ski mask item.

Fred replied, as he scribbled his signature on the last page of the purchase and sale agreement, "Well, Wanda typically male clients use those masks but yes, when women use them we do need to make sure all cosmetics have been removed first. Some use a hair net before putting on the mask."

"Humpf, ain't that something. You know Fred, Alex and me found one of these here bank robber hat things just yesterday. Belongs to some Mistress Xtc. You reckon she put that thing on, or is it probably used by her clients? Be awfully hard to look all womanly and mean in your leather do-dah's, without some make-up on. Might be the make-up they wear is a little Goth? Make her look all Morticia Addams and all. But still, a girl gotta have some goods on her face, 'specially if she is acting."

Fred handed me the final page and smiled, "Wanda she's not acting and I do know some mistresses who don't wear makeup and in fact their clients prefer it. There are a lot of varieties of apples, if you know what I mean."

I had to jump in now, "So Fred I've got your paper work covered here. The listing agent wants me to present at 1:00 pm and it looks like we are all set to go with this. Switching from our real estate business, we spoke the other day about the handcuffs at Catherine Tilberts' house with the *Mistress Xtc.* imprint on them. Wanda found some other Mistress Xtc. items yesterday. We are pretty sure they belong to Mary Beth Hilson. I know you have client confidentiality, but it just seems odd to me that Catherine's daughter would leave her special handcuffs in her mother's laundry room, under the washing machine. Call it intuition, but something just doesn't add up."

Fred's pants squeaked a bit, as he held out the plate of lemon bars to Wanda, who promptly took another one. Fred cleared his throat, "I admit it does seem an odd coincidence. As you know, I can't reveal if I have worked with someone or not. I can tell you that if I thought anyone's life was in danger, I would let you know. If you are really curious, you might want speak directly with this person you think is Mistress Xtc."

We thanked Fred and I assured him I would call him as soon as I knew if the seller would accept his offer. It was clear Fred was not going to budge and tell us what he knew about Mistress Xtc. Talking to Mary Beth would get us nowhere. So, we decided to let it be for now. I dropped Wanda off at her office and went through the rest of my day. There were a few calls from agents about Catherine's house and one who promised to show it, a prospective buyer calling to make an appointment, and that was it for real estate. Fred's offer was accepted and he was clearly excited. We arranged to have his inspection done the next day. Always better to get the inspection done as soon as possible, keeps those hummingbirds of doubt and worry from completely ruling your brain.

I arrived home around 7:00 p.m. and it was still light outside, thanks to the recent time change. I heard Clyde barking in the back yard as I pulled in my small sliver of a drive/parking space. When Clyde barks, something is definitely wrong. Thankfully he's never been a dog to just bark at the drop of a pine cone or to get attention. I bolted from the car and let myself in the back yard through the gate. Clyde came running up to me, looking happy and then growling. This was very unusual behavior for my canine trickster. I asked him what was wrong but he wasn't ready to speak in English. I looked around the yard, everything seemed in place. I didn't see the squirrels hanging out by the big oak tree in back. They get Clyde riled up but he rarely barks at them. He usually just chases them and tries to climb up the tree after them. I had given up on what triggered Clyde's barking and was about to enter the house, via the french doors, when I spied a yellow, plastic, dog bowl next to the living/kitchen outside area. I feed

Clyde indoors and his bowls are stainless steel. When I went over to the bowl, Clyde immediately ran up to me and bumped my legs. His way of letting me know, "Now you got it, you human idiot—the odd bowl, stupid!" Inside the bowl, were broken pieces of glass and a small notebook piece of paper with letters cut out and glued. The charming love letter read, "Next time with food for Fido."

I felt an icy trickle run down my spine. Someone had been here. Someone had left a bowl of glass to scare me, by threatening Clyde. They had walked through my back yard gate and left a calling card. I immediately went to my car, got out my brief case, pulled out Detective Davies' card and dialed.

17

Detective Davies came by and assessed the situation. He spoke with the neighbors on my dead end street. No one had seen anything out of the ordinary. He quizzed me about Clyde and asked if he bothered my neighbors. That was a negative and I explained the cult of Clyde. He then asked if I had any enemies, any business deals that went sour, nothing there. He asked if I had any ex-lovers who wanted to scare me, or if I was having an affair, nada. With my boring life, who would threaten my dog? I concluded it had to be Mary Beth or Mary Beth related, who else? "What about Mary Beth Hilson? She threw the iron door stop through my car window, she hates me. I think the handcuffs in her mother's laundry room belong to her. What were they doing in there? Nothing adds up. I believe Mary Beth is trying to keep me out of things, because something is going on that she doesn't want revealed."

Detective Davies sighed and said, "I can see how you would reach that conclusion about Mrs. Hilson. However, we can't prove that she hurled the iron door stop through your car window. We can suspect that she did and connect dots. For now, legally I have nothing to go on. I'm going to take the bowl and note and keep it in case we need it for evidence in the future. I want you to stay alert. Put a lock on that back gate. Maybe keep your dog in while you are away and call me if anything suspicious or out of the ordinary occurs."

That was it for now. I brought Clyde inside, made a quick stir fry dinner, checked the locks on the doors and settled in. The rest of the night, the slightest sound and I was wide awake looking around.

97

Clyde slept peacefully however. Dogs tend to know when something is worth waking up for or not. The next day was overcast. Clyde becomes a hermit when it is overcast. So it was easy to take Clyde for his walk and then leave him in the house for the day. He hopped right back up on the bed, did his walk around in a circle thing, and then plopped down. He sighed and looked up at me as if to say, "Anything you need here? I'm kind of busy trying to take a nap. Don't you have human stuff to go and do?"

I hit the road. I had a showing for the pregnant couple, some paper work to file, and I wanted to check on the Tilberts' listing to make sure the flyers were plentiful and no bimbo agents had left doors unlocked, windows open, or god only knows what else. One of the worst bimbo agent stories I have heard recently, involved an owner occupied house. The buyers' agent allowed her clients to literally re-arrange the furniture in the living room while showing them the house. Not just a moving a chair (not that that would be acceptable) but moving the rug, all the big pieces of furniture, lamps, etc.... They then left it re-arranged. The owners were less than thrilled and the listing agent was ballistic. The wonders of real estate never cease.

While out and about, I had a call from Wanda. She was meeting with Fred that afternoon to lock in his loan. I assured her that his deal was signed around. She invited (ordered) me to come to her house for dinner and bring a copy of Fred's signed around deal with me, so she could file it at her office and get to work on securing his loan. I had called her last night and filled her in on the bowl of glass and she was pissed. "Make sure you bring Clyde with you too. I'm gonna personally bust the ass of the person that put that glass out for him. I'm telling you, Detective Davies or not, ain't nothing right about this and if he don't figure it out we are going to. I got a client waiting for me, I'll see you and Clyde around 7:00 and Lexi is coming too. I told her she best bring me that hair extension back that I left over there. You don't know anything about that, do you Alex?" Wanda's hair thing-- the "bird's nest" on Lexi's latest creation. "Why no Wanda, I don't know anything about your hair. See you tonight." A little white lie for self preservation.

I stopped by the Winterfrost office at 2:30 and was happily breezing through the office, when the vapor cloud hit me and then Stinky swooped in. "Well Alex, just getting started on your little day in real estate? I'm taking clients by Mary Beth's house this evening. I just know they are going to love the house. I'll let you know when I've sold it." Stinky said this with her usual smirk. Today, her smirk was glittery maroon colored and she was fiddling with a chunky piece of citrine which was hanging on a thick gold rope chain in her tit valley. Her orange hued hair was even spikier today and blended in nicely with her fresh spray-on "tan." Her ensemble was a tad blah by Stinky standards. She wore a taupe and citrine striped pant suit with the suit top cut low to accentuate her inflatable friends, naturally.

"That's nice Share. I wish you luck with your clients tonight. Let me know how it goes."

"So Alex, have you spoken with Marc Hilson? Mary Beth seems highly annoyed and I'm wondering if they had some kind of run-in at the open house."

"No, I let Marc know how the open house went and he was pleased. I haven't heard from him since then. Did Mary Beth let you know why she might be annoyed or give any hints?"

Stinky gave a dramatic sigh and replied, "Well, you are too new to know how this works I suppose. Anyway, when you have been in the business as long as I have Alex, and you are as spiritually connected as I am, you develop your sixth sense. My sixth sense is always accurate. I can tell you that Mary Beth didn't say what was bothering her, but my sense tells me that she and Marc had some kind of tiff about the open house. Anyhow, it won't matter much longer, because I'm going to sell their house tonight. By the way Alex, you don't know where my custom A-board is from the open house, do you?" Stinky insinuated in this last query that I had taken her A-board.

"No Share, I don't know where you A-board is. You only put out one. I assumed you picked it up, because I don't recall seeing your A-board by the driveway when I left. I did remove your name rider from the top of it. As you know, that is against Winterfrost policy. I put that on your desk."

"Yes, I saw that. I've always place those riders on my A-boards and never had any flack. But I guess some of you new people are sticklers for Winterfrost policy. Oh well, I can be big about these things. I know what it is like to start out and live on salads while big agents like me have all the steaks. Well, if you find my A-board please drop that on by desk too. Oh, I've gotta run! I'm meeting with a developer for lunch as Basco's to discuss handling his new project and I was supposed to be there ten minutes ago."

With that she bitch booted her way out the back door. I was fuming. Calling me a new agent, insinuating that I took her ugly A-board. Some day Stinky, some day! Of course my reaction is exactly what a calculating bitch like Stinky lives for. If she makes me angry, then I make her happy. Perverse but true.

18

Nothing was amiss at the Tilberts' listing. The flyers were plentiful and the house looked like a show pony. I took the pregnant couple through a newly listed 1960s split level and they went home to sleep on it. I dashed by Sasser's Bakery and got a chocolate cake to take to Wanda's and apologized to Daynia for not bringing Clyde with me. I promised her I would give Clyde the treat she wrapped up for him. Talk about spoiled. I pulled in my parking spot, checked around the yard, and luckily there were no bowls of glass or other fun gift items left today. Clyde was doing circus dog leaps, showing me how much he missed me and how much he needed to water the back oak tree. I quickly flipped through the mail. Nothing of great importance. Just another solicitation from the cable TV company trying to get me to subscribe to the pleasures of their mind numbing crap, available on over two hundred channels. Talk about a racket. I have only heard horrible things from my clients about the cable TV company, their lack of service and their unsavory billing practices. With their local market monopoly, the cable TV company doesn't have to provide customer service or even pretend to care. They've got the number one mind numbing drug of choice in America. The subscribers may complain, but they consent and most important they pay. I made sure my little ranch was all locked up. Lights left on, radio turned on, to make it sound like someone was home, all the anti-prowler touches. Off Clyde and I went to Wanda's.

Wanda lives about ten blocks away from her salon in a neighborhood called Highmont. Highmont has a lot of 1880s to 1930s era clapboards and bungalow style houses. For a brief spell, in the early 1900s, Highmont was Clinton's new elite neighborhood. It sits between the interstate and downtown and is situated on a steep hill overlooking the downtown, hence the name. Views from certain parts of Highmont are of the downtown area and the sound. Highmont has experienced the ups and downs of Clinton's many economic boom-bust cycles. A large black population lives in Highmont, but it was ethnically diverse from the start. In the 1960s and 1970s, it was Clinton's version of Haight-Ashbury. Today there are still very brightly painted houses and quite a number of communal households still functioning. Highmont has an insider's feel and a respect for diversity and artistic expression flourish. Highmont High School is the local alternative arts school and occasionally, Lexi lectures there to sculpture students. Some people are afraid of Highmont (color and creative expression can be such a heart stopper) and so the house values are some what lower than other areas in Clinton. Very ironic, considering the housing stock is generally more historic and often of a better quality than other more expensive neighborhoods. Wanda's house is a late 1920s, turquoise painted, three bedroom, stucco, bungalow. It sits up off the street, has two eyelet windows up top, a small grass patch front yard and a mid size back yard encased by ten foot high Camellia bushes. From the west side of her house, you can see downtown and slices of the water below.

Once I turned onto Wanda's street, Clyde's tail began to thump with ever increasing enthusiasm. He knew where we were going and he loves visiting Wanda. I parked the car on the street and was unlocking Clyde's doggy seatbelt when Wanda appeared through her

Camellia hedge. She was in one of her at home, lounge-wear outfits. A sweeping hot pink and orange psychedelic swirl muumuu style dress or house dress as she refers to them when she is feeling old fashioned and proper. Complete with matching head wrap and her bare feet. "Baby, how are you doing? I haven't seen my precious sweet pea in too damn long! Alex, you don't bring him over her near often enough. Hurry up and get him out of that thing! Can't you see he is excited to see his mama?" Finally, the doggy seatbelt released and Clyde flew out of the car in a single, leaping motion. Up onto Wanda he went. Front legs extending straight out, paws resting on her cleavage, stubby tail moving like helicopter blades on full steam. Now the mutual slurping and ooh-hing and aah-hing would begin. Frankly, it always grosses me out. The fact she encourages Clyde to prop himself up on her, really plays on my last nerve. Wanda loves to take his paws and dance with him and tonight would surely involve a Clyde and Wanda living room tango show or two. She claims he knows music and that he prefers to dance to tango or salsa style music. I say Wanda needs to meet a traditional style, Latino man and go on a proper date.

Wanda was in the midst of her Clyde greeting ritual, when Miss Lyla from down the street chimed in, "Honey, you gonna have to get a room, you keep that up with that dog! How you been Alex? Ain't seen you round here in forever. You still sellin' them houses?" Miss Lyla is one of Wanda's neighbors and she has lived in the Highmont her whole life. In fact, I don't think she has ever left the neighborhood once, literally. I asked her about it one time and she said to me, "What I need to go down from the Highmont for? Ain't nothing down there that I cain't see from up here, baby." She is somewhere into her mid eighties or maybe older. Wanda looked up, "Oh, hey lady! Where you be headed this time of night, girl? Don't you know only the hoochie mamas come out this time of night? Is you turning hoochie mama on me Miss Lyla?" That started a loud round of cackling laughter from Miss Lyla, Wanda, and other assorted neighbors out on the street.

"No baby, no hoochie mama left in me! I'm on my way up to the church, part of my bargain with the devil and lord. See I'm a going up to his house to worship, but when that get through, you know I'm a gonna tear through that after service buffet and eat my fill. Want me to brang you some of them wings that Loretta Thompson makes?"

"OHHH, baby, you do that for me? Lord that enough to make me go to church. Hell yeah, Miss Lyla bring me some of them wings. We eat 'em for breakfast at yo place, round 7:00 tomorrow?"

"Okay then baby, see ya in the mornin'. Alex don't let her get all jiggy with that dog —ain't right what she do with him, you know that's true! Dancing with him like he some man! Humphhh! Good thang she ain't never had no kids, got enough bad ass brats out here as it is."

19

Wanda led Clyde and me up the cement steps to her front door. Currently her front door is painted a bright lemon yellow. Last time I visited, the door was lime green. On average, Wanda's changes her front door color at least a couple of times a year. The exterior has been turquoise for many years now, but Wanda has been threatening to have it painted hot pink for some time. Even for the Highmont, Wanda's color choices are a bit bright but better that than endless beige and brown. "Like my new door color Alex? I was gettin' tired of the green, it's getting on into spring, time to liven it up, make it say somebody *lives* here! Let's let Clyde out in the back yard, he gotta sniff all his places and make sure they still his. Lexi should be here by now but you know 'Lexi Time.' You tell her 7:30 and she shows at 8:00." Naturally Wanda forgets "Wanda Time," which is always later than "Lexi Time" but who is keeping track? Odd thing about Wanda, if she's late then it is not an issue but show up late to her house or one of her events and she's counting every minute.

I handed Wanda the Sasser's box with the chocolate cake. "Thank you baby. We havin' an early spring fiesta here at House Wanda tonight. I already have two pitchers of Sangria in the fridge, take one out for me while I go hunt up my Sangria glasses. I think they in my mama's old breakfront." Wanda stepped out of the kitchen into her dining room. Wanda's house interior is mostly original but somewhere along the way someone opened it up. The kitchen, dining, and living rooms are defined by wide open arches. The arch between the dining and living area still has the original, old growth, wooden pocket doors which Wanda keeps intending to restore. Her dining room has nice arts and crafts style paneling, a box beam ceiling, and the original brass and milk glass globe chandelier. A large window seat looks out onto the side yard over the tops of the tall Camellia hedge which runs the perimeter of the property. This window seat provides a direct view of Clinton's downtown and the water below it. Wanda practically lives in her window seat. It is filled with custom pillows in various gem colored hues. Her kitchen has been redone but still has the original deep porcelain sink, next to which she installed an enormous Viking range last year. The expensive range is definitely put to good use in House Wanda. Unlike many of the listings I show, she actually uses her $10,000 range. Of course, Wanda didn't exactly pay retail for her chef's range. In fact, she barely paid anything, monetarily that is. She dated the appliance sales rep for Viking and he gave her a deep discount. He didn't last too long once she'd installed her new range. Some who are catty, would say nasty things about that. I say, it's Wanda's business and besides Wanda changes boy friends about as often as she changes hair and door colors.

We were pouring Sangria when Lexi arrived, letting Clyde back in as she burst through the front door. "I know I'm late but you two are just going to have to deal. Here Wanda, the happy hostess gift," she said while thrusting a bunch of tulips in Wanda's hand, "The real flowers haven't come up yet and these were all the yard had to offer, so I hope you like them. God, pour me one of those red drinks please! I've been dealing with the Clinton Arts Commission jackasses all afternoon. If I have to attend one more of their supervisory meetings regarding my installation piece on Jackson Street, well there's just not going to be a fucking installation!" Lexi plopped down on Wanda's chocolate brown, leather sofa, knocking over a bowl of corn chips in the process, which Clyde promptly began to lick but not actually eat. "Oh shit, sorry for the mess there. What a snotty dog Alex. Look, he licks the chips but won't eat them. More finicky than a cat if you ask me. Thank you for this dear." Lexi said, taking a glass of Sangria from Wanda, "Now what have you two been up to? Hopefully something more fun than tangling with pompous art commission pea brains, who think a major in art history at Vassar thirty years ago entitles them to rule your artistic sensibilities."

We proceeded to fill Lexi in on the bowl of glass, the Mistress Xtc. enigma, and life in general. We moved to the kitchen island and helped Wanda as she started deep frying some kind of Mexican burrito thing, a Wanda creation. "Alex, get out that other pitcher of Sangria I got ready in the fridge and pour up some more glasses. Lexi you get the sliverware on the table girl and I'm gonna have these ready for us. Put that bowl of Mexican rice on the table too, honey. Don't you worry precious Clyde, mama frying you up some gizzards and other non-white boy food for you to munch on, baby." The frenzy of serving was soon over and we were all munching away, Clyde included. It makes me a bit peeved, the way Wanda prepares a special plate for Clyde and then sets it on the floor right next to her chair. He gobbled it up, and then looked up at Wanda with his big, brown, pleading eyes. She popped bits of her chicken burrito thing in his mouth and he gave me sly, *look what I'm getting away with look.* Lexi continued to quiz us on the bowl of glass, the note, and the goods we found at Mary Beth's house.

"God, Nancy Drew and Sherlock are at it again. You know that bowl of glass? That sounds mob-like to me. What would make this Mary Beth woman be so afraid that she would start to threaten you?"

I swatted at Clyde, trying to get him away from the table. "For starters, Mary Beth Hilson is married to a big business leader, who tells me he wants to run for city council. He has great development plans for our humble downtown. He's not going to want everyone to know that he has a dominatrix wife known as Mistress Xtc. Even if they are divorcing, it would ruin him in a medium size city like Clinton. Plus, she is way into her whole silver spoon, social standing. If her little quirk gets out, then her Muffy-the-debutante image is ruined."

Lexi nodded in agreement, while taking another long draw on her Sangria but Wanda started shaking her head from side to side. "No babies. You two got it wrong. What I always say to do Alex? Follow the money, honey." She let out one of her loud laughs and quickly slipped another sliver of chicken in Clyde's gaping mouth. "Let's see here, what does Mary Beth stand to gain from all this here mess?"

I pondered a bit, "You are right Wanda, money is usually a part in misdeeds. I would venture to guess that Mary Beth has an inheritance coming from her mother's estate. She would be getting half of Marc's net worth from the years they were married, and that should be a chunk of change. Seems like she has lots of money coming in, not a lack of it." I pushed Clyde away from the table again, his nails making a swooshing sound on the hardwood floors. He promptly shot me a nasty look and went around next to Wanda on the other side of the table, where I could not reach him.

Wanda patted Clyde's shaggy head, "Yep. From what you say, it would appear she is fixing to get herself a whole heap of money. But just like her little spanky-spanky show, appearance and reality are sometimes two different things."

Lexi nodded, "That's for damn sure. You know, I think Mary Beth's brother owns the Wharf Rat. That's the skank bar I go to sometimes, when I'm shopping for new metal pieces for my creations. I have to get some new scrap metal for my summer projects. I'll make an appointment to meet with my metal boys this week and see what the street has to say about this Tilberts family. Maybe someone at the Wharf Rat knows about Mistress Xtc? Somebody is leaving you broken glass and love letters, Alex. We know they are playing for keeps." With that Wanda brought out the chocolate cake and we proceeded to gorge.

After cake, Wanda samba'd with Clyde to the Salsa music. Then she switched over to some old Parliament CD and proceeded to really get down with her shaggy dance partner. It was around midnight, and Lexi was mixing up a batch of some kind of drinks, using Wanda's new home shopping channel bartender-blender gadget. I spied a grossly familiar face near the front window in Wanda's living room . Off to the side of her chocolate sofa, tucked in the corner, next to the front window with its leaded panes, was Stinky's smiling mug shot. I nearly spilled my Sangria. What was Share's A-board doing in Wanda's living room?

110

Wanda began to cackle, "I wondered how long it would take you to discover that bitch's board. I managed to lift that at the open house. Ain't she something, over there in the corner? Make me wanna get some eggs and take her out in the back yard. What you say Clyde? You up for egging that smelly, white bitch's, face?" Next thing I knew, we were all in Wanda's back yard throwing eggs at Stinky's mug shot.

20

The next day was a blur. Three of my clients wanted to see houses right away. Another client kept calling me every hour, asking me the same questions about a condominium he was thinking about purchasing. This gem of a buyer is a fifty-five year old, with the emotional maturity and decision making skills of a special needs-emotionally disturbed seven year old. He was pissed at life. He felt that being fifty-five entitled him to at least a two bedroom, thousand square foot condo, with balcony and a swimming pool in the complex to boot. With his budget, the only thing he can afford is a three hundred square foot studio and he is damn lucky to find that. I suggested numerous times, that perhaps he would be better off continuing to rent but he wasn't having any of that. Life owed him and it was my fault or Wanda's fault, that he could not afford or find exactly what he wanted. In the most recent round of his neurotic questioning, I had pawned him off to Wanda, advising he speak with his lender about his spending limit. Wanda left me a message around noon, "That white dumb ass calls me one more time Alex, I'm gonna take a two by four upside his fat little head! By the way baby, Lexi says she gonna catch up with you later. She wants you to go to that skank bar with her. Lord, I gotta run. Miz Liz called me this morning to tell me that my statue done sprung a leak. The water ain't comin' out of his big dick no more. She say it coming out his ass! Lexi swear it ain't got nothing to do with her welding skills. But I'm telling you, this here is an aggravation, playing on my very last nerve today."

I took the pregnant couple out again and showed them another split level. Once more, they were going home to think. They were now pondering whether or not they should raise their soon to be hatched prodigy in a suburban split level or in a downtown condo. She had read some sociology study online that reported on the psycho sociological development of children raised in the suburbs versus children raised in the city. Now they were in a complete knot, as to whether their child would turn into some deranged, isolated, sociopath in the suburbs. Then they worried about the schooling options and the violence in the city. I say spit out the baby and buy what you like. The rest will take care of itself, if you are an attentive parent. They weren't interested in my take on child rearing, so off they went to torture themselves.

I did two more client tours and at 5:00 I checked my messages again. Lexi wanted me to meet her at 5:30 at the Wharf Rat. I managed to find the address in my city map book and took off. The Wharf Rat is in an area near the old port terminals. It is an industrial warehouse area focused solely on shipping freight. Since Clinton's ports declined in the 1970s, this area has gone steadily downhill. Many of the buildings are boarded over and or burned out. The Wharf Rat sits right on Dock Street. At its best, it was a longshoreman's hang out in the 1950s. Now it was a drunk's play house. Only the "W" in the old neon sign out front lit up and it flickered a frail red at that. Inside, the black cement floors were sticky with booze (I hope) and the air was thick with cigar and cigarette smoke. Clinton banned smoking in bars five years ago. I guess the Wharf Rat never got the notice. This is the kind of place the police would avoid and the mob reportedly controlled. A decaying juke box was haphazardly spewing out "I Walk the Line," two dilapidated pool tables sat underneath a thick blue haze of smoke. One was in use, the sound of pool balls languidly cracking. A gold speckled, Formica topped, bar ran along the back wall, with a cloudy wall length mirror behind it. Assorted, dusty liquor bottles ran alongside the dirty mirror. In the middle of the counter sat a beige, non-electric, key punch style cash register, probably fifty years or older. A salty looking guy somewhere over forty-five, with mullet style hair and a patch over one eye, was slowly pouring a shot of what appeared to be crème de menthe.

One woman, somewhere over sixty, sat perched at the bar. She had a box of Kent 100 cigarettes placed next to her empty shot glass and was tapping her slim gold lighter on the counter, waiting for salty-the-pirate bartender to hurry up and pour. She looked like a poor version of Judy Garland, circa her final years. Overdrawn ruby red lips, pancake makeup. She wore an aquamarine swirl patterned, pajama looking, pant suit. A few stools down from her sat a couple of real Harley biker types. These bikers were not to be confused with the pseudo Harley guys. The pseudo Harley boys are fat, white, boomers, who have worked as corporate tools all their lives and are now suddenly cool and born-to-be-wild on the weekends. Thanks to clever marketing (brain washing), they are ready to let it all hang out forty-five years too late. At the very end of the bar, sat a dark haired man in his fifties sitting straight up. His big ruby ring glimmered in the haze while he pawed through what appeared to be a sizable stack of cash. I spied Lexi in the corner, perched on a cracking, red vinyl, bar stool alongside

114

a high metal bar table. These wall stool-table sets had probably been very smart in 1948. They were rusty and gross now. Lexi held up her Budweiser bottle to guide me through the smoke. "You made it Alex, cheers! I was beginning to think you had gotten stuck with some god forsaken suburbanites, showing endless cul-de-sacs and other split level nightmares."

"Something like that Lexi. You are having a beer, unusual for you. Sorry to have kept you waiting."

Lexi held up the bottle to salty the bartender and gave a loud whistle, "I've just ordered you one of these. Trust me; you only want to drink something out of a bottle in this place. I doubt they ever wash the glasses. You are having a Budweiser, that's all they serve in a bottle." Salty gave a loud whistle back and Lexi nudged me, "That would be your beer, dear." I stepped over to the bar, my shoes making sticky ripping sounds with each step. I felt a bit uncomfortable in my corduroys, checked blazer shirt, and grey cashmere sweater. Real estate drag was not part of the Wharf Rat's dress code. However, as I walked back with my beer and the jukebox switched over to one of Patsy Cline's numerous wails, I realized no one even looked up at me. They were all lost in their own personal haze and could give a rat's ass (no pun intended) about my perky real estate agent attire. At least the Bud was cold. I hadn't had a Bud since high school when we would pay the local drunks to make a run for us at the 7/11. I took a pull on the Bud and considered sitting at the table's other bar stool, but it had what appeared to be a spring poking through its cracked, red vinyl, so I opted to stand.

"Welcome to the Wharf Rat Alex." Lexi said with an ironic smile, "Jesus, what a pig sty and I'm not even a neat nick person. So, you know this place is run by the mob? That guy at the end of the bar counting out his money is Tony. I kid you not, Tony is his name. He's pre-*Sopranos*. Anyway, Tony is the man I talk to when I need some major metal scraps for my pieces. We've already had a chat about what I'll need for this summer's projects and like a true gentleman, he'll deliver on time. He'll be over here in a bit to settle up the metal order. I was thinking you and I could hopefully get Tony to give us a little info about your situation."

I took another long draw from my Bud and Tony appeared at our bar table. "Hey lady, I got your order all set now. No worries Lexi, it'll all be prime steel, none of that Chinese shit. The cash is good. Youze a good woman. Me or Ricky gonna give youze a call when we got shipment."

Lexi smiled and sat up a straight, "Ohhh, thank you so much Tony. You are always such a pleasure and help. Why, I was telling my friend Alex here, I don't know what I would do without your help in procuring the steel for my works. You know, Tony, I invited you to my last public works dedication back in September. The mayor and all those public shits were there. Your company was sorely missed. Oh where are my manners, Alex Campbell this is Tony my steel man."

I shot Lexi a quick look. I was a bit astonished at how fast she could pour it on, she was building up Tony like there was a smoke blowing contest. I stuck out my hand, "Glad to meet you Tony. Lexi always raves about what a help you are to her and her art."

116

Tony beamed and rocked up on his heels a bit, while pumping my hand up and down with a crunching vise grip, "Oh this lady is real classy Alex. Any friend of hers, would be a real friend of mine. Ya' know this chick really knows how to make the goods? Youze seen her stuff and now all them big wigs are buying it. I'm telling you she's on the way up. Top floor all the way baby! Me and Ricky is gonna make sure she gets all the steel she needs to keep them pieces of art coming."

"Ohh, Tony you are too kind. Anyway, Tony, my friend Alex here, well he's a real estate agent here in Clinton, he sells the whole damn city. Anyway, he's got this client situation going on. I can't tell you all about it, but there is this kinky aspect. You know as in whips and chains, that sort of thing? Actually, in this case it's more handcuffs. Well specifically, it is Mistress Xtc. cuffs." Tony's eyes widened and he looked at me and then at Lexi and seemed intrigued.

"Oh no, don't get it wrong Tony. Alex, he's not into that kind of thing. Why my friend Wanda and I, we would be positively delirious if he were! You know he is just too damn young to be a celibate bisexual, don't you think so Tony?"

Tony gave me an appraising up and down look. I almost choked on my sip of Bud. "Anyhow Tony, it's a long real estate agent story but Alex stumbled across some handcuffs that belong to this Mistress Xtc. We are trying to figure out who they belong to so we can return them."

Tony nodded his head a couple of times, "I don't know Lexi this is a new one. I mean youze know, we boys might know a thing or two about well, let's say the street scene. We have some knowledge of the, shall we say, getting your needs met business. Youze know the

117

man who runs this place for us Lexi? Old money kind of guy. Let's just say this mistress youze talking about, well she might know the manager real well, as in brother and sister. Not somethings youze wanna go talking about, especially with your art buyers Lexi. Best to keep it all zipped." Tony was fingering a thick gold chain around his hairy neck, "Youze know, I would not worry about getting them cuffs back to the owner. I'm sure she's got a back-up pair. Best if youze and Lexi just forget about all this here. And youze one of them bisectional types, huh? Well youze know, I gotta brother that's a fairy. He lives in Miami, he'd think youze was hot. I can hook youze two up sometime, if youze are ever down that way."

I didn't know whether to laugh, cringe, or both. Tony gave each of us pats on the shoulders, "Youze guys are alright. Hey, I'll have your steel to youze real soon Lexi. If we need some land or buildings, maybe we will look youze up Alex. Better yet, maybe my brother will want to buy something here sometime. He's always talking about quitting Miami and moving back. Take it easy, youze two and just let the whole mistress and her cuffs slide. Youze two don't need none of that. Hey, youze guys follow me to the bar. I'll make sure Leo sets youze up real nice. Enjoy your night, know what I'm talking bout?"

With that Tony led us over to the bar and put us on stools next to the Judy Garland twin. He banged his hand on the counter to get Leo's (a.k.a. Salty's) attention, waved so long to us, walked down to the end of the bar, and began a meeting of sorts with the two Harley guys.

Leo plopped two more Buds in front of us and we started drinking free beers as Leslie Gore's "Judy's Turn to Cry" began wailing from the jukebox. Two sips into my beer I noticed the jukebox song was in surround sound. Seems the Judy Garland's twin knew all the words and wasn't afraid to belt them out. "Say, you two don't come here. What's brought you here this evening folks?"

Lexi gave a big smile, "Oh, we are here doing some business with Tony, same as everyone I suppose."

"Hahhaa! You got that one right sister. I suppose I'm the only regular here who doesn't deal with Tony. Yep, weren't for my tab, the Rat would go under. Sandy's the name and I've been coming here regular since, what ohh god, 1962 or was it '63? You know this song was a top hit back then and I can remember singing it right here at this very bar when it was first put in that jukebox. Yep, I've had my turn to cry many a times since those years." With that, Sandy held up her shot glass of green stuff and gave a cackle before downing it. She slammed it down on the counter and shouted, "Hey Leo, hit it son!" and popped another Kent 100 in between her red ringed lips.

Lexi introduced us and proceeded to quiz Sandy about her years at the Wharf Rat. Sandy began a long drawn out monologue about her years at the Rat, what she'd seen, how she'd worked at the Filbert's dime store until it went under, then she was a secretary, how the Wharf Rat used to be respectable, highly doubtful. "Yes sir, this new kid they got in charge here has just been running the place into the ground. You know he's one of them Bluff trust fund kids, daddy gave him everything and he just pissed it all away. Now he's one of Tony's front people. Owns the place on paper, but don't do nothing to keep it up and going. I hear he is in some serious debt, can't keep his gambling under control. Now he's Tony's stool pigeon. Owes Tony's guys a huge pack of green from all his bad gambling. Reminds me of my second husband, Rick. The man couldn't keep his hands off the damn dice and cards. Cost me my Thunderbird and the little house I'd busted my ass to save for. Damn pig that man was."

Lexi looked very interested and leaned in towards Sandy, "Oh I hear you on the ex's honey. Sounds like your second was as bad as my third! So who is this guy that's running the Wharf for Tony?"

"Your second, my third—no wait you had it the other way! Hahh—Leo give me another round or I'll have to flash you again!" Sandy went off into a hacking of smoker's cough induced by her deep laughter. "Oh yeah, the so called owner here is that Bluff family's boy—Tim, oh what's the name? Tim. . ."

"Tilberts?" I said abruptly.

"Yep. The very one. He don't come in here much. I suppose he's afraid Tony is going shake him till the change falls out of his pockets. Yes sir, he got himself a big gambling problem and now he's running this joint to cover for Tony. Nice pay back scheme for Tony I suppose, but you know this place used to be respectable—really. Not at all like it is today, but you know that's the way with everything, ain't it?"

Lexi and I gave each other the eye. Tim Tilberts owned the Wharf Rat and Tony just told us that the guy who owned the place was the brother of the Mistress Xtc. So Mary Beth did have her kinks and we'd confirmed it. Now what? And what did it mean that Tim was up

to his eyeballs in gambling debt and ran a skank bar for the mob as a
payback for his debt?

21

"**O**kay, I wanna know what the hell that Tilberts lady son be running that skank bar for?" Wanda asked while typing client financial information into her laptop. "Damn, you know these nails ain't meant for no key board. They need to make us a good computer key board that's got keys to handle a woman's nails. You know what I mean Alex? I bet I could even get my buddy Harlan to make us a prototype. Yep, get us Harlan to design us that special nail key board Alex then you could--"

I gave her my mock horror, rounded eyes look. In the past few years Wanda has come up with more "entrepreneurial" ideas to outlast both our lifetimes. Quite a few, she has tried out over the years but thus far, I've managed to avoid any of her brilliant schemes and just kept her focused, literally, on the numbers.

"Hummph, well okay Mr. Real-ahh-tor, but next time I hear you mouthing 'bout some lame-ass client of yours, don't be dialing me to complain. Damn nails. Let's just see you try and type on this here key board with these nails stuck on your fingers Mr. Alex. Then we see what you think." Wanda resumed her typing, while muttering to herself. It never occurred to her that those stick-on nails of hers were optional items? I never understood why she wears them, but as she so often likes to tell me, it's a "woman thang."

"Wanda, what do you think about Tim and his mob connection? It all seems very odd to me."

"Ohh, me too. But then again you rich white folk have always been odd in my book." Wanda chortled and patted Clyde's shaggy head. "Don't get all up on me. I know you ain't rich Alex, but you come from it and damn you sure *is* the whiter shade of pale that Procol Harum band sang about. No offense though. It's a whitey thang! Ain't right for me to say but hey, dye your hair jet black Alex and you got yourself an instant Goth-boy look going on, without no makeup!

Seriously, I think this whole Tilberts thing all smells like a big pile of rotten fish to me. Don't make no sense, that old lady laid up dead in her laundry room. Now one of her daughters is some kinky ass, spank-yo'-butt hooker. And her only son is upside down on his butt in debt, and runnin' some skank bar for the M-O-B? Shit, black folk know enough to stay away from them people Alex! Nope, it don't smell right to Miss Wanda, not one bit. What you say we call up that hunky Pete Davies and see what he says? Maybe it's his day off and he would come over here and he'd have on some them really short running shorts? Then we'd see what that package of his looks like in shorts and then---,"

"Shut up Wanda!" I said while covering my ears. "Not listening. Get your mind out of the trousers and help out here." Clyde again looked up at me, his tongue hanging out of his mouth, hoping I was going to give him some food.

"Damn, you don't let me have no fun Alex. What are you the imagination patrol? Did them born-again's hire you to police people like me? Then again, the shit them born-agains been caught with lately, hell they got more going on in the sheets than you or me combined. 'Course that ain't saying much, considering your end of the sheets. You know since you are not into this imagination stuff, why don't you get off your boney white butt and get me another one of these here slushy drinks? Only this time, bring the Bacardi to the table, you don't hardly put any in! Ain't that right Clyde? And while you up, feed this poor dog some food. I bet he ain't seen no food since early this morning, have you precious?" Clyde immediately got up, rested his shaggy head in Wanda's lap and glanced back at me with a smirk on his face.

I grabbed the cocktail glasses and went in through the rolled up glass garage door into my compact kitchen. I was dumping some ice and frozen strawberries in the blender, when there was an enormous crash in my living room area. Clyde came galloping into the house, with Wanda behind him, "What the hell is that sound---,"

Wanda was cut short. I stepped into the living area, noticing that the big front window was broken. On top of my small coffee table was a brick wrapped with a piece of white paper. I stepped up to window and looked out through the broken glass. My dead end street was silent, nothing moving. Wanda picked up the brick and read the note, "*Stop asking questions. Do your job and sell. Next time it is you.* Whoever wrote this sure don't read no Miss Manners. Damn Alex, we gotta call Pete Davies after all."

And that is what we did. Detective Davies arrived twenty minutes later and proceeded to quiz us both. He bagged the brick and wrote up a report. "If this happens again Alex, I am going to call in the evidence unit and have pictures taken. You say you and your friend Lexi asked around about Tim Tilberts at the Wharf Rat last night and now this? Doesn't prove anything of course, but common sense says you are stepping on some toes Mr. Campbell. You might want to consider walking more softly. This Tim Tilberts is one of your clients, part of an estate sale you are representing?"

I replied yes and explained what Lexi and I had learned about him, his debt, and mob connections. Detective Davies agreed, Tim, Mary Beth, and their mother's death, it all didn't really add up. But he cautioned me about getting too involved. This set Wanda off.

"What you mean he shouldn't get too involved? Hell, they his clients aren't they? Something ain't adding up right here, we all know it, even you said it. So we gotta figure it out. Find out who be knocking off a little old lady in her laundry room. Why did that bitch throw the door stopper through Alex's car window? Who is tryin' to feed this precious dog a bowl of glass? Who throws a brick through a front window for a late afternoon thrill? And is this Mistress Xtc., Mary Beth? If so, what does her spanky-butt business have to do with all this? That's what we gotta figure out Davies."

Clearly the search for the bulge in his trousers was over. That's Wanda. Set her off and away she goes. Detective Davies appeared a bit taken aback. People usually are when they first encounter one of Wanda's blow-ups. He cleared his throat, "You are correct Ms. Billings. Mr. Campbell does have some clients whose behavior is questionable. However, we cannot prove that the glass in the bowl, or the brick through the window has anything to do with his clients. Mrs. Tilberts' death was ruled accidental. Until we find some evidence that directly disproves this, then we have to go with accidental and leave it at that. I will admit, off the record, that it does appear to be odd, but for now we have to take these things as isolated incidents and treat them as such."

"As such my ass, Mr. Po-po!" Oh god, I know she didn't just refer to the policeman as the *po-po*. "Look here Davies, my family from way back had stupid white men in sheets burning crosses in they front yard. I know where this brick through the window shit can lead and honey it ain't pretty. So listen, I hear you. I know you gotta do the whole po-po, department thang, act all official, but let's get real. We all know something's going on here and it ain't no Avon Lady callin'. No sir, this some crazy, rich, white people shit. We all need to work at this together and get this one figured out."

Detective Davies appeared a bit shocked but amenable, "I hear that Ms. Billings and I have told you both unofficially that there could be more to this. I will keep my eyes open. You call me if something like this brick incident occurs again or---,"

"Or-- my fat black butt! Now take that po-po stick out yo' ass and talk. And cut that Ms. Billings crap, it's Wanda—W-a-n-d-a. Now Alex and me gonna be doing some of our own Nancy Drew on this and we gonna put you on our speed dials. We gonna call you up when we find out anything. You okay with that? You gonna help us out? Cause I ain't got no truck dealing with no dead dog or worse yet a dead Alex."

Detective Davies smiled meekly, "Okay Ms., ahh-- Wanda. You all have my number. You know I am keeping track of these incidents and you know you can call me when you need help. I guess I can't say or do anything to keep you two from looking into this on your own, but you really need to be careful and call the police if you find anything substantial or if something dangerous happens."

"You got that right slim. We gonna speed dial yo' sexy ass right up whenever we find something. Gonna make you our backup angel. When we need that gun in your holster, you best not be shootin' no blanks! Not with Wanda baby." Wanda then tilted her head and tried to appear demure.

Between the brick through my window, and Wanda's routine, I couldn't get my head around the whole afternoon. Right after Detective Davies left, my cell phone rang and it was my latest clients. They wanted me to come as soon as possible and show them a house for sale that they just drove past in Rosedale. Wanda said she would get someone out to replace my window and keep an eye on Clyde until I returned.

22

It turns out the house in Rosedale was somewhat of a false alarm. My clients, Tiffany and Bart, are late twenty-something's in a great hurry to be part of the big time Clinton social set. Tiffany is a public relations VP. When she is not whoring herself out by getting paid to tell lies for big corporations, she enjoys micromanaging Bart's career trajectory in the telecom industry and plotting ways to get asked to join the Clinton Junior League and the Bluffs Country Club. I hate to tell them but neither one has what it takes to make it in those stuffy circles. They would be better off getting over themselves and enjoying life or at least being realistic and aiming for inclusion in the annual Beaumont Ball. By the time I arrived in Rosedale, Tiffany had already decided the house would not do. It was not the right starter house for a couple that was destined for greatness and the Bluffs. I tried to be diplomatic, but the hard truth is her voice annoys the living hell out of me. What is up with grown women who consciously talk like they are fourteen years old and trying to do a bad Marilyn Monroe impression? The baby talk routine is flat out disgusting. Does it make Gloria Steinem want to hurl as much as me? The irony is, most grown women who do the whole baby talk routine are absolute back-stabbing bitches; especially when everything does not go one hundred percent their way. Bart still wanted to see the 1960s rambler, so I took them through, ignoring Tiffany's pouty sighs and sulky looks. I left Bart to pacify his little castrator in Prada. She was whining about how the Bluffs was the perfect neighborhood for them and why couldn't he just make more money or get cash from his parents so they could move there now.

As I pulled into my little parking pad, I noticed the front window was replaced and the window repair van was pulling away from the curb. Wanda met me at the door, "Hey, the window is fixed. Now get your fancy tux duds and bring Clyde. We going over to my house to change and Clyde is going to stay at my house. We got us a big kiss-ass art event to attend with Lexi. Don't you just stand there staring at me, get yo' ass in gear honey!"

Turns out Lexi had an art event at the Clinton Civic Center and she was one of the featured artists. She called Wanda after I left, to ask us to attend. This is typical Lexi. She probably forgot she had to attend the event until one of the sponsors called to remind her. She then naturally called Wanda and me to come along for moral support. Lexi hates promotional events and always requires that we show up (with hardly any notice) to be her support group. Not that I can criticize. I would rather hammer my thumb all night than go to some bullshit black tie function. But Wanda always ropes me in. Before I know it, there I am smiling blankly, holding a sweaty, tepid, glass of cheap white wine, and listening to Wanda make small talk. There was no use feigning illness or giving the standard "I'm too tired" excuse. No excuses work with Wanda when she's on a networking roll. I didn't even bother to protest. I just grabbed my ugly penguin suit, locked up the ranch, and put Clyde in the car. Off we went to Wanda's to change.

23

When Wanda hits a networking event, it's a production to behold. "Your name? What's that say on your little gold name tag there, baby? Ahh, Ricardo. Well Ricardo, your green is in keeping my car here as she looks right now. No, scratches, dents, changing my seat setting, or playing with my radio. I KNOW what the mileage is. So no quick drag races in Miss Emerald here while I'm inside talking with the do-dah's. Got it? You don't think I'm playing for real? Then just ask my penguin boy here what I did the last time a car jockey messed with my ride. Better yet, give a call over to the Coliseum parking staff. I know they'll remember me from last January." With that Wanda handed over the keys to her precious ride and we followed other penguins and their variously dressed female counterparts into the civic center. "You got your ten business cards with you in that nice case I gave you?"

"Yep, right here Wanda."

"Good, you get over to the cash bar and bring us something to make this go easy. They won't have no slushy drinks, so bring anything back but the nasty wine. You can pass out a card while you are getting the drinks. I want to see that case empty by the time we leave this event." Wanda said while waving off the *Hello My Name Is* stick-on tag the check-in volunteer was trying to give her. "Here baby, let me put your name plate on for you." Wanda opened her purple sequined evening handbag and clipped on my laminated *Hello My name Is Alex Campbell*, name tag. Wanda had custom, clip-on, name tags made for us a year or so ago. The usual stick-on name tags are worthless in

Wanda's opinion and worse would be the ones that are pinned to your clothes. Wanda doesn't agree with sticking pin holes in her clothes. I suppose her logic is correct and it is pretty organized on her part, but I still cringe every time she pulls out our name plate badges. The worst part is, she put our company names and contact information on the name tags as well. I have yet to see a sale or any business come from wearing my custom name badge. Just a late night phone call from an over-the-hill horny housewife who thought I might provide escort services of the pool boy sort. To Wanda, that was proof the name badges work and it is just a matter of time before some huge sale and a loan originates from her clever name badges.

The Clinton Civic Center is a huge white concrete blob built in the mid 1980s and it hosts all sorts of cultural/arts events. Tonight's whirl was celebrating thirty years of Clinton arts and kicking off a month long drive to fundraise and create a better awareness of arts in our community. The reception hall was elbow to elbow penguins and their sequined counter parts; all smiles, all ha- ha- ha. The kind of event that makes me want to go home and give Clyde a bath or cut my toenails, get out the toothbrush and clean that build-up between the kitchen faucet and the counter top lip.

I had barely retrieved two vodka tonics from the cash bar when Wanda appeared and snapped her drink from my hand telling me to follow. Through the maze of people, Wanda flashed her big fuchsia lipped smile, her eyes all wide as she, "Excuse me honey, nice to see ya' baby, on your left,..." our way up to Lexi's side. Lexi was near the podium part of the art event. Evidently (and thankfully) we arrived after some big wigs made speeches and handed out various medals and

131

awards. Lexi was wearing a green satin ribbon around her neck with what appeared to be a medal of recognition. Next to her the Mayor of Clinton was smiling big and wide as the event photographer snapped away. In a matter of seconds, Wanda was positioned between Lexi and the mayor and ordering the photographer to snap their photo. Before I could think, she had pulled me along side of her and the mayor and another photo was taken. Wanda then clasped the mayor's arm and began telling him how nice it was to see him again. Would he be attending the next business networking breakfast for the Highmont Business Association, of which Wanda is president. The mayor, a chinless three hundred pound wheeler-dealer, wasted no time in cajoling Wanda and assuring her he wouldn't miss their breakfast. As the mayor waddled off, Wanda muttered, while smiling big and wide, "Not one to pass up on a free breakfast put on by the coloreds and hippies. He don't wanna miss out on any chitlins and eggs or Mavis Johnson's pan size Johnny Cakes! That fat cracker better bring his damn check book this time, the park needs new play equipment."

Before I could respond, Lexi popped up and was flashing her medal asking us what we thought. While we were ooh-ing and ahh-ing over her award, Lexi spoke in a low voice, "Don't look now you two, but Sally Anne Tilberts is over there admiring my installation. Perhaps we should see if she has any information as to the handcuffs or knows anything else?" Before I could answer, Wanda was forging the way to Lexi's installation. "Installation" would be a polite term in my world. This art piece appeared to consist of the front end of a burned out Cadillac wrapped in rusting barbed wire with various cow bones and

132

other oddities attached. She called it "Moonlight Drive Number Four" and god only knows what or where one, two, and three were.

Sally Anne perked up as we approached, "Oh Lexi, this piece is so interesting and congratulations on the award! You know, I too used to do installation pieces way back." Lexi thanked her and they chit-chatted some more while Wanda and I nodded demurely. While they art talked, Wanda muttered to me, "Shit, how she gets them fat cracker pigs to pay real money to put this rusted crap on display is a mystery to me Alex. I mean damn, that Lexi is one woman who can work it. Hell, I know of at least three rusted-out cars like this here in the Highmont. Ain't nobody paying me good money to wrap 'em in no barbed wire." I admit I tittered a bit before replying, "Wanda, the art world is not like our world. I'm sure you and I could go find rusted out cars, but would we have the vision to wrap them in barbed wire, attach cow bones and who knows what else?" Wanda nodded, "Hell no, you are right. Lexi is some kind a magician as much as she is an artist. You know Alex, that girl should go into sales. Course she'd best steer clear of the mortgage and real estate arenas unless she wants us for competition."

Sally Anne and Lexi finished their art talk and Lexi mentioned that Wanda and I had recently done an open house at her sister's. Sally Anne gave a serene smile and sighed, "Oh, so you ended up co-listing Mary Beth's house Alex? Well, that is great for your business and for Marc, but I can only imagine what Mary Beth must be like to work with. Do you have to deal with her directly?" To that, I told her no and explained that Marc was my contact and that Mary Beth did not appear to live in the house any more. Sally Anne did not look surprised, "No she moved out a while back and I have always thought something must be off. For her to voluntarily vacate that house is not her style. No, I warned mother about Mary Beth moving out, told her I did not think it added up. She must have done something that Marc could use against her. Mother of course, saw none of it. Why, she was still mother's prized horseback riding daughter. I shouldn't say that. I mean she is upset about mother's death and as you know Alex, Mary Beth is not exactly at her best right now, what with the divorce and all. Still, I could have predicted this story line years ago. But mother and father would have none of it. Must be the youngest child syndrome I suppose."

"Well baby, all siblings got some kind of complex." Wanda said while adjusting her bra strap. "I understand your younger sis, she likes to throw things through windows? She broke Alex's car window 'cause she didn't get her way. And wouldn't you know it, just earlier today, some fool went and threw a brick through Alex's living room window!"

Sally Anne's eyes widened, "Oh no, you aren't serious?" She said looking at Wanda then at me. I started to respond but Wanda cut in, "Serious as a heart attack. And let me tell you, the brick had one nasty note attached. You wouldn't know anything about this, would you Sally Anne? You know, like where your sister Mary Beth was earlier this afternoon? I don't wanna go throwing out no wild stories or nothing, but we already know younger sis got herself a mean pitchin' arm."

Sally Anne cringed, "Oh god, I hope this doesn't have anything to do with Mary Beth. She has always been the wild child in our family. Was anyone hurt? What did the note say?"

I cleared my throat, "Ah, nobody was hurt and the note basically told me to mind my own business and sell houses."

"Well, that's putting it politely," Wanda muttered. "His living room window was destroyed and the previous note left with glass in the dog's bowl, told him to quit asking questions or they'd off his dog, Clyde."

Sally Anne gasped, putting her right hand over her sternum, "That is terrible! What questions are you asking that would cause someone to throw a brick through your window and leave glass in your dog's bowl? God, I really don't know what to say. I hope this is not another one of Mary Beth's episodes. Did you do something to set her off Alex?"

Before I could respond Wanda cut in, "I don't think Alex was asking any questions that would make someone go wild with a brick and broken glass. What kind of questions about your sister or family could be asked that would set someone off like this, Sally Anne?"

Sally Anne let out a sigh, tossing her long hair back over her shoulder, "God where would we start Wanda? Every family has its problems and mine is definitely no exception. Mary Beth's pending divorce is a bad situation. She was awfully angry with mother for not letting her have the house. And we all know she was seriously upset that mother intended to list the house with Alex. I know there are some personal issues between Mary Beth and Marc that are better left quiet, especially since Marc plans to run for public office. I have never been told exactly what those issues are. I have just offered Mary Beth my emotional support, but I don't think she's interested."

Wanda moved in closer to Sally Anne, "I would say your sister might have herself some personal issues of a real private nature. Issues that her husband would definitely not want the public to know about. Alex and I stumbled upon some information and nothing is set in stone, but it ain't looking pretty for Miss Mary Beth."

Sally Anne shook her head, "Yes, it is not a pretty picture Wanda. I thought she had gotten over her problem but from what I'm hearing maybe that is not so. Her love for cocaine started when she was in high school and mother and father just buried their heads in the sand. You see Mary Beth was always the perfect one. For them to admit their little angel was snorting coke on a regular basis, that was something they couldn't accept. I tried to help, but when people are not ready to face a problem, there really isn't anything you can do. I thought the cocaine was long behind Mary Beth but maybe not. Especially with her mood swings of late, it seems like some kind of drugs might be involved. God, mother would be so upset. You know families and siblings are really something else. A soap opera we are written into and really have no control over."

Without missing a beat Lexi chimed in, "Yes, Sally Anne siblings are something else; you should meet my younger brother, the entomologist. He was the prize of my family, what with my father being a college biology professor and mother a wanna-be Madam Cure. No, they never understood me, that's for sure. Of course maybe that's a good thing for an artist? Sally Anne I know your sister is having her problems, but what about your brother, Tim? Is he still in the bar business these days?"

136

Sally Anne again flipped her long hair back over her shoulder and smiled, "Ohhh, that! So you know about Tim's business? Mother never found out he was front-running that bar. I kept my mouth shut and for some reason Mary Beth never spilled the beans either. Which come to think of it, is not like her, but I guess she is too consumed with her divorce. She really wanted to get mother's house and I guess bad mouthing Tim didn't rank on her list of mother manipulations. Or maybe, Tim knows she has started up with the cocaine again? Tim has been at the Wharf Rat for some time now. I'm not sure what compels him, but I can assure you my father would turn over in his grave if he knew about it. The ideal son, in a business like that? Ohh, I hate to rush off but I see Sharon Munzer signaling me over there and she's my ride. I would love to talk more but when Sharon is ready to leave, there is no delaying. It was great seeing you all, congratulations again Lexi. Alex I'm sure I'll be seeing you soon, hopefully, with an offer for mother's house. Please let me know if anything else happens, any more items going through your windows, etc.... It might be wise to report it to the police. I don't think Mary Beth is a physical threat to you Alex, but gosh with a note like that, and the glass in the dog's dish, and her cocaine use, who really knows."

Off Sally Anne went, her long grey and sage colored dress flowing behind her and what appeared to be grey Birkenstock sandals beneath it. Wanda let out a sigh, "Damn, least her dogs gonna be feeling alright once this hoo-ha is over with. I didn't know white children from good homes wore them hippie shoes with formal dresses."

"Wanda," Lexi replied, "you just wouldn't understand it's a white girl, rebellious, artist thang!" With that they peeled into hysterical laughter so loud that heads turned. Naturally, I was a bit peeved. Wanda looked up at me, "Oh go on and laugh or finish your drink. Or else let us get someone here to lay you so that crow bar up yo' ass can be safely removed. It sounds like we just got ourselves some more information about Miss Mary Beth. Who knew the bitch had a thing for snow? Interesting, that Sally Anne didn't say a word about Mistress Xtc. Seem like she don't have clue about her little sis' spanking business. Humph--- this is one to sit on a while. Okay, we need food and we need to get them business cards passed out Mr. Alex. What time are you leaving Lexi?"

"Well, I've picked up my medal but I suppose there are some people I should schmooze with before I leave. Why?"

"You have to ask? Hell, once we have all done our duty, its back to my place for a real party---the after party! You wanna ride with us or did you fly here on your broom tonight?"

"I had an escort who picked me up and I guess he'd take me back but I'll just tell him no need and leave with you two."

"Escort, is this the kind I'm thinking about or some pasty art intern the Art Council sent to pick you up?"

"That would be choice number two. Actually he's not too pasty, he might be someone Alex should meet."

With that they turned toward me, but I quickly disappeared into the crowd. I had business cards to unload and I was not about to stick around for a Wanda and Lexi matchmaker event.

138

24

I woke up the next morning with a pounding headache and incessant nudging from Clyde's wet muzzle against my forearm. The art award event had gone on too long and Wanda's after event celebration went on far into the night. By the time Wanda dropped me off, I had consumed too many vodka tonics and too little food. While I was stumbling around the bathroom trying to find an old bottle of aspirin, (it is not often that I wake up hung over or feel the need for over the counter pain killers) I checked the voice mails on my cell. One message was the pregnant couple, letting me know they still had not made up their mind yet as to the "appropriate neighborhood venue" in which to raise their future genius spawn. Major yawn. Next, was a message from my broker letting me know I needed to take one of the upcoming state classes before renewing my real estate license. Nice of him to feign concern, but I took care of the required state class last month and in fact he'd signed off on the completion certificate. Guess he too, had trouble finding his bottle of pain killers this morning.

The final call was from an agent with Sunshine Realty named Caitlin Spears. She was letting me know that she was going to meet with her clients this morning and write up an offer on the Tilberts' house. While this was good news, I could not help letting out a groan which caused Clyde to emit an empathy whine. The prospect of an offer was great. However, when I replayed the message, Caitlin sounded like she had eaten a balloon filled with helium and was maybe twelve years old. Also, Sunshine Realty? What the fuck was that? I had never heard of the company.

"Ahmm, hi this is ahmm, Caitlin Spears with Sunshine Realty? I've got like these buyers who totally want to buy your listing… ahhhm in the Bluffs, you know the old rich neighborhood? You know the place with the pool out back and like the views of the water? So, we are gonna meet for breakfast and do the, you know, ahhm paper work and so I just wanted to know like where ahhhm you are gonna be at, so I can like get the offer to you and all?" I swear I could hear bubble gum popping in her mouth as she left her phone number. Doubtful that Caitlin was a recent liberal arts college graduate with a useless degree in English Literature, trying to make a stab at a living by selling real estate. From the sound of her voice, her last job probably involved a pole, a platform, and very loud music. Call me cynical, but experience led me to believe this agent could be fresh off the turnip truck, with little to no experience dealing with clients and real estate offers. These newbies seem to appear daily. Newbie agents who heard about all the "easy" money to be made in real estate. They are giving up their pole jobs, their stints at the used car lot, or their future life in the call center, to make their millions as a "real estate professional." I suppose you can't knock them from trying, but the vast majority end up paying a fortune in company fees and within six to eight months are bounced on their butts, flat broke and worse off than they were before they drank the real estate Kool-Aide. However, I suppose Caitlin deserves a point for at least calling me to let me know an offer would be forthcoming. Most agents can't be bothered to even do that.

After uncovering two lint covered aspirin tablets from the bottom of my old toiletries kit, I called and left Sally Anne a message letting her know an offer might be coming in and informing her we would all need to meet to review it. I then managed to paste a smile on my face and call Caitlin back. I let her know she could drop the offer off at my office (I had my doubts she could work a fax machine much less email a PDF) and I told her how excited we would be to review her client's offer, blah, blah, blah.

True to intuition, the offer was a complete piece of shit. I literally thought it was a joke, when I first opened the manila packet left for me at the Winterfrost will-call desk. Another point for Caitlin, she did have a loan pre-approval letter (albeit a letter which appeared to have coffee spilled all over it) for her clients' offer. And when I called the loan person listed in the pre-approval letter, it appeared the buyers were legitimate and could actually purchase the Tilberts' place. Point three for Caitlin was she had dropped off the offer. However, the three points in her favor were completely out scored by all of the rest of her incompetence. The purchase and sale forms are available to any agent online at the local multiple listing service. An agent pulls them up, types in the offer information, or so you would think, and prints them out. Unfortunately, many agents have never mastered the fine art of typing information into pre-made forms provided online. Instead, ditzs like Caitlin print them out and then attempt to fill in the blanks by hand. In this case, she had used a variety of what appeared to be children's magic markers. The first set of forms was filled in with a light purple ink, the next set in a spring green and to complete her color wheel, she had her buyers sign everything using a sky blue marker.

Brilliant work on Caitlin's part! These marker colors do not copy on a Xerox machine and do not appear on a faxed or scanned copy either. State law requires copies of the offer be provided to all parties. So there was no way I could Xerox or scan Caitlin's clients' offer and provide copies to each of the Tilberts kids. But the ink color choices were the least of Caitlin's problems. She had used one form that was two years out-of-date (state law requires all offers be written on the most up-to-date forms). How she even had access to a form that was two years out of date was a wonder to me. Then there were the numerous blanks she had neglected to fill in, nineteen of them to be precise. Assuming I filled them in for her (in black or blue ballpoint ink of course), by law I would have to get each of the Tilberts kids to initial and date each of the nineteen blanks I had filled in. Then, the two buyers would have to initial and date each of those nineteen changes as well. There is no way the offer forms would end up legible, much less legal, by the time all that extraneous and unnecessary initialing had taken place.

Rather than call Caitlin or her designated broker at Sunshine Realty and try and get her to do her job properly, I took the path of least resistance. I pulled up the forms online and proceeded to key in and print out the offer paperwork myself. Technically, this would be an offer from the Tilberts to sell to the buyers. More than likely, the buyers would never figure out that their agent was incompetent, even when she presented them with the sellers' offer to sell and had them resign everything. I added a clause, stating that the buyers would sign the documents using black or blue ballpoint ink only. Hopefully, that would not be too much of a challenge! Once again, I would be doing the work for both agents and yet Caitlin the ditz would still be paid in full for her stellar incompetence.

I sat down at one of the computers in the Winterfrost work room to write up the Tilberts' offer to sell. I had worked my way through the first two forms, when who should I smell but Stinky. Around the corner she came, the strong scent of freesia, rose, musk, and god knows what else, hitting my nostrils like a heavy fog bank. Her jangling jewelry and shrill voice assaulting my ears next. "Ohh, it's our Mr. Bluffs listing agent, live and in person," Share said in a stage voice, looking around the room to see if she had an audience. While clattering up to the computer terminal I was using Share exclaimed, "A little bird tells me that you have an offer on the Tilberts' house Alex." Just smelling Share was enough to make my skin crawl. I mentally bunkered down and barely glanced up while continuing to type and replied, "Oh, it's you Share. Your little bird must be pretty nosey to know about the offer or did you peruse the will-call box up front again?"

"Peruse? Oh, that must be one of your big college graduate vocabulary words Alex. Pardon me. It takes me a while to catch on to big words. I'm just a hard working high school graduate gal, you know?" Spare me the Loretta Lynn hard knocks story woman. "Well, Alex you know my sources are everywhere, that's what it takes to be a real estate pro! Good luck with that offer. I sure hope all of those Tilberts children can agree. Oh, but I'm sure you know how to handle that kind of thing. You are a Bluffs listing agent after all! Don't worry though," she said with her sneering Joker-esque smile, "once I get a buyer for our co-listing, I'll make sure everything is done right. You won't have to worry a bit. Just sit back and play your pretty college boy part and I'll do the real work." Her cell phone *Yellow Rose of Texas* ring tone started and before I could respond, Share was cackling away into her cell and wobbling off out of the work room in her ten inch, pointy bitch boots.

25

I swung by my humble abode and took Clyde out for a quick walk prior to heading off to the Tilberts to go over the revised offer. I knew Clyde would probably be okay, waiting for his walk until I got back from the offer review. However, I did not want to sit there with three antagonistic siblings while my mind whirled like a hamster wheel wondering if Clyde was okay. Did he needed to go out? Would he have an accident, etc.... Clyde has not had an accident in years but the worry machine in my head never ceases when it comes to Clyde. I can only imagine what it would be like if Clyde were a child. Clyde marked his favorite spots, tried to pull me down the way to Sasser's Bakery but gave up once he intuited that I had other business to attend to. I put some fresh kibble in his bowl, made sure there were no new bricks thrown through the window, or a bowl of broken glass left, no assassins out in the big oak tree. Then, I loaded up the paperwork in my brief case. Clyde plopped down on the crusty leather sofa, looked up sullenly at me, trying to make me feel as bad as he could. "Nice try shaggy, but no cigar. I've got a friggin' house to sell and kibble to keep in your bowl. I'll put on some music for you." Clyde gave a loud pouty sigh. I turned on the radio to a jazz station and left Clyde to chill with Coltrane and what sounded like some feeble white chick (in dreadlocks no doubt) trying to do some sort of spoken word/rap over one of Coltrane's famous rifts. I guess this was my revenge on Clyde for acting so pouty. He could suffer through the woman's poetic oozing.

Winding up the hills into the Bluffs, I wondered what kind of scene I was about to enter. I spoke with Sally Anne earlier and she told me she and her siblings would be available and meeting me at her mother's house at 6:30. I pulled into the white pebbled drive and noticed two cars were there; Mary Beth's late model Range Rover and Sally Anne's mint green 1984 Volvo station wagon. I rang the bell and Sally Anne greeted me, "Come in Alex, you are right on time as always. Mary Beth and I are hanging out in the kitchen. Tim just called and he is not going to be able to make it. He wants me to phone in once we have reviewed things. If you don't mind, you can take whatever paperwork he needs to sign to him later on this evening."

"That will not be a problem." I told her as she led me into the kitchen and over to the antique pine table where Mary Beth was sitting with a glass of what appeared to be white wine by her side. "We can review the offer and if you two agree and sign, I will take it over to Tim for review and get his signatures."

"Well aren't you just Mister Delivery Man! Have you even checked to verify this is a legitimate offer?" Mary Beth snorted as her way of hello.

Sally Anne shook her head while indicating a seat for me at the table. "Alex, why don't you show us the offer and we can go through it together. Would you care for something to drink, soda, wine, water?"

"No thank you, I am fine." I took a seat directly across from Mary Beth and Sally Anne, pulled out the offer paper work and placed it in front of them. "I did review the buyers' offer Mary Beth. I checked with the buyers' lender and they do have a legitimate pre-approval to purchase this house. Unfortunately, the offer paperwork was not filled out correctly by the buyers' agent. So I printed out an offer for you to sell to the buyer, in order to save us time and aggravation. Now, let's go through this page by page and ask me any questions. I'll do my upside down reading routine." By that, I meant the offer paperwork was right side up on their side of the table. I, like any good agent, know the forms backwards and forwards. I can sit on the other side of the table and go through the forms while they are literally upside down. Such a talent. I am waiting for my trophy.

Sally Anne smiled in response while Mary Beth snorted, literally, took out a lavender handkerchief with her initials embroidered in red and wiped her nose. The offer was full price with no seller pre-paid items, always the sign of a robust seller's market. Multiple offers had cooled off somewhat but were still out there. However, with a house this size and in this price range, multiple offers were somewhat rare even in our booming market. As we went through each page of the offer, I had each of them sign/date/initial where appropriate. Mary Beth continued to sniff and wipe her nose. At one point, she took a break and went to the bathroom while complaining that her seasonal allergies were acting up. Sally Anne gave me a knowing look while we waited for Mary Beth's return. When we had finished going through all of the pages, Mary Beth let out a big sigh, "Well, I suppose that is it. We have sold mother's house for less than it is worth. I still think Share could have gotten us a much better deal. But since you and Tim always out vote me, I guess I have no choice but go along. It just isn't my year, what with mother's death and my divorce and you two bullying me to agree to a sale I know is a rip-off."

I consciously kept my face stone neutral. The offer was full price, the list price had been chosen based on statistics I provided for active comparable listings and sold comparable listings. The offer was legitimate, the price fair, but some people have to always complain. Sally Anne gave a wistful smile, shook her head and passed the paperwork back across the table to me. "Thank you for writing this up properly Alex and for walking us through it."

"You are most welcome. I will give Tim a call and try and meet up with him this evening to get his signatures. Then I will get this back to the buyers' agent and make sure she has them sign where needed. So, hopefully by tomorrow evening we will have mutual agreement and then the buyers will start their seven day inspection contingency period and we will go from there." I stood up, put the paperwork in my brief case, shook Sally Anne's hand, and held out my hand to Mary Beth who responded by sniffing into her handkerchief. With that, Sally Anne followed me out to the front door.

"I hope Mary Beth has not offended you. Trust me, it is nothing personal Alex, she has acted like this since I can remember. Be happy you didn't have to grow up with her."

I gave her a sympathetic smile, "Thanks again for your help Sally Anne and I will call you once everything is signed around." I checked my car windows as I got in, no iron horses or bricks. According to Sally Anne, Tim was not going to be available for at least another hour. I thought I'd kill the time by meeting up with Wanda. I rolled over to the Highmont. My old two-door chugging slowly up the very steep Tenth Street that is the main access street for the Highmont.

I parked outside Wanda's and gave a brief "shave and a haircut" rap on her lemon yellow front door. Wanda quickly answered, motioning me inside while yammering away on her cell. "Okay then, we got ya down mayor and I'll make sure they save you some of the Johnny Cakes!" Wanda clicked off while walking back to her kitchen, "Hear that Alex? The fat cracker is gonna show up for the Highmont Business Association meeting. I'm gonna feed his fat ass. And he's gonna sign off on the new playground equipment before he can waddle himself back into the black limo that will bring his sorry ass over here. Here, have some of this margarita I mixed up and have seat while I tend to my chicken." Wanda pushed the blue pitcher of margarita in my direction, pointed to a counter stool and went over to her million dollar stove to turn the chicken she was frying up.

I took a seat, poured myself a small margarita and savored the smell of Wanda's famous Cajun fried chicken. If Clyde were here, he'd be whining and no doubt, she would be feeding him first. "This here chicken is gonna be a good snack for us. Didn't you say you had to find that Tim Tilberts man and get his John Hancock on the offer papers? We can go out for a real dinner once we are done with him. I guess I don't have to ask, you didn't bring my baby along? Oh well, I guess you can't take Clyde everywhere with you. I'll wrap him up some choice pieces of this bird for you to take back to him. I won't worry; he'll know it's from me."

The chicken looked good enough for lunch and dinner combined as far as I was concerned. Come to think of it, I'd forgotten to have lunch today. Not smart, but so far the low blood sugar had not reared its ugly head. I was savoring a sip of margarita when Wanda turned to me and thrust a set of tongs in my hand, "Here, you turn the chicken while I go put on something else. I can't have a good chicken appetizer and dinner with you unless I get out of these boring mortgage clothes." With that she headed off down the narrow hall to her bedroom. I stood next to the stove somewhat perplexed, staring down at the low sizzling chicken pieces, afraid I'd ruin it all. "And I know what you are standing there thinking, just turn the damn bird pieces every few minutes and I'll be back with you in no time. There ain't no way you can ruin my chicken now, so don't sweat it!" Sometimes Wanda is psychic like that.

I couldn't wait to see what was less boring than her mortgage clothes. Boring for Wanda today, had been a bright lime green and blue blouse with a long sweeping black skirt with shiny things on it. I dutifully turned chicken pieces with the provided tongs and Wanda magically re-appeared. She wore orange slacks and what was either a very short magenta and orange striped mini dress or a long blouse. She also added some long multi-piece mirrored, ear rings which flounced back and forth as she sauntered into the kitchen. She took the tongs out of my hand and pointed them at the stool. I quickly sat down and proceeded to salivate, while waiting for the chicken to hurry up and cook.

When we finished eating several pieces of her delicious chicken and she polished off her pitcher of margaritas, as if on cue, my cell phone began to ring. It was Tim and he wanted to know where I was. I told him I was visiting a friend in the Highmont but could meet him wherever was convenient to go over the offer. Tim told me he could easily make it to the Highmont and asked if I knew a place called the Ridge? It is a private club in the Highmont. I asked him to hold on and asked Wanda if she knew where the Ridge was located. Wanda's eyes perked up and she nodded yes. I told Tim my friend could direct me to the Ridge. He said to bring the friend along and meet him at the Ridge in a half an hour.

Once I hung up, Wanda was all over it. "That man wants to meet you at the Ridge? What is he black? No he can't be, he's that Tilberts boy right? Well did the Tilberts adopt a black child back in the 1960s Alex, because no white man goes to the Ridge to hang out."

"I'm just telling you where he wants to meet us in a half an hour. He said to bring you along."

"White man settin' up a real estate meeting at the Ridge; don't that just beat all. I don't know if I've mentioned the Ridge to you before or not Alex. It's this private blacks only, club up there in an old house at the dead end side of Clayton Street. Used to be a blacks-only whore house back in the early 1900s. Then it was a black speak-easy. Since the 1950s, it has been a private, members-only, black club or bar is more like it. For a while there, it was Clinton's only private black club and let me tell you it has been through its various phases of respectable and not respectable. I've only been there a few times myself. Only way to get in is to be a member or be invited by a member. How does this white man have a membership at the Ridge and how can he invite his real estate agent to meet him there? I guess you and me is gonna find out."

With that Wanda kicked back the last of her margarita and began loading the plates into her dishwasher. A new dishwasher it appeared. Stainless and god only knows how expensive. The kind you need a rocket manual to operate. Wanda looked back up at me, noticing my eyes appraising her new dishwasher. "Yeah, you like my new dish licker here Alex? I think it is new since you were here last. One of the best European dish lickers there is. I ain't gonna tell you what I licked to get this here stainless dish licking bundle of joy!"

I could only guess who and what. My bet was that the upper end appliance boy friend was back in the picture.

"You know I had to upgrade the dishwasher Alex. What with this expensive Viking range here. The range made the old dishwasher look tacky."

I didn't say a word, just smiled. Wanda fired up her new dishwasher and turned on some lamps around the house. She collected her sizeable fuchsia colored hand bag and out the door we went in search of the Ridge.

26

U p the narrow streets we wound. We finally hit Clayton Street which was still paved in cobble stones and mostly a steep and windy, one lane affair. Tall oak trees clung to the bordering hills and we abruptly reached the dead end of Clayton Street which ended in a high bluff overlooking the downtown and water far below. There were a number of assorted cars parked along the side of the street and in the turnaround part where the street ended. We finally found a spot that would fit my aging two-door and got out. It was just turning dark. I could make out a few early 1900s era houses farther up the street nestled in the wooded hillside. I looked around the dead end area. No house and no club sign. "Wanda, where is this Ridge place? I don't see anything, are you sure we---,"

Wanda put her hand up to silence me and motioned me forward, "Do you dare doubt I know where we are?" Wanda said while letting out one of her little chortle laughs. "Follow me, baby and I'll get us to the Ridge. I still don't see how some white man is meeting us here, hell I've only been in this place a few times, well that I can recall at any rate." I followed Wanda to the guard rail that announced the street's end and steep drop below. She moved past the hazy orange street light's glow and came to a row of tall, ancient holly bushes. Tucked deep inside of them, away from the street light was a cut through. And deep inside that was an ancient wooden door with an aging black iron electric lamp at the top. Wanda pushed it open, the hinges creaking. Down some moss covered stone steps we went. Just around a curve on the steep hillside path, lit by electric lanterns on black poles, there it was, the Ridge.

The Ridge was indeed, an 1890s clapboard. It was a three story house complete with a turret and period appropriate, stained glass windows scattered about. It appeared to be literally hanging off the wooded hillside. I suppose it was built on a ridge but to my way of thinking, cliff was more accurate. We stepped down onto the wide wooden wraparound porch and went past a couple of curtained windows, faint peach colored lighting barely showing through them. The porch surrounded the curved window turret (they don't make curved windows like that anymore my inner real estate agent noted). The view from the porch overlooking the woods, downtown, and the glistening water far below, was amazing. A massive, ornately carved, oak door was on the other side of the turret. Next to it hung a shoe box sized, green neon sign stating in buzzing 1950s cursive lettering, *Ridge*. Below the sign was a small brass plaque, *Members Only*. Wanda twisted the large brass dial, built into the massive oak door. A loud ring let out as the old style, manual door bell announced our arrival. While waiting for an answer, I noted the green "d" in *Ridge* flickered and I turned to take in the view. View real estate did not get more superb than this, except maybe in the Bluffs. I doubted the house could even be constructed with today's building codes, given that it appeared to literally be built on air hanging off a cliff. I was taking it all in, when the massive oak door's lock clicked and the door slowly opened. There appeared a white and blue, ornately tiled, vestibule with a cherub brass chandelier above, each of the six cherubs holding up ancient stained glass globes. The globes gave off a warm peach colored glow. Between the solid oak door and the leaded cut glass door with white gauze curtains, stood a six foot five, black man with a short grey afro. He was dressed all in black and had the kind of blank face perfected by British butlers. He could have been anywhere between thirty five and sixty five years old. "Good evening, welcome to the Ridge. May I have your names and the member's name with whom you are meeting?"

Wanda didn't miss a beat, "Oh, hey honey. You might remember me? Wanda Billings of Safety Mortgage and of course you probably know Salon Wanda! It has been a long while since I was here last. See you still looking fine, Lurch, and keeping the door all locked up tight." Wanda let out a low cackle, "Me and white boy are here to meet another white boy. Say, I thought the Ridge was blacks only? When they start letting the crackers join?"

The doorman's impartial face, winced as Wanda spoke, especially at her cracker reference. "Yes, hello Ms. Billings. So nice to have you at the Ridge again. What did you say is the name of the member you and the gentleman are here to meet?" Grey top said this while stepping in closer to Wanda and me, causing us to step back towards the oak door. Wanda appeared a bit flustered, so I piped in, "Ah, hello we are here to meet Tim Tilberts."

"Yes. Very good, then. Mr. Tilberts did phone and let us know to expect you. Please sign your names in the registry book." He indicated an ornately carved registry table off to the left in the tiled vestibule, upon which sat an ancient, black leather bound book. Several names had already signed in under today's date and Wanda and

I followed suit. Wanda muttering, "I forgot all this sign in your name stuff they do here. Seems like something they'd do at the department of corrections." While I signed my name I muttered back, "What was that cracker and white boy reference all about? You'd shit a brick if I referred to you as a black girl." Wanda let out a sigh and whispered, "Yeah, you got a point there Alex."

The doorman glanced at our signatures and then proceeded to open the leaded glass door. Inside was a large living room area with assorted Victorian furnishings, some probably there since the house had first been built. A coat check room was off to the left in a wooden nook. To the right, was a large curved open arch entryway with ancient dark green velvet curtains pulled back on either side. Through the archway was a dining room with about twelve or so white cloth covered tables. There were three tables occupied by various middle aged black couples, all well dressed. "Oh, a room full of Clinton's Huxtables. Bet they don't go upstairs much." Wanda whispered. Set back from the glass entry door and curving around the living room was a massive oak paneled stairway with an ancient oriental runner down the middle of its wide, glossy brown steps. Halfway up was a wide landing complete with another brass cherub, stained glass globe, chandelier. The massive, carved, newel post was a larger version of the vestibule and landing chandelier cherubs. Wanda took a look and said to me, "Oh that big cherub must be those other little fat kids' mama." I had to laugh out loud at that. The doorman remained neutral and said, "You all may wish to go upstairs to the bar and lounge. I am sure Mr. Tilberts will be here shortly."

Upstairs was another world. At the top of the stairs was a short, narrow hallway, with a large window at one end which overlooked tree tops. The other end was a black leather, padded, swinging door. Wanda pushed it open. The wood floors creaked under our feet as the door swung shut. This was a continuation of the narrow hallway, except now there were brass wall sconces lit with low wattage, flickering amber bulbs. An old wooden phone booth, complete with a glass door was built-in on the left side of the hallway. An ancient, electric green "telephone" sign buzzed faintly. It was straight out of 1940 or earlier. On the right, was a wooden door marked "gentlemen" and farther down the hall, another door on the right marked "ladies." At the end, was another black, padded, swinging door. As we approached it, the soft muffle of voices and music could be heard. Once Wanda pushed it open, we were in the Ridge's bar and lounge. This consisted of a very large, open room which must run the entire length of the house. At the far end of the room, the side which faced the wooded hillside and the dead end street, was an enormous late 1800s built-in bar. The bar spanned the entire end of the house complete with hand carved panels, more cherubs acting as columns and holding up stained glass globes, "See that mama on the stairs be making these here fat babies work extra hard since they get to hang out with the booze." Wanda commented. A huge, hazy with age, and spidery mirror, hung behind the bar. Hundreds of gleaming liquor bottles lined the elaborate built-in shelves. The area around the bar consisted of dark hardwood floors and the bar held twelve red leather stools, five of which were currently occupied. The lounge area was carpeted in very thick maroon carpeting and there were gaming tables with chairs scattered about, and various Victorian sofa and chair sitting areas filled up the huge room. At the opposite end of the bar, in the big bay window nook, was a period pool table with worn green felt and again four carved cherubs were on duty holding up the pool table. A large, green glass, concave chandelier hung low over the pool table and four elderly black men were playing. The view from the large bay window was incredible. The outlook was over the tree tops and the steep hill, the downtown and then the water glistening under the moonlight out to the horizon. There were several muted conversations, the quiet clacking of the pool balls, and piped in softly from above, was the sound of Billie Holliday.

"Good evening, Mr. Campbell and Ms. Billings. Mr. Tilberts has not yet arrived. Would you like to have a seat at the bar or in the lounge while you wait for him?" This from a middle aged, non-descript, black waitress, also dressed head to toe in black like her doorman counterpart. "Damn sister, either you and Lurch are psychic or he done phoned you the 4-1-1 before we hoofed our butts up those bad ass stairs. Hey girl, why don't you put us over there in that window to the left of the pool table boys?" Wanda didn't wait for the waitress to respond. She started walking across the plush maroon carpeting over to a seating area that consisted of two very large empire style chairs and a medium size matching, sofa seating arrangement. All faced a large window looking out over the hill.

The waitress slightly shook her head as Wanda took off in front of her, she turned back to me, "Certainly, please follow me." Once we had been seated in the large empire style chairs, covered in thick light blue, velvet fabric, (which appeared to be comfortable but were in actuality not too kind on the lower back) Wanda placed an order for some kind of frozen cocktail for herself. I ordered a tonic water with lime. Wanda gave me the eye and I replied, "You know I never drink while working and I have a purchase and sale agreement to get signed Wanda. Just having those few sips of Margarita at your place was really bending my work rules."

"Always mister business first, Alex. Oh well, hell look where you are. You are in Clinton's most exclusive, oldest, blacks-only club and you got the best damn view in the house. I hope once those papers are signed, you will at least celebrate with something from one of those one hundred plus shiny bottles back there."

"Perhaps, but if this club is still only for blacks then how is Tim Tilberts entertaining us here? It would appear the help knows who he is." The waitress reappeared with our drinks and a silver bowl filled with cashews, complete with tiny silver tongs to retrieve them. While we sipped our drinks and waited for Tim, Wanda filled me in on some of the history of the Ridge. It was a highly successful whore house, complete with a bar when it was first built in 1890. The Ridge was built and run by a fierce black woman named Safrina Wright. She had been a prostitute and folk lore had it that she black mailed the then mayor of Clinton and some other big time city fathers and built the Ridge on white peoples' hush money. Cops stayed away and Safrina made a fortune on the place. Safrina Wright Elementary was built by her money and named for her in 1922. Once Safrina passed away, her cousins took title and by 1930 it was a speakeasy, mostly for blacks. By the 1950s The Ridge was on hard luck and then several prominent black pillars of the community purchased it and turned it into the exclusive blacks-only club it is today.

A small open doorway off to the right of the bar led to the third floor where the original working girls had their rooms. During prohibition, the bar sold bathtub gin and since Wanda was a little girl, the third floor was reportedly where a huge numbers racket was run and some say drugs were dealt.

"The respectable black folks keep mostly to the downstairs, but some do come up here as you can see. The third floor has always been off limits. I can recall all sorts of stories about the number running going on up there. You know Alex that might be why Tim can invite people here. We already know he is the front man for the mob at the skanky Wharf Rat. And number running and the mob seem like a close match to me. Also, ever since I was little, the word on the street was a lot of them Huxtables we saw eating downstairs, ain't nothing but upper end drug pushers. Heard tell, a lot of horse and pot used to come out this house's third floor. Never interested me. So I don't know 'bout the truth of that story. But I can bet you that there's still something naughty going on up there on that third floor."

Naughty or not, we were on our second round of drinks and still no Tim.

27

With her second slushy drink nearing its end, Wanda decided it was time to make use of the facilities or as she put it, mocking the Ridge staff, "Alex, I do believe it is time I avail myself of the woman's lounge and powder my nose." I was zoning out on the water far below, glistening beneath the moon light, lulled by the soft clacks of the pool balls and the lilting Billie Holliday piped in all around. "Do tell our lovely waitress that I would like another one of these peach concoctions and to put some extra rum in this one. Or perhaps, I'll let the charming bar tender know how I want this one made in person. Now let's see, I believe the ladies is right by the bar up that stairway---,"

"What? No way Wanda! You know where the ladies room is, out in the hall way. Don't go upstairs; I don't want to get in trouble. Tim hasn't even shown up and I have a deal that has to be signed by him in order to be complete. Don't go and muck---,"

I shut up since Wanda was already gone. I glanced over my shoulder and watched as she skirted the edge of the bar, dropping her drink glass off, smiling at a man on the nearest bar stool, while apparently giving the bar tender her drink specifications. Then, once she had engaged them, she turned, did a quick three sixty around the room and quick as a mouse, ducked around the corner to the dark stairwell off to the right of the bar. The waitress returned with Wanda's new drink and another tonic and lime for me, even though I didn't order it—how's that for private club service? I asked her if there had been any word from Tim and she said no sir and would there be anything else. By this point, the view and the exotic private club ambiance were starting to fade on me. It was getting close to 9:00 pm and I needed to get this offer paperwork signed around and back to the buyers' idiot agent so we could have mutual agreement and move on. I pulled out my cell phone and dialed Tim's number. It went straight to voice mail. I left a message letting him know that we were at the Ridge and waiting for him. I had just hung up when Wanda reappeared, eyes a bit wide.

She sat down on the edge of the big empire style chair, took a long pull through the straw on her slushy cocktail, looked to either side of her, and then leaned in close to me. In a soft voice, well soft for Wanda, she said, "Alex you will never guess who I ran into upstairs. What they say about the Ridge's third floor is no lie! You know I was just curious about that third floor and once I got up there I was checking out all these little rooms off this long hallway up there. Those little rooms were where the hookers did there thing way back. Anyhow, the room at the end of the hallway, the door was open. There was a light on. In there was this big white man and two black men, one dressed all in black just like the help wears here. They were sitting around this card table, stack of green on it and what looked like some kind of numbers spreadsheet. They were none too happy to see me in the doorway. But you know me. I thought real quick and asked if they could direct me to the ladies room. Well, they got all up in my business, wanting to know who I am and what I was doing at the Ridge, etc.... Once I mentioned Tim's and your names and why we were here to meet him, the big white man smiled. He say his name is

Tony and he's met you. I think he is that man Lexi uses for metal and you two met him at the Wharf Rat. Anyway, Tony says to me that the ladies room is on this floor. That you and me should just go on home, because he doesn't think Tim is going to make it over here tonight."

At this point my heart started to beat a bit faster. Great, the mob boss was up on the third floor and he is letting us know Tim won't be making it here tonight. I took a gulp of the tonic, now wishing there was some vodka in it. "Okay, Wanda then that's it for us here. Let's go. I have to get Tim to sign these damn papers so I can get this deal completed. I have the client file in the car with Tim's home address, do you mind if we head over there now?"

"Mind? Hell to the no, this is starting to get real interesting. Okay, let me finish old slushy here and then let's see if we can track down Mr. Tim. Mummmph, I'm telling you, the third floor at the Ridge is what they say it is. They have a white mob boss up there and a white man meeting guests at the club. God, what is next? They gonna let the Jews and Asians in here?" With that Wanda let out a mean chuckle and out we went.

Down the grand stairway, at the bottom of the stairs the doorman was waiting. Wanda handed him her now empty glass, "Okay baby, here's my empty slushy glass. Don't want you to think I'm walking out of here boosting none of the Ridge goods. Anyway, you take good care of the mama here," Wanda said patting the large cherub newel post, "and make sure her babies behave." Wanda let out a loud chortle and headed out the door. I lingered, thanking the doorman and telling him to please have Mr. Tilberts call me if he showed up. The doorman gave me a tight smile, while focusing on Wanda moving out the door, "I will certainly let Mr. Tilberts know. I hope your drinks were satisfactory. We look forward to serving you again in the future, when a member invites you to join us. Good evening." With that he ushered me out to the porch and shut and locked the big oak door.

Back in the car, I looked up the address Tim had filled in on my client contact sheet. From the address, I noted Tim lived in the Lee District, certainly not the ritzy Bluffs where he grew up but the Lee with its trendy doctors and lawyers was not shabby. Down from Highmont we rolled, through the downtown and over to the Lee. Tim's address was on one of the side streets in the Lee. It was one of the mixed-use streets, meaning there was a local coffee shop with apartments above, old buildings that had been turned into trendy condos, some gift and clothing shops, a small book store, and then there were a smattering of clapboard one up-one down duplexes. Tim's address indicated his was unit B of a fading white, 1920s vintage one up and one down duplex. It was a small city lot with a little front yard and a screened-in porch ran across the front of the building both up and down. The duplex was shot gun style or what I refer to as living in a shoe box.

To access Tim's apartment, we took the wooden stairs on the side of the screen porch. His screen porch door was unlocked; we entered the porch and walked over to the glass paned front door. Light peeked out from behind the bamboo blinds, covering the glass door. I knocked but no answer. I dialed his cell phone number but it went straight to voice mail again. I knocked again but nothing. Wanda grabbed the glass cut door knob and the door opened, she stuck her head in and hollered out, "Yoo-hoo, anybody home? Tim are you in?" With no answer, Wanda opened the door more. Inside the living room, the lamp shade on the brass floor lamp was askew, there were papers on the floor, an old pizza box on the coffee table, beer cans and used glasses scattered all about. It looked like the stereotypical bachelor's pad. A mostly dead fichus tree sat in a black plastic planter. A dingy, once white, futon with an equally dingy Mexican throw rug, a large newer style black TV appeared to be the one high-end item in the apartment. A grungy blue corduroy covered bean bag chair was in front of the TV and next to it was an orange Bic lighter and a blue glass bong, much used based on the grey film that covered its interior. A narrow, dark hallway ran from the front living room all the way to the back of the apartment. The small kitchen located behind the living room was an ancient, green pea soup color. A yellowish florescent bulb blandly blinked above the chipped white porcelain sink, which was piled high with dirty dishes. A blue Formica topped, metal table with two broken down matching chairs were off in the corner of the kitchen. On top of the table was an open box of Lucky Charms cereal. A crusty bowl with congealing milk and soggy Charms sat next to it. Old newspapers were stacked up off to the side, a calculator and a sheet of paper with calculations scribbled on it were next to the cereal bowl.

Wanda was calling out Tim's name as we moved farther back into the apartment. The bathroom was next after the kitchen. No one was in there. It consisted of an old white claw footed tub with improvised shower fixture added, a white sink with a dripping faucet and spots where the white enamel had worn away and the iron below was rusting. The steady dripping faucet provided an annoying sound in the otherwise silent apartment. The dry, cracking, unpolished, wooden floor boards creaked as we approached the back of the apartment. Off the narrow hall, was the bedroom. Its door was half way closed and on the other side of the hall another glass rear entry door was ajar. The glass door opened to an outside set of wooden stairs which led down to a two car parking area off an alley. I was sticking my head out that door when Wanda gasped, "Oh damn Alex, call 9-1-1!"

I looked back inside and Wanda was standing inside the bedroom door. I dialed 9-1-1 on my cell phone, as Wanda moved over to a mattress that sat on the floor. On top of the minimal bed was Tim. He was face down, dressed in blue jeans, running shoes and a blood covered polo shirt. His head was turned to the side, eyes closed and there was a large knot/wound on the back of his head. The dingy white sheets beneath him had quite a bit of blood on them. Lying across his bloodied back was what appeared to be a car tire iron, obviously what hit him in the head. Off to the side of the bed, on the floor, turned on its side was a cheap blue ceramic lamp, with no shade. Its fifty watt bulb was glaring sideways, casting shadows and making Tim's bloody head appear even more creepy. Off to the other side was a cheap four drawer dresser. All of its drawers were open and overflowing with various pieces of clothing. Next to the dresser was a small closet, its door was wide open. The naked light bulb with a dangling pull string inside was turned on. There were some clothes hanging on the rod, boots and some other shoes on the floor. Next to them was a grey floor safe, its door was open and the interior was empty.

Everything was a blur. I spoke with the emergency operator, while Wanda placed one of her cosmetic mirrors next to Tim's nose to see if he was breathing; it appeared he was, barely. The fire department arrived first, checked Tim's eyes with a flashlight. They applied gauze to his bleeding head wound, and then the ambulance and paramedics arrived. Wanda and I were ushered to the front porch. The police were just walking in. From there, it was a flurry of questions and Tim was carried out on a stretcher. So much for getting my deal signed around tonight.

I called Sally Anne and let her know what was going on and told her they had just taken Tim to Clinton General. The cops questioned Wanda and me, wanting to know why we were there, what was our relation to the victim, how did we get in the apartment, etc.... Wanda started asking the cops questions right back. "Looks like you got a robbery and attempted murder scene here. You going to dust for prints? That safe in the bedroom appears empty to me. What do you think they took from it? Who do you think hit him on the head? Do you know Detective Davies? He has been helping us, you can check with him about us. Do you know that this Tim Tilberts is the front man for the mob down at that Wharf Rat bar? You think the mob is trying to off him? You know he has a sister who is big on throwing things. You think she threw something at his head, like that tire iron?" On and on Wanda went, the officers appearing more weary. They finally told us it was okay to go. They would check in with Tim's family over at the hospital and would call us in if they had additional questions. Once again, I was told not to leave town without checking in with the police first. As we left, the investigators were pulling up and starting to unroll the yellow tape, while another officer was questioning the neighbors. As I was dropping Wanda off, I received a call from Sally Anne and she let me know that they had Tim in the intensive care ward. She was still waiting to hear a report from the doctor. I offered to come over to the hospital but she said she and Mary Beth had it covered.

28

When I finally got home late in the evening, poor Clyde was about ready to burst his bladder. But loyal soul that he is, he managed to hold it. The minute I turned the key in the lock he ran past me like white lighting and drowned the small magnolia tree in my front yard. I know I could not have held it as long as Clyde did, so as a reward I cooked him half a steak at 1:00 a.m. I emailed the buyer's agent, letting her know what had happened with Tim and that I would keep her posted as to the status. I also emailed Sally Anne and suggested we may need to do a power of attorney for Tim to keep the deal together. Crass I know, but as they say in my business "time is of the essence" and it is my job to be the tactful, hopefully, task master. I took Clyde for a quick walk, gave him a couple of doggie treats to thank him again for his bladder control and finally hit the sack at 2:30 a.m.

The next morning I had a 10:00 a.m. showing with the couple that has the genius spawn on the way. They now decided they were going to home school and have the little tyke in college by age fifteen, so the concern over the inner city versus the suburban environment was no longer a major issue. We toured some houses in Rosedale and one in the Lee. Nothing was quite hitting them, so back to the drawing board. Sally Anne left me a message letting me know that Tim was still unconscious in the IC unit. They were not sure when or if he would be regaining consciousness, it was not looking good. For now, the police had classified it as a robbery and assault. She asked if I could meet up with her later to discuss getting a power of attorney so the deal could still move forward. She wanted to meet at Tim's apartment as she had to find some papers and identification for the attorney to draw up the power of attorney letter. The police had given her permission to enter the apartment to get the paperwork she needed. I pulled up in front of Tim's duplex at 2:00 p.m. I noticed Sally Anne's car out front, walked up to his porch, and gave the glass door a quick rap. Sally Anne appeared, "Hi Alex, thank you for coming by. Come on in. His place is its usual mess, as I am sure you noticed last night. The lawyer wants me to bring in his driver's license or passport and a copy of his Will if I can find it or any document that would help provide a basis for a power of attorney during his incapacitation.

We started going through various piles of papers scattered about his apartment. When we reached the sheet of paper with the calculations on the kitchen table, Sally Anne looked up at me, "I guess you might know about Tim's gambling problem. It's been a long ongoing issue and as I told the police I am not sure who or what is behind this robbery and assault. Hopefully, Tim might shed some light when he wakes up but I doubt he'll spill the beans given the circles he swims in."

I nodded in sympathy and replied, "I know it must be difficult with your mother and now Tim. You know I have heard that Tim has some gambling issues and to be honest, I have heard a few things about Mary Beth as well. Every family has its unique set of problems. I am not sure why someone would be brutally attacking Tim and apparently robbing him."

Sally Anne sighed, "Yes, this family certainly has its issues. Tim has always been the rebel so to speak. He never mooched off my parents but he paid his own way in not so legal ways. He dealt pot for years but I think he got out of that racket years ago. I told the police that his closet door and that grey safe were usually left open so that's not too alarming. I don't think he ever used that safe except maybe back when he was dealing pot but that's been at least a decade or more. But as I told the police, I did notice that his white laptop appears to be missing. He moved from pot into the gambling and numbers racket. Mother never figured that one out and that is probably best. I know Mary Beth knows about his gambling problems and they have always been at each other like cats and dogs. Mary Beth was the spoiled one and I know she is pissed because Tim wanted or needed the money from the sale of mother's house to stay afloat. Mary Beth wanted the house, since she is apparently not going to get anything in her divorce. Which I think is odd but I make it a policy to stay out of my siblings' affairs, focus on my art. I suppose that is the chink in my armor. I always escape through my art."

We had moved on to Tim's bedroom and Sally Anne was going through the overstuffed dresser, "You know Sally Anne, I have heard some odd things about Mary Beth. It could be that she is agreeing to a divorce with no alimony because her husband has embarrassing information about her."

"Ahh, here is his passport and there is a file here marked "Will." Let's see if there is anything about a power of attorney in here. Yes, Alex, I know what you are saying. I do think it is odd someone as selfish as my sister would agree to a no alimony divorce. I also would not put it past my sister and brother to be after each other. I could easily see Tim holding information about her life over her and vice versa. Like I said, I try to maintain a distance, not get involved. Ohh, look here is a Will he wrote up a few years ago. It is one of those do it yourself ones but that should still make the lawyer happy. There is a power of attorney clause and he appointed mother and then me. Okay, I think this is what we need. If you want to follow me to the attorney's office, I can hopefully get the power of attorney created and can sign the purchase and sale documents on Tim's behalf.

"Well, that's a relief to know the real estate deal will still be afloat at least. Any word from the police yet as to what they think was stolen, finger print evidence, etc…?" I queried.

"Nothing yet. Years ago I would have said it was pot in that safe that got stolen but I don't think that is the case. I am not sure what was so important in there that warranted someone attacking Tim. One could guess it might be related to his gambling problem but who knows. I just hope they can figure out who attacked him by lifting prints or something from the tire iron." Sally Anne turned to leave the bedroom and said she was going to use the bathroom before we left. While she was in the bathroom, I glanced in the drawer where she found his Will and noticed another file that was stuffed in and hidden behind some of the clothes. The very tip of its file tab appeared to read, "xtc." I quickly opened the file folder and inside there were copies of emails with dollar amounts. I noticed one of the email addresses was Marc Hilson's, Mary Beth's husband. I did not have time to read anything as the toilet flushed and the bathroom sink

started to run. I had to high tail it down the hall to the front room.
Sally Anne reappeared, locked up the front entry door, and while she
put the spare key under dirt filled but empty flower pot, she sighed,
"This is really so surreal Alex. First mother's death. Now this
happening to Tim. And then, Mary Beth's odd behavior. I tell you, I
don't know what to think anymore." I nodded in sympathy.

I followed Sally Anne to the lawyer's office and it took some
time but Sally Anne was finally able to sign the purchase and sale
agreement on Tim's behalf. I faxed over the sellers offer to sell. I then
called Caitlin, the buyers' agent, and left her a voice mail asking her to
let me know once her buyers agreed and to make sure they signed in
blue or black ink this time. I then asked her to fax me back the
completed, signed around deal, and please let me know when the
inspection date and time was scheduled.

While driving back to my office to check my mail file, I thought
about Fred. His inspection was scheduled for tomorrow. If all went
well, the suburbs would have its very own official S&M coach. I
remembered how he said if he thought someone's life were at stake
then he would reveal who he worked with. I wondered if the assault
on Tim would qualify. If I could take a closer look at the Xtc. file in
Tim's dresser drawer, then I might be able to find out if there was a
link and if so, perhaps Fred would be willing to tell what he knew
regarding Mary Beth and her role as Mistress Xtc.

I breezed through the Winterfrost office. No Stinky in scent or
sight, just the usual gaggle of former nine to fivers. Next, I stopped by
Sasser's Bakery and was reprimanded for not bringing Clyde with me.
I ordered my usual Italian espresso and some warm fresh sourdough

bread with butter. Then I stopped and picked up Clyde, no bowls of glass or other oddities were apparent around the ranch. I drove first to a doggy park located on a ridge to the south of downtown. Clyde went totally nuts and enjoyed running wild with the other assorted dogs. I was half listening to some woman tell me the long pedigree of her fluffy looking dog. Who incidentally, was busy humping some mongrel mutt literally behind her back, as she was gushing on about her dog's long, proud bloodline. My cell phone thankfully saved me and I quickly apologized to the woman and told her I was expecting a business call. The woman then noticed what her fluffy dog was up to and she completely lost it. She started running after fluffy screaming, "No, No, No! Bad dog, you come over here right now!" Naturally, that just encouraged her dog. Fluffy obviously liked an audience, humm--- maybe he had a future as a dog porn star? With that I picked up the phone.

"Okay, so did you get the power of attorney, is the deal going through, any word on Tim?" Wanda barked in my ear.

"Oh, yes, so nice to speak with you Ms. Billings. Yes, quite a lovely day we are having. Me? Why I am okay, thank you for asking. Right now I am with my cute dog at the dog park on the south ridge. And how may I ask, is your day going?"

"Oh, alright I get it. I have had a bit too much coffee today and let me tell you, I have kicked some major ass around this office today to get these loan processors and underwriters to do right! So, what's going on?"

I filled Wanda in on the day's details and when I mentioned the file in Tim's drawer she quickly cut me off.

"Okay, so here is what we gotta do. We need to get back in that apartment tonight and take a close look at that file. I am telling you my sixth sense is going off something fierce on this Alex. Something is off on all of this and we got to figure it out. And I know you are going to protest, try and say no we can't but here is where I'm gonna trip you up. Someone is doing harm to folks out there now. I don't know if it is that mob man, Tony, or if that Mary Beth hit Tim in the head but a tire iron upside the head sure wasn't meant to be a life affirming action. You know the lord would say we gotta get out there and protect those who—awe hell you know what I mean. So are we going back to Tim's tonight and doing some Nancy Drew/Hardy Boys?"

I smiled as I listened to Wanda's comic pitch and because fluffy's owner had hit a mud slick, fallen on her pink jogging suited ass and fluffy appeared to be mounting her leg as she flailed about in the mud. Fortunately, Clyde was nowhere near this scene. There were obviously squirrels in the trees on the edge of the park, because Clyde was camped out under some oaks looking up, ignoring all of the dog park action. "Oh you should see this Wanda, ahh well never mind. Sure I guess you are right, we should try to see what that file has in it. I am not thrilled about the breaking and entering aspect involved in satisfying our curiosity. But, I don't think we are going to literally have to break, in order to enter. I saw where Sally Anne put the spare key to Tim's apartment when we left today."

"Damn, I am always missing out on something. Must be something you are seeing at that dog park, always some kind of strange goings on down there. My Clyde aint in no any trouble is he? Okay, so come pick me up tonight around eight, we can get us some food and then go do some B and E—that's short for---,"

"Yes, Wanda I may be white and uptight but I didn't ride the short bus to school. See you at eight and you can rest easy, Clyde is not involved in this fracas over here, he is too busy staking out the squirrels.

29

I drove over to Wanda's around 8 p.m. As I pulled up, what appeared to be her boyfriend/high-end appliance salesman was leaving. Wanda met me at the door, her hair was all frayed up, one of her long silver earrings was missing, and she was definitely flustered. "Oh, Alex, hey! That was my Romeo leaving and let me tell you---,"

"Ahh, no don't. Just keep it zipped. Glad he makes you happy, don't need to know any more."

"Hummph! No surprise there. Hell, if you were a TV network your call letters would be TMI, too much information. Damn your news division would be less informed and balanced than that Fox outfit! Go on in the kitchen baby and make yourself something to drink, I'm gonna dash on back and finish getting ready. I was thinking we could go get some seafood or maybe tonight's more a Mexican night? Then again, I wouldn't mind me some of that Frenchy stuff they make at that place down on Cole." Wanda wandered down her hall and I departed for the kitchen.

Upon entering the kitchen I knew why the appliance salesman/boyfriend left so satisfied. Wanda's kitchen was now sporting one of those ridiculously expensive, glass fronted, full size, refrigerators. Was she completely out of her mind? Wanda's refrigerator is a constant pigsty-catastrophe and now she is going to have its contents on full display for everyone to see? This style of refrigerator was invented for OCD, anorexic, rich, nuts who never use their kitchens. They can keep a few selected items on prominent display in their overpriced refrigerator/display cases and life goes on as one continual, sterile, magazine spread.

I was pouring myself some tonic water and squeezing in lime juice when Wanda emerged. She had decided to keep the frayed up hair and made it even higher and more spread out. She was decked out in a subtle Wanda casual dining and B&E ensemble; fuchsia slacks, a large loose top with swirling black and fuchsia patterns and black spiky mule shoes. "My, aren't we all in character for our B&E Wanda? I guess the black shoes are meant to keep us unnoticed, not that the fuchsia isn't a nice sedate and blend-in color."

Wanda was mixing up a drink for herself and proceeded to let the vodka bottle spill into my own concoction. "Oh loosen up for damn's sake! If I'm gonna B&E, then I'm gonna do it in style. Besides, no one will hardly take notice of me in such a bland outfit. I don't even have on jewelry and no never mind anyway, who is gonna be watching us walk into some dull ass duplex in the Lee?"

"Ohh, I don't know, the neighbors perhaps?"

"Hummph, neighbors my ass. You leave them to me if we have to talk or get spotted. Besides, you told me that you know where the spare key is and that means this probably don't even qualify as a real B and E."

"Jesus, how much vodka did you pour in my tonic water Wanda?" I said coughing up the sip I had taken. "And what is up with the new neurotic display refrigerator? I know how and where you got it, but are you insane? Do you know how hard it will be to keep the insides of your now always-on-display refrigerator looking clean and orderly? And there is also the window and finger print smudge issue."

"Yeah, I thought about that. I'm thinking now that it has to always look good, it's gonna mean I will eat more healthy food and probably lose some weight in the process. Not that I'm about losing weight! You know I'm a proud full figure woman and…"

"Oh, not the full figure diatribe. You can go have that gab fest with Marie Osmond or Jenny Craig or whoever else is on cable TV hawking their diets."

"You know Alex, I think you might be the perfect spokesman for that I'm-not-a-gay-man-because-I-diet ad they got running 24/7 on cable. All them pot bellied, middle aged men, washed up sports dummies, talking about how they order these packaged meals and they lost weight. But lord knows, just 'cause they went on a diet don't mean they are gay. As if they need to be concerned 'bout people thinking they are gay. They all such dumpy, middle aged, pigs, they don't have to worry a bit about being mistaken for being gay. No self respecting homo would ever let themselves look that flabby and old. Damn, they pot bellies so big they probably ain't seen their tad pole wee-wee's in decades."

With that I had to laugh, "Ahh yes the infamous I am-not-a-fag-because-I-diet ads. Have you noticed the spokesmen are still pot bellied, flabbies in their "after" shots? And the whole, I'm a former sports star angle is pathetic. Obviously they stopped the sports part and started the chow train decades ago. No true athlete would allow themselves to become pot bellied and flabby."

"Tell the truth Alex! Okay, so on that note honey I'm starving and I'm figuring we can do that Frenchy place or go get some seafood over at Mama Honey's. Your call but I'm personally leaning toward some of Mama Honey's Cajun crab and shrimp jambalaya."

That settled, we downed our drinks and I poured half of mine down her drain since it was so strong. We took off in my two-door beater to the edge of the Highmont. Mama Honey's is situated on a small side street that borders the official beginning of downtown Clinton and the lower edge of the Highmont. It has been in business since the 1980s and is situated in what used to be a local hardware store, a yellow bricked one story building from the early 1920s. Mama Honey's has a loyal following of downtown workers who keep it full and overflowing for lunch five days a week. Their dinner hours are limited and not so busy. Mama Honey, is in fact, the name of the owner. She's a sixty-something, Creole, woman from New Orleans and her non-stop infectious laughter fills the small restaurant. Wanda and I are on a first name basis with Mama and she immediately asked me how Clyde was the minute we set foot in the door. We got a table by the big plate glass window, not that it matters because the windows at Mama Honey's are almost always steamed over. Her open air kitchen sits right in the center of the restaurant, literally cooking in the round. There are always enormous pots of gumbo steaming away. In the summer, the air conditioning window units in the transoms strain to keep the heat from the stove at a minimum. In the winter, it is like eating in a steam bath and I swear I have stopped many a cold simply by dining at Mama Honey's on a chilly winter's night. For dinner, she usually offers five or six dishes but it doesn't matter because we always get the same thing, seafood jambalaya. She offers four kinds of bottled beer and one red and one white house wine. I always get beer. "I get you jambalaya. You be lucky ones, we gone to close within de hour. Miss Wanda be lookin' her usual pretty self and Mr. Alex ain't nothing to strain de eyes neither."

After stuffing our faces with seafood jambalaya, Mama Honey brought out two slices of fresh coconut cream pie. We never ask for her famous coconut pie, she just automatically brings it. Sometimes, I stop by Mama Honey's just to have a slice of her coconut cream pie. It is beyond description and I am not someone who typically enjoys sweets. Usually when I come for a slice of pie, it is after the lunch rush and Clyde is with me. That's how Clyde and Mama Honey became such chums. She always dishes up some seafood for Clyde to munch while I am comfort fooding myself with the coconut cream pie. "Now I want to be a seein' you two lovelies back here soon, ya hear me? And bring me the dog Alex, it's been far too long for him not to be havin' some of Mama's jambalaya."

With that, Wanda and I made our way to the car and drove over to Tim's apartment. His street appeared to be dead. No people out and about. A few apartments and house windows sported the blue glow of television sets but that was about the only sign of life. The lights were all off in the apartment below Tim's and no cars were parked in back. Wanda led the way up the stairs to Tim's porch. Everything was completely dark but luckily the blue-ish street light provided us enough light to see the empty flower pot on the screened porch's ledge. Sure enough, the key that Sally Anne placed under the flower pot was still there. I approached the glass entry door and we were inside Tim's apartment in no time. Inside it was dark, the street light glaring in at odd angles through the ratty bamboo blinds. There was a faint hum of the old refrigerator but beyond that it was spooky quiet. I turned on the mini flashlight I had taken out of my car's trunk and led the way down the hall to Tim's bedroom. Everything was as it had appeared before except, the once brilliant red, blood, stained sheets were now a blotchy rusty brown. The dresser drawers were still open and I quickly located the "Xtc." file, handing it to Wanda. I was about to tell her to open it up, when we heard a rustling sound from the back entry door. Someone was definitely outside and quickly coming up the back stairs! Wanda's eyes bugged out. We did not say a word, just turned and high tailed it down the hallway to the front door. I could hear the back door being opened as I quietly shut the front door. I put the key back under the flower pot and we tip toed down the entry steps as fast and quietly as we could. We made a bee line for my car parked a couple of houses down the street.

Once inside the car, we both let out audible sighs. "Who the hell was that coming in his apartment at 10:15 at night?" Wanda said with exasperation, as if anyone should dare to interrupt our B and E.

"I don't know but thank god we escaped. I don't think whoever it was knew we were there do you? Oh good, I see you have the file."

"Yeah, I got it. We should go around back and see if we can check out who is in there. That's what a real PI would do Alex."

"But we are not private investigators Wanda. We sell and finance houses. I guess you are right though, but we need to hide so no one sees us."

"Not a problem, I always knew I could be a great detective. Follow me." Wanda said while getting out of the car and slipping down a driveway that led to the alleyway. We were just outside of Tim's duplex when a dark figure appeared on the rear entry stairs. We ducked behind a metal dumpster bin and watched as the hulking figure lumbered down the wooden stairs. Whoever it was, did not appear to be too concerned about being seen or caught. They paused at the bottom step and lit what smelled like a cigar. There was a cell phone jingle, it sounded like the soundtrack music from the movie "Jaws" to me. The dark figure then flipped open the phone, "Yeah. Nope. Ain't got nothing. Might as well, be there soon." He snapped the phone shut and slowly ambled off down the dark alley. Wanda got up as if she wanted to pursue or follow the figure but I quickly pulled her sleeve and shook my head. After waiting a bit, we went back to my car, no sign of the big hulking figure anywhere.

Once in the car, Wanda picked up the "Xtc." file. "Damn, I wonder who that man was in Tim's apartment. Sounded like he didn't find what he came for. We got what we wanted, let's take a look." Wanda opened the file. There were several printed out emails to and from Marc Hilson. The person writing to Marc was obviously black mailing him, demanding $300,000 in hush money. There was a reference to his wife's "bad behavior" and his future chances of winning elected office. I could not tell from the email address, who the extortionist was. It was a generic, free, email account consisting of random letters and numbers. No name or cute nick names, etc....

"Wanda it appears we were on the right track. Someone, I'm guessing Tim, is black mailing Mary Beth's husband. This would explain why Mary Beth is not getting any alimony. If she is the Mistress Xtc. dominatrix, then it appears her brother knows this and is using it to make some money."

"That's just cold. Course family can be that way, sometimes worse than friends." Wanda slowly shook her head, "What else is in there?" I flipped through some more emails. The first batch was a back and forth between Marc and who we guessed was Tim. The next batch of emails was paper clipped together. This pile was from the same anonymous extortionist's email account and was sent to a "mistressxtc" at another free server's email. These appeared to be quite emotional in content. "It looks like Tim is black mailing Mary Beth too! Look he's demanding she pay to keep his mouth shut and pony up $400,000 or else he'll go public with her dominatrix business. In this email, she says she can't get that kind of money. Here he's saying she should take the proceeds from the sale of her mother's house and pay him off that way. She seems surprised the black mailer knows about her mother's death, asking how he knows about this. The response is pretty cutting, telling her that unlike some socialite ditzs, like herself, he can read the newspaper. Look, he says since the mother has passed away, he now wants $700,000 total from her. Says here, since she is going to get money from her house sale with her husband, he's upped the price to include the money she is going to get from the sale of her mother's house. This email is another reminder that he'll go public with her business and a custody battle over the kids won't go her way if everyone knows she is a dominatrix."

"Do you think she knows it is her brother demanding this money?"

"That's hard to tell from these emails. But wow, Tim has been a busy man Wanda, separately blackmailing Mary Beth and her husband. I bet he is trying to get money from them both to cover his gambling debts."

Wanda shook her head, agreeing. "Okay, we now know we were right about Mistress Xtc. and Tim's gambling problems are bigger than we imagined. Guess it's time to for *Cagney and Lacey* here to end. I got me an early day tomorrow, baby. You hold on to that file Alex and we'll see what's what." By 1:00 a.m. I had dropped Wanda off at her house and was heading back to my little ranch. Clyde was waiting by the door, but this time it was not a full bladder emergency. I did not notice anything amiss, took him outside to squirt some bushes in the back yard, and was in bed by 2:00 a.m.

30

The next day was off to an early start. I showed up at 9:00a.m. for Fred's home inspection. Fred was waiting outside the house, dressed in sedate chinos and a white button down. As soon as I unlocked the house, his inspector got to work. The inspection was going fairly well. The inspector found a bit of dry rot in the back porch and laundry room. As the inspector set up the ladder and began to go up to take a look at the roof, I figured it would be a good time to see if Fred might provide more information, in light of Tim's attack and robbery. I quickly summed up the situation and let Fred know that it now appeared peoples' lives were at risk. Fred let out an audible sigh, "Well Alex, I have always maintained a strict client confidentiality policy but you are right. It sounds as if this person named Tim, his life is at risk. He was beaten and robbed and you strongly suspect there is a direct link between this Mistress Xtc. and Tim? They are brother and sister right? So here are the beans, all off-the-record. I will never admit to anyone that I gave you this information. You are correct, in your assumption that Mary Beth Hilson is Mistress Xtc. She and her husband actually trained with me a number of years ago. They came to one of my couple's weekend workshops, part of my *Exploring the Other Side* series. Seems he wanted to spice up their marriage and he saw my workshop ad in the free weekly. She was very shy and obviously did not want to be there.

However, after two workshops he lost interest but she definitely got the bug so to speak. In fact, she became my star pupil in training. She began learning about all the facets of the business from

186

me. I did supervised sessions with her and with her first clients. I know her husband Marc did not know about this. Mary Beth struck me as the type of person who does everything to its full extent, very competitive in nature. So once she started her dominatrix training, she had one goal, to be the very best dominatrix in Clinton. For a while, she really was the best dominatrix in Clinton. However, I believe the Tim person you mentioned found out about her secret business and from what you have described he was black mailing her. By this point, I was not seeing Mistress Xtc. very much. She had established herself and had her own space to work from. I ran into her once about a year ago at our annual tradeshow and she alluded to some problems. Seems her husband found out about her new profession and filed for divorce with no alimony. He told her if she sought any alimony, he would go public with her dominatrix work and ruin her chances for getting joint custody of their teenage children. Not to mention, ruin her social standing in Clinton. Then, I guess it was six months ago, she closed shop, referred all of her regular clients out and I have not heard a word from her since."

The home inspector was folding up his ladder and he let us know the roof was in about its fifth year of a fifteen to twenty year cycle. That sounded promising. I thanked Fred for his off-the-record confirmation of facts and we waited in silence as his inspector wrote up the inspection report.

It looked as if there would be a few minor items Fred would ask the sellers to repair, via his inspection contingency. If all went according to plan, his deal would close in three weeks. I was pondering the confirmation that Mary Beth really was the Mistress Xtc., when my cell phone gave a chirp. I pulled the car over to the side of the road and answered. It was Sally Anne. She proceeded to tell me that Tim had passed away that morning in the hospital. He had not regained consciousness, was discovered not breathing by the morning shift nurse and pronounced dead at 11:00 a.m. The police were now considering his robbery and assault a murder. Tests were underway at the morgue to determine the actual cause of death. I gave Sally Anne my condolences and asked if there was anything I could do to help. She thanked me and said at this point, there wasn't much anyone could do. She had been trying to contact and locate Mary Beth all morning but had not had any luck. She asked me to have Mary Beth call her ASAP if for some odd reason she contacted me. She mentioned the police would probably have some more questions regarding my finding Tim unconscious, now that this was classified a murder. I said I would be available and we hung up.

I had one showing to do and then Wanda and I were scheduled to meet for lunch. I called Wanda on the way to my showing and left her a voice mail letting her know I might be a bit late for lunch depending on how long the showing took. I pulled up fifteen minutes early to what brokers now like to call a "mid century charmer." In reality, this usually means a 1950s dump with molding aluminum windows and the cloying odor of the recently deceased grandma owner prevailing in the unfortunate press board paneling and sculpted aquamarine wall-to-wall carpeting. Tiffany and Bart had now decided they wanted to redo a mid century rambler. There must have been a recent special on TV extolling the virtues of white, upwardly mobile, wanna-be's rehabbing America's mid century housing supply. They were right out front waiting for me. Tiffany chirping away on her cell phone to some other grub in her office, while Bart, looking as pussy whipped as ever, stood by her side kicking at the cracked cement front walk.

For better or worse, I was right about the house's odors and décor. However, grandma did not appear to have passed away yet, as the house was still occupied by someone in the over seventy age bracket. The tour was going okay, Tiffany babbling on and on about the potential and how cool 1950s houses were. I just smiled and let them wander. We went down to the basement, and entered a rec. room. It sported faux pine paneling, popcorn textured ceiling panels with glow-in–the-dark speckles, and a black vinyl covered bar complete with a gold, marbleized, mirror backdrop. There was a closed door off of the rec. room and Tiffany was struggling to get it open. I was on my way over to help her, when she finally popped it open. "Ohh, it seems to be another room Bart. Where is the light switch? Oh, right here on the wall. You know we could make this our-- AGGGHHH, OHHH, SHITT!!!!" Tiffany screeched as she fled the room. Before I could respond, Bart was backing out of the room sputtering. They both fled to the stairs leading up to the kitchen. I slowly approached the room and poked my head in. The brightly florescent lit room left no margin for hallucinations or shadows. I think I even momentarily levitated, because inside this small room with brown mottled carpeting was a very large snake. A python to be precise. Mr. or Ms. Python was loose in the middle of the room and looked none too pleased to have been so rudely interrupted. The snake was beginning to uncoil and move toward the door and this was no baby python. He or she appeared to be at least ten feet. Off to the stairs I fled. I don't recall my feet hitting a single step on my way up to the Richard Nixon era kitchen. I slammed the basement door shut and found Tiffany and Bart already outside standing on the cement walk. Tiffany sputtered, "What the hell? I mean who would have, why would they not lock--?"

I nodded in agreement as I found the listing agent's number on the listing report and proceeded to dial. Her line's voice mail was full. So I called her main office number and asked for the designated broker. He was all sunshine and fresh as a daisy, until I explained his agent had a listing with a loose python inside. I also let him know that his agent had provided no notice whatsoever that a large snake lived in the basement. It was apparent that Tiffany and Bart were no longer interested in 1950s mid century ramblers with pythons. I apologized for the incompetent listing agent and we agreed to meet again. Tiffany was already saying that perhaps this was a sign. They needed to rethink the type of place they wanted. Oh god!

When I arrived at lunch, for once Wanda was there first. She was waiting with a slushy drink and none too pleased that I had dared to roll in five minutes past our appointed *rendezvous* time. "Well damn, if it ain't Mr. Always On Time walking in late. I ordered you one of these banana, mango, rum things but he ain't bringing it out until he sees your boney ass."

"Hello, to you too Wanda. I am sorry I am late and kept you waiting. I had a loose python in the basement to deal with and—"

"Yeah, ahh hum. Only python you need to be talking about is the one you just found in some man's pants. It is men today right? We haven't flipped back to beaver patrol have we?"

"Wanda I would appreciate it if you would learn more about bisexual---,"

"Hup!" Wanda said putting her hand up. "In your case, let's just get to the 'sexual' part, period. No need to concern ourselves with bi, homo, hetero. Put any or all of them prefixes on that sexual part and then you are in business Alex! I mean damn, if you gonna sit around and waste it all these years, then you might as well get in with one of them religions that requires no sex and earn yourself a nice church pension."

"This is a nice plan you have for me Wanda but I have more interesting news. Sally Anne called and told me that Tim passed away this morning and his death has been classified a murder. Fred confirmed Mary Beth is Mistress Xtc." Wanda's mouth dropped open and my slushy drink arrived, purple umbrella and all. "Alex, you and me may have us a smoking gun with those emails."

31

Before the realization could sink in that Mary Beth probably killed her brother and proof of her motivation, via the emails, was in our hands, my cell phone rang. I barely got out a hello.

"Listen Alex, it's Lexi. I have a bizarre message to pass on to you and Wanda. You know my contact Tony at the Wharf Rat? Well I just got a call from him and he requests the pleasure of Wanda's and your company this evening. Says you all have some business to discuss and he will be expecting you two at the Rat around 9:00 p.m."

"But Lexi, we don't even---,"

"Look, I wouldn't even consider this invitation optional Alex. When Tony and Company calls, you go, period. What have you and Wanda been up to anyway?"

I quickly brought Lexi up to date and we arranged to all meet at my place first and then all three go over to the Wharf Rat together. Lexi would at least be a good witness and she did know Tony, so perhaps she could help out if needed. Wanda and I quickly finished up our lunch, wondering about various reasons as to why Tony would want to see us. I had to go show the lovely pregnant couple a house that just listed. We agreed to meet up at my house around 7:00 p.m. to discuss things before going to the Warf Rat. I phoned Lexi back and told her to be at my house at 7:00 p.m. and she said she'd bring some take-out from Dim Lung's. I reminded her to get extra fortune cookies or Wanda would be pissed. I swung by the Winterfrost office to quickly print out a listing report for the house I was showing and after

doing the usual polite agent/designated broker bullshit routine with
Todd, I sped off to Rosedale to meet the clients.

This time, the pregnant couple was seeing a vacant, 1935
vintage, Tudor style house. Obviously the whole educating the child in
the inner city fantasy had completely worn off. Now we were going to
see if Hansel and Gretel were alive and well, in their mock Tudor
cottage. The house was very cute and priced well, so I had no doubt it
would sell quickly. The inside of the house was pretty dark, which is
not a surprise, as mock Tudor style houses from the 1930s usually are.
They also typically come with very small, chopped up, rooms and this
one was no exception. The dark woodwork, moldings, and coved
ceilings were period and cute. The fused green tile fireplace with its
small stained glass window in the middle of the mantel's chimney and
the wrought iron wall sconces on either side could have been from a
movie set. However, it appeared that only the Munchkins or some
character from Harry Potter, were the only people who could actually
live comfortably in this house. Regular size furniture was out of the
question, given the "quaint" small room dimensions. This was where
the story book Tudor look meets reality. I could see the expectant
couple was not going to compromise on their bulky Restoration
Hardware treasures. Thus, no way were things going to fit or work out
with this house. At least I did not encounter any unexpected pets on
this tour.

I got home by 6:00 p.m. and took Clyde for a long walk. We
went to the rotting piers, sniffed endless bushes, trees, tried to chase a
couple of squirrels, stopped by Sasser's and said hello to Daynia (who
of course fed Clyde a lovely snack). As we were approaching my little

ranch, Lexi pulled up in her aging yellow, Chevy Bronco. "Well perfect timing. I see my friend Clyde has been for a walk. Here, help me with these take-out bags Alex." Once inside, Lexi and I dropped the bags of take-out on the counter. Clyde proceeded to do his welcome dance for Lexi, while I took out some cold Chablis and proceeded to pour us both a glass. Lexi was looking out of the glass garage door wall, commenting on the progress I had recently made on my gardening out back when Wanda arrived.

"Hey babies," Wanda chimed as she let herself in and rushed to pick up Clyde's front paws and dance with him toward my open kitchen. "Lexi, you are looking fine girl. Did you lose some pounds or no, it's your hair isnt' it?"

Lexi smiled, "Thanks Wanda but I've gained three pounds and my hair hasn't changed in at least ten years. You look model perfect as ever Wanda."

"Oh thank you honey," Wanda said while taking my glass of Chablis and slugging back a big sip. "Damn, that is the cheap shit Alex. Eww, even that two buck Chuck taste better than this here crap. Can't say I'm surprised. No offense, but you are tight with that wallet Alex. Thank you anyway, you can refill my glass and oh look, we got us some Dim Lung for dinner, don't we Clyde."

"Well, yes Wanda I guess we all can't date high end appliance salesmen and splurge on every little indulgence." I replied while topping off my glass and pouring a new glass of wine for Wanda. "Besides, what's wrong with a little two buck Chuck? Table wine doesn't have to cost a fortune to be palatable."

194

"Humph…that is true, but what you pouring is more from the vinegar family if you ask me. And you know, dating a high end appliance salesman might be just what you need Alex. Why, I bet Dave knows someone over where he works that swings your way. Look you could have a nice see through refrigerator in here too Alex, if you put your mind, well no actually your pelvis, to work."

Lexi quickly interjected, "Now children, enough. Let's dish out the Dim's and then figure out why in the hell you two are going to the Wharf Rat for a special request meeting with Tony for god's sake."

My place does not have a dining room, so I dished up the take out and we all sat at bar stools around the concrete counter discussing Tim's death or now murder. We'd finished all of the main courses. I hate duck, so that dish was just for Wanda, Lexi and Clyde. Wanda opened the small bag of fortune cookies and started handing each of us a cookie, while cracking open a couple for herself. "I still don't think Tony could know that we did a B and E at Tim's and why would he care about those black mailing emails? Only thing Tony would care about is the numbers and it sounds like Tim owed them some big ones." Wanda said while cracking open a third fortune cookie.

Lexi tossed her fortune on the table, *Life unfolds for you in your own way* and laughed, "So much for me getting one that promised love or lots of money. I guess you two will just have to see what Mr. Tony has to say. I would guess he is after something Tim had related to the numbers business, but who knows."

Wanda tossed the small fortune cookie bag at Lexi, while cracking open her fourth cookie, "There baby, find another cookie with a fortune you like. Look I finally found me one here that I like,

Others see you as the kind soul you are. See there, just this afternoon I was told I was a kind person at the Highmont business meeting. Course, that was after I threatened not to back their annual fund drive anymore if they wouldn't allow me to hand out promotional coupons for Salon Wanda. Anyhow, we best just get over to the Rat and see what's what. After that, we gotta figure out what to do with those emails Alex what with this now being a murder investigation and all. How are we gonna let on that we have them and not have them figure out we did our B and E? Hey, open up your cookie there Alex, what's your fortune say? *All will be revealed in time,* no kidding.

32

We piled into Wanda's big boat of a car and soon pulled up to the Wharf Rat. Inside, it was still the same worn in "ambiance." No one was playing pool, the juke box was lit up but slient, and only about five people appeared to be there. "Damn, these floors is sticky! Look my mules are really sticking to this floor. What you say about drinking in this place Lexi, only get a beer? Oh, check that out, they got a pirate working the bar." We walked up to the bar and Leo was there with his eye patch pouring a drink for our old friend Sandy. Sandy was perched on what must be "her" stool, blue eye shadow perfectly in place and wearing another pajama looking ensemble, this one in orange and yellow swirls. She coughed out a cheery hello, while lighting another Kent 100 and I introduced her to Wanda. Wanda proceeded to talk Sandy up, asking her where she bought her clothes, if she owned or rented, and had she ever considered a reverse mortgage. From there, they were discussing hair and Wanda promptly handed her a Salon Wanda card, "Girl I know Miss Liz gonna wanna meet you! Give her a call, tell her I said so. You gotta come by and see my salon honey, it's the bomb." Lexi asked Leo to let Tony know we were there for our appointment. Our bottled Budweisers had just arrived when Tony appeared.

"Oh, hello so good youze could make it. Come join me in da office, we can discuss things there. Thanks for deliverin' them the message Lexi. You make sure Leo here treats you right, while I have a word wid our friends."

Wanda gave me a wide eyed look and off we went after Tony, our shoes making little ripping sounds on the sticky cement floor. Tony led us through a door next to the restrooms and inside was a makeshift office. The ten by ten, florescent lit, room had boxes of liquor stacked against the walls. A dented, grey, metal desk sat in the middle with two metal fold out chairs on one side and an ancient wooden swivel desk chair on the other side. A black rotary dial telephone probably from the 1950s sat on the desk, along with a brown coffee mug and a clunky, dark green, glass ashtray. Behind the desk, squeezed in between liquor boxes, was an old four drawer, wooden filing cabinet. Above it a faded wall calendar from *Durby's Tire and Re-Treds* with the month of March 1962 on permanent display. Tony indicated the metal chairs for us and parked himself in the wooden swivel chair.

"So's, just to thank you two for coming in and havin' this little meetin' with me", he said while offering us a cigar from a wooden cigar box he had taken out of a desk drawer. We both politely declined the stogies and he promptly lit one up, letting off a cloud of smelly smoke which curled up above us and wrapped around the desk. "Youze," he said looking at Wanda, "I believe we met the other night at the Ridge. Guess youze found the ladies room, huh? And youze, I know from Lexi. Hey, youze know my fairy brother from down south? He's coming to visit next month. We gotta get youze two together, ya know? Anyways, I had us here tonight so we could review things. I understand youze two know Tim. Youze must know he is dead, they say it's a murder. Imagine that, will ya? Some gaboon clubbed him in the head with a tire iron. Say they emptied a safe he had there too. Now a little byord told me that youze two might know something about all this here."

Wanda looked at me and then smiled sheepishly at Tony. I gave a quick smile and proceeded to concentrate on making sure my hands were perfectly folded in my lap. "I guess I's should tell ya, I had a little business with Tim, you see? He ran some things for me. Now I know youze two didn't off Tim, but I don't know what youze was doing over at his place the other night. Could you fill me in?"

I cleared my throat, Wanda shifted in her chair, "Well," I said, "Wanda and I were checking on some paperwork. You know, ahh, Tim was part of a real estate deal I am working on and---,"

Tony leaned back in his chair letting out a smoky exhale, "Yeah, I know all about the real estate deal there. Tim coulda used that money from the sale see? Cause he owed us some money. So's I can appreciate youze making sure the sale is going along and all. What papers was youze getting from his place?"

Wanda piped in, "Oh, we had to go and check on some papers we thought Tim might have. See, we got us a theory about his mama's death and all. What we were checking on had nothing to do with none of Tim's business with you. Not that we know anything about his business with you Mr. Tony. No, Alex and me just trying to figure out what happened to Tim's mama and why his sister act like such a bitch."

Tony smiled, "Glad to know you ain't all up in my business. Youze know the cops are gonna start asking a lot of questions now that this is a murder. Youze two wanna make sure youze got your stories straight."

"Word, I hear that Mr. Tony. And I tell you, like I said, Alex and me just trying to figure out the--well I guess you'd call it the family dynamics here. See, we think Tim was blackmailing his sister and her husband. We think his sister Mary Beth, she the bitchy one, anyway we think she done spanked people for a living. And you know, with her wanna-be, politician husband that type of biz don't fly."

Tony sat up a little straighter, "Well youze don't say. Tim was blackmailing his own family to pay off his debts? That's inter—esting, ain't it? So youze two was at Tim's place getting what?"

I cleared my throat, "We were at Tim's apartment because I saw a file while I was there with his sister Sally Anne. The file had emails which appear to show that Tim was blackmailing his sister Mary Beth and her husband Marc Hilson. This explains why Mary Beth has been so hostile to me about the sale of her mother's house."

"Youze two got yourselves emails that show Tim was blackmailing family? Youze gonna share that with the cops? See they might wanna know something like that, seein hows Tim got killed and all. But youze two didn't run across Tim's laptop did youze? Tim's laptop is missing. It would be good for me to have that, seeings how I purchased it for him. Ya know, so he could do his business work for me and all."

Wanda and I looked at one another and I piped in, "Oh, Tony we don't know anything about a missing laptop. We saw some hand written calculations on a sheet of paper in his kitchen but no laptop."

"Well I tell ya what, youze keep your eyes open for that laptop. It's a white, Mac version. Ya find it, let me know. I gotta a little numbers business on there that I need to keep in my possession. Youze guys help me out with this and maybe I can help youze out with something later on, ya know? Also, best if ya just keep your mouths shut. Don't go talking bout no business of Tim and me. Like at the Ridge, best if you just find the ladies room without finding me, *capiche?*"

"Ohh, I definetly got that one Tony! No more searching for the ladies for me. No way, humph—gonna just get me some Depends if it gets that bad. No, you won't be seein' me Mr. Tony. Course if Alex and me find this laptop, we gonna be in touch with you."

"That's nice, real nice. So who do youze two think off'd Tim? I'm thinking maybe they might know something about this missing laptop. Ya know, a blow to the head with a tire iron, well that really ain't our style around here if youze know what I mean."

Know what I mean? Christ, this really was a Tony Soprano moment and his name was really Tony. "Well, I'm sure it's not. I would guess the police will be trying to figure out who hit and killed Tim."

"You know, seems awful nasty, a hit on the head now don't it?" Wanda said thinking aloud. "Course it reminds me, you know that Mary Beth smashed out Alex's car window by throwing some statue through it. And then, someone threw a brick with a note threatening his dog through his living room window. Seems like an awful lot of throwing and hitting going down, and it ain't baseball season yet."

Tony asked some questions about what Wanda mentioned and we filled him in. "Sounds to me, like youze got a whack job on your tail Alex. Nothing youze two describe sounds like a professional. Really could be that sister of his, the spanker. Sounds to me like she might have slipped a gear. Maybe she needs a little talkin' to, ya know? Wouldn't hurt to find out more and see about collecting some of Tim's debts. Just an idea I have. Youze guys keep me posted, what I really need is that laptop. I would be very appreciative if you found that for me. Sort of an informal job for youze two, get what I mean? See I can't be goin' around no more looking for no laptop with our friendly cops all involved. Youze two, well that's a different story. See what I'm saying?" A cell phone began to ring in Tony's pocket, it played the theme to "Jaws" when it rang. "Oh, so's I gotta take this here call. Nice talkin' wid youze, let's keep in touch."

With that, our appointment with Tony ended. We found Lexi at the bar yakking away with Sandy. Lexi had her recorder out on the bar, taping the soundscape as she calls it. She had suddenly decided her next installation needed to include sound. So now wherever Lexi went, her tape recorder seemed to magically appear. Sandy was having another crème de menthe and told Wanda she was definitely going to stop by Salon Wanda.

We left the sticky floored bar and were walking back to Wanda's boat, I mean car, "Damn, least I got the salon a new potential customer out of that sticky floor bar. Lord knows that woman needs a little Miss Liz's magic in her life. By the looks of Sandy, if I didn't know better, I'd swear that it was 1968 and some Andy Williams special was airing on the TV. She sweet though. Anyway, look like us two got a new job and Mr. Tony for a boss. Damn, doing some freelance work for the mob, that's rich! And did you hear that 'Jaws' music playing on his phone Alex? That's the phone we heard the night

202

someone busted in on us at Tim's apartment. Must have been big
Tony there looking for his laptop. You know we get all tight with
Tony and I can see me helping out him and his other comb
over/toupee wearin' peeps. You know, get them set up with some real
hair at Salon Wanda, maybe start me a Clinton hair club for men kinda
thang and then me doing some investment mortgages for our mob
friends." Mob "friends" I'm sure.

We piled in the car and filled Lexi in, while Wanda drove us
back to my house.

33

The next day, Wanda and I met at Doris Havlon's office. Doris is a local real estate attorney. We wanted to see about passing along the emails we had boosted from Tim's place to the police. Doris is a no nonsense woman who is very polite and nice, but cross her path and you will come out looking like you had a spin in a Cuisenart. Doris was dressed in a tailored, taupe, pant suit with a single strand of choker length black pearls and black flats. Her graying hair was styled in a perfect bowl cut. "Looking at these emails Alex, I can see you and Wanda have some information you would like to pass along to the police which may or may not be helpful in the Tim Tilberts' murder investigation. Is that correct?" We nodded in agreement. "Fine, I will invoke attorney-client privilege in this matter and forward the email copies to the investigating officer."

"Yeah, when we were there getting those files, you know that mob guy---,"

"No need to elaborate Wanda. I have all I need. I do not want to know anything more. You did say something about a mob guy. I would warn both of you to stay away from organized crime, as I do not do criminal litigation defense work."

"Nuff, said." Wanda replied. "Say who's doing your hair these days, lady? You know Salon Wanda---,"

"Same person as the last time you asked about my hair Wanda. Me. I am proficient with hair cutting scissors and I see no reason for me to waste valuable time and money visiting a salon. Although I admire your business model and am sure you make quite a profit."

With that, we left Doris' office. "Gee, Dorothy Hamill there sure ain't open to updating her look is she Alex? Might get herself a man and quit sleeping with her work if she got a hair style that don't scream 1976. Anyway, we got to get a plan on finding that laptop Alex. I'm betting that Mary Beth has got it. I am also thinking she offed her brother. Hit him upside the head and took off with that laptop. Got rid of her black mail problem, solved her cash flow problems, all in one whack."

"Well that sounds like a reasonable assumption to me but what do we care about Tony's laptop? It's not our job to go out of our way and find it."

"No it's not Alex. But see, you don't watch yourself enough *Sopranos*. When big Tony there was 'suggesting' we help out, he was more like ordering us to help out. I ain't planning to get in bad with the mob, no sir-ee. Miss Wanda gonna do what she can to help out Mr. Tony and you are too. Hell, they can be some bad ass protection if we need it someday Alex."

"Oh yes, with all the nefarious deals we do and circles we run in Wanda. Gosh yes, mob protection may be just the ticket for us. But okay, we could try and locate the laptop. Besides, if Mary Beth is the murderer and has it, we would be helping out my would-have-been client, Mrs. Tilberts. Even if it is post mortem help, and it turns out her own children kill each other."

Later in the day, I received a call from Sally Anne letting me know that she had spoken with Mary Beth. They managed to plan a funeral for Tim. It would be a private, simple service at the same church as his mother. She also let me know that his death was ruled a murder from blunt trauma to the head. The weapon used, appeared to be the tire iron which they were currently testing for finger prints or to see what type of car it might have come from. The police did not say they had any leads. I inquired as to where Mary Beth was living these days but Sally Anne said she did not know. She only had her cell phone number. So, looks like I would have to check in with Stinky and try and weasel from her where exactly her client Mary Beth was now living. If we could take a quick tour of her living accommodations, then perhaps we could locate the missing laptop.

As fate would have it, an offer came in for Mary Beth and Marc's house. I contacted Marc and arranged to meet with him at his office to review the offer. I left a couple of voice mail messages for Share letting her know an offer was in but did not heard back from her. The offer was straight forward and full price. Marc quickly reviewed it and signed off. We still needed to get Mary Beth's signature on the documents. Marc said that Mary Beth would agree to everything and I told him I had been trying to reach Share. Once I had the documents completely signed around we would have mutual agreement. After I left Marc's office, I sat in my car and chilled for a few minutes. I dialed Share's cell again and she actually picked up. "Hello this is Share Shelton, Winterfrost Real Estate's premier agent, how may I assist you in buying or selling?" Gag me. "Uhh, yes, hi Share it is Alex. I left you several messages. We have a full price offer for Mary Beth and Marc's house. I just met with Marc and he has signed. I need to get the documents to you, so you can meet with Mary Beth and have her sign. The buyer's agent has the offer expiring tonight, so we need to move quickly."

"Ooohh, yes Alex-- the new wonder listing agent! Did you call me? Gee, I didn't see any messages. Oh well, you have me now. A full price offer for Mary Beth's place, that sounds good. You know I am not available today or tonight. I guess you will have to meet with Mary Beth and get her signatures. Let me give you her cell number and address. Of course I will put a call in to her first and let her know you will be bringing the paperwork by. Try not to annoy her. She really is not a fan of yours."

Fucking, lazy bitch. "Well Share, you are working with Mary Beth and we are co-listing agents. It is up to you to meet with Mary Beth and get her signatures. I have done my part."

"Ohh, Alex don't be so naïve. Why, I am not even in town. I am rejuvenating my mind, body, and spirit at the fabulous Mermosa Spa. You do know I go to the spa at least every other month. Why Janet Jackson was just here and there's a rumor that Paris is going to be coming tomorrow! A good agent has to maintain their appearance, but I guess that is something you obviously have not yet figured out. So, anyway, you will have to meet up with Mary Beth. I will put the call in to her. You let me know how things go. I'll be back in Clinton in a day or so."

Before I could respond, Share rattled off Mary Beth's number and address and hung up. I was fuming. I pondered calling Todd Blund, our designated broker, and let him know what Stinky was doing or rather not doing. Then I realized, that would be a waste of my time. Todd would not stand up to Stinky and make her do her job.

Winterfrost never makes its big name, diva agents follow the rules. I decided not to waste anymore time seething, just find Mary Beth and get the job done. I dialed her cell and left her a message. I let her know that Stinky was unavailable and I needed to get her signatures and have the offer completed by tonight before it expired. I called Marc to fill him in and he promised to leave Mary Beth a message as well. I told Marc if I had not heard back from Mary Beth by early this evening, then I was going to go knock on her door. Maybe I could scout around for the missing laptop?

34

By 5:30 p.m., I had walked Clyde and killed time by re-arranging my utility closet. I had left two more messages for Mary Beth and still no response. I was going to have to go to her house and try and track her down. I called Wanda and asked if she would tag along with me to Mary Beth's. I wanted back up, in case Mary Beth went loco with a brick or tire iron. Also, perhaps Wanda could see if the missing laptop was in Mary Beth's house, while I had the nut sign the offer paperwork. Wanda was all gung-ho, the looking for the laptop part anyway. I picked her up a bit after 6:30 at her office.

"Hey baby. I am telling you there is some serious shit going down with these low-ball lenders out there Alex. You would not believe the type of loans they are putting folks in. Folks who got no business renting, much less buying are jumping in these deals--humph. They handing out those no income verification loans like candy; putting folks in negative amortization and three year adjustable rate mortgages, left and right. This is a time bomb, I'm telling you. Where Clyde at?"

"Ah, Clyde is home guarding the ranch. I didn't want to bring him along to Miss Psycho's house. So let's review Wanda. I need to get Mary Beth's signature on all of the offer paperwork and not have her try and kill me. While I am doing that, you can make sure she is not going loco and perhaps see if you can find the missing laptop. If you see it, just leave it and we can figure that out once we leave."

"Sounds like a plan Hardy Boy. So, Miss Stinky is too busy getting her ass waxed at some spa to take care of her business. No surprise there. But this is good, gets us in Mary Beth's crib and lets us help Mr. Tony out. Humph, this Mary Beth sure must be low on the funds; this is one skanky 'hood. Miss Bluffs-Beaumont done fallen into the Skytown 'hood, ain't that a pill!'"

I counted off the house numbers and sure enough, there was the address that matched Mary Beth's on the right. Skytown is a modular housing, low-rent, community built on the outskirts of Clinton near the airport, in the early 1950s. It is comprised of one story, flat roof, duplexes with single pane aluminum windows and fading aluminum siding. It had to be skanky when it was built and the intervening decades have done it no favors. Sure enough Mary Beth's bright red Range Rover was parked in front, glittering conspicuously amongst the assorted beater cars. "Damn, now you know her mama would be in a world of pain if she saw this dump her psycho daughter be livin' in." Wanda said while accompanying me up the cracked cement front walk.

A busted out aluminum screen door hung limply. I reached through it and pressed the black buzzer, next to the fading orange front door. The door abruptly popped open, a brass chain lock in place. Mary Beth peered out, with her smudged raccoon eyes. "What the fuck do you want? You cheated my mother, conspired against me, and stole the listing of my house from Share." I explained why I was there and that I had left her several messages. She abruptly slammed the door. I looked at Wanda and then called Marc. I explained the situation and that Share was not available. He agreed to meet us there in twenty minutes. Wanda and I went back to my old Volvo and listened to the radio and discussed what might be a good food venue for dinner later on tonight. We decided having pizza delivered to Wanda's house was the best option.

Marc Hilson arrived twenty-five minutes later in a shiny, late model, black, Lexus sedan. He immediately began banging on Mary Beth's front door. When she cracked it open, he told her to let him in or he'd bust the door down. She complied. Less than five minutes later, he opened the door and motioned us in. The rental was a very simple, one bedroom affair. The front door led right into a brown shag carpeted, musty smelling, small living room/dining area. There was an ancient olive green sofa, a broken, three legged coffee table and one metal folding chair. The dining area had an aluminum, single bulb, chandelier over a white, circular table which was surrounded by four white, lime green vinyl, cushioned swivel chairs. Mary Beth was seated in one, glaring up at us. Behind her was a very small galley style kitchenette in fading yellow. To the left of the living area was a narrow hall with a bathroom and the single bedroom.

Marc was standing next to Mary Beth, "Here Alex, put the paperwork on the table and Mary Beth will sign where you need her to." I put the documents down and Wanda piped in, "Could I use your bathroom?" Before Mary Beth could respond, Marc nodded and off Wanda went.

The document signing went fairly fast. I turned each page and showed Mary Beth where to initial and date. We had just finished up the last page when Wanda re-appeared in the living/dining room. I told Marc and Mary Beth I now had everything I needed and that I would get the mutually signed around deal back to the listing agent.

We would then wait for the inspection date notification. Marc showed us to the door and thanked me, while Mary Beth sat slumped at the table bawling about how everyone always cheated her and her life was in ruins.

Wanda and I drove off, speeding out of Skytown to the Winterfrost office. I needed, per the law, to fax over the signed around deal and notify the buyer's agent it was done. "Damn, Alex that white laptop sure 'nuff is under that whack bitch's bed. I had to move fast in there but luckily that place is so small you can hardly turn around. I say we get Mr. Tony notified of this."

"Tim's laptop was under her bed? Okay, so while I fax this deal to the buyer's agent, why don't you call Lexi and see if she can let Tony know where the laptop is. I guess we should tell Tony that he has to work fast and get what he wants off of that laptop, because we have to notify the police as well. I am thinking we will let Doris tip the police off anonymously again."

While I faxed the deal, Wanda reached Lexi on her cell and she was in an artists' co-op meeting. Lexi said she would contact Tony and relay the message and Mary Beth's address. She would also let Tony know that we planned to have Doris contact the police tomorrow afternoon regarding the laptop, so Tony needed to work fast. Lexi mentioned she would stop by Wanda's when the artists' meeting was done. Once the faxing was complete and the fax receipt was in my hand, I called the buyer's agent to let her know the signed around deal was there. I copied the deal paperwork, filled out an office transaction sheet and dropped the copy off in Todd's in-box. We left Winterfrost and headed back to Wanda's for pizza.

35

Lexi arrived after we had almost finished the pizza, "My looks like you two had a pizza with every imaginable topping available. What is that Romero's delivery?" Lexi said while Wanda put a slushy drink in her hand. "Thank you. Oh Wanda, I like the new magenta sofa cushions, ahh good to sit down. Anyhow, I passed your message along to Tony. Sally Anne was at the artists' co-op meeting. She was quietly telling me and a few others that her sister Mary Beth may be in trouble. Everyone was offering her their condolences for Tim's murder. She was gracious as ever. She told me that she was talking with the police and that she had let them know Mary Beth had items that were missing from Tim's apartment. Said she had seen them at Mary Beth's apartment when they met there to plan Tim's funeral. She felt torn, but figured she was better off letting the police know. I got some awesome street sounds today for my sound installation, wanna listen?"

Fortunately, my cell phone rang. It was Tony and he said he was parked outside of Mary Beth's house. He wanted to know if we could help him out tonight, getting the information off of the laptop at Mary Beth's. Tony thought it would be in "our best interest" to accomplish this ASAP. We talked a bit and I tossed around ideas with Wanda as well. Bottom line, Tony needed about ten minutes with the laptop to copy and erase the files that pertained to his business. I thought the best pretext for entry would be for us to pretend we needed to get Mary Beth's and Marc's signatures again. Once inside, Wanda could pass the laptop out the window to Tony's computer guy and hopefully hide it under the bed again while I got the paperwork re-signed.

I knew what I had to do. I called Marc and explained that unfortunately the fax machine had mangled the signed paperwork and I would need to have Mary Beth and him re-sign. He did not seem annoyed, just said sometimes machines screw things up. I told him, to make it is less of a problem for Mary Beth, I would be happy to stop by her place in a half hour, as I was on my way picking up Wanda from a meeting she had with another client. Marc said he would let Mary Beth know and would see us over there soon.

Back out we went, Lexi decided to head off for her house. She was all excited about her new street recordings and needed to get back and work on her installation project. Wanda and I rolled over to Mary Beth's again. We did not see Marc's car but a black Cadillac Escalade down the street flashed its lights, so I pulled my car up. Tony leaned out his black tinted window, "So, youze gonna hand the laptop to Mick here through that side bedroom or bathroom window, right?" Wanda nodded in response. "Good deal. Shouldn't take too long and youze can stash it back under her bed and we are done with our business." Sounded good to me. I parked my car in front of Mary Beth's rental and just as I turned off the headlights, Marc pulled up. This time, getting inside was no issue. Mary Beth opened the door wide, turned around and parked herself at the white table. "So looks like my agent Share was right Marc. Retard agent here, can't even manage to work a fax machine." Marc held up his hand to Mary Beth, "Just can it Mary Beth. Accidents happen, machines do not always work properly. You should be thankful Alex here is decent enough to come out and fix this. Hell, your agent isn't even around. I haven't seen her lift a damn finger."

"How dare you---,"

Wanda interrupted her, "Baby, is it okay if I use your facilities?"

"What? Yeah, go ahead. You should know where it is, you used it the last time you were here. As you can see, I don't live in a palace like my soon to be ex-husband here. No, I'm in a tenement dump until we can get this all worked out. Lord, if it is not my siblings screwing me over it is my husband, some life! Why I never would ---,"
I cut her off by putting the pile of paperwork in front of her and motioned for Marc to sit down as well. I sat down and pretended I had to organize the paperwork, anything I could do to distract them and stall for time. We were moving along with the signatures and it had already been over ten minutes when there was a loud crash from the bathroom.

"What the hell?" Mary Beth said as she got up from her chair and walked over to the tiny hallway. Marc and I followed behind her. Mary Beth reached the bathroom door and pushed it open, "Hey, what's going on in here? You got some kind of problem? What was that crash? Hey, why are you in my bathtub?" I looked over Mary Beth's shoulder and there was Wanda flat on her ass in the pink bathtub. One leg was hanging over the tub's edge, the suction cup style bathroom shower curtain rod was part way down the wall and part of the gray plastic shower curtain was draped over Wanda.

"Oh, mercy baby! Don't you worry. I just fell in your tub here. Was washing my hands and you know, these shoes here is new and real

216

high. So I lost my balance and well, here I am. Don't worry I'll put your curtain back. I am so sorry I interrupted your signing."

Mary Beth glared at Wanda and then back at and Marc and me. "Fell in my tub? I suppose that is possible, since you are wearing hooker heals. What are you a Tina Turner wanna-be? God, did you break my shower curtain? You better not have hurt yourself because if you did, it was your own damn fault and I'm not liable, nor is my landlord. Gee Marc, your people here are causing damage to my crappy rental. Guess I'll have to have the landlord take it up with you, ha! What's the window open for?" Mary Beth pointed to the small aluminum window that was inset in the bath/shower wall.

Wanda propped herself up, moving her legs, "Well, I just opened it for some fresh air. I mean you know, fresh air in a bathroom is good after your company has had some digestive problems due to the extra spicy chicken enchilada I had for dinner tonight. Now, I'll fix everything up. If you don't mind?" Wanda said looking directly at Mary Beth and bugging her eyes out, while she muttered, "Spanky ho' calling me a ho' in Tina Turner heels, don't that beat all."

"What?!" Mary Beth exclaimed glaring back at Wanda, "Did you just say something about me? Did you call me a spanky whore?"

"Say what? Baby you are hearing things! I was wondering if I had my hanky with me. Didn't anybody say nothin' 'bout no ho'."

Mary Beth let out a humph of disgust and slammed the hollow core bathroom door shut. "That's the last time she uses my bathroom! In fact, this better be the last time I ever see you two and hopefully soon I can say the same for you as well Marc. Now, what the fuck else do I have to sign? I'd like to go to bed before midnight if that's all right with everyone!"

She huffed back to the white table and I got them both back to signing. Wanda was still in the bathroom when we finished the paperwork. There was nothing else I could do to delay things. Marc stood up, followed by Mary Beth. I tried to pack the paperwork as slowly as I could in my brief case, pretending I was checking each page.

Mary Beth let out a loud sigh, "Do you all plan to leave tonight or should I have the concierge make up extra beds for you? And what's the problem with your fat friend? Is she having more digestive issues? Or perhaps she's decided she likes my lovely apartment so much she wants to take a bath in my *deluxe* pink bathtub? Of course, she'd be much happier tagging along with Marc and parking her fat ass in the Jacuzzi soaking tub that is in what used to be my private bathroom suite." Mary Beth, walked to the bathroom door and gave it a loud bang, "Finish up toots and get the hell out of here!"

Wanda exited the bathroom ignoring Mary Beth and said she'd wait for me outside. Mary Beth rolled her eyes and said, "Let's hope she doesn't break the front door on the way out." Marc and I followed Wanda out the door and Mary Beth ceremoniously slammed the front door shut behind us. I thanked Marc again for being so cooperative. He replied, "No, thank you for making sure things are taken care of Alex. Wanda, I am sorry Mary Beth is such a bitch. Guess you can see why we are divorcing."

Marc drove off and Wanda and I sat for a few moments in my car. Wanda said we should go to the Tiki Bar over near the airport, since it was close by. She wanted a drink and she said she wasn't going to fill me in until she had one. The Tiki Bar is exactly what it sounds like, an early 1960s pseudo Polynesian themed bar. It sits right off the main highway, a block away from the entrance to the airport drive. We went inside and sat in one of the faux bamboo shrouded booths. Wanda proceeded to order us both some gigantic Polynesian rum, slushy drinks. They arrived in turquoise ceramic glasses shaped like mini smiling Buddhas. Wanda took a long slurp of hers through the red straw. "Damn Alex, almost had to belt that bitch. Good thing she ain't throwin' no bricks and what not tonight. She gotta lot of nerve for a woman who used to spank people for a livin'. She now gonna probably be busted for offing her own brother."

I took a small sip of my slushy concoction. It wasn't too horribly sweet. "So what happened, Wanda? Did Tony's guy get the laptop info? Did you get the laptop put back under her bed?"

"Yes and no." Wanda mumbled while slurping at her slushy.

"Yes and NO? You are kidding me? The laptop did not make it back under Mary Beth's bed? I cannot believe we are out here faking paperwork to keep a mob boss happy, so he doesn't report us for breaking and entering in what is now a murder and robbery crime scene. Now you tell me that Mr. Tony the mob boss did not return the laptop?"

"See, first I was gonna pass that laptop through the bedroom window, but that damn window would not open, it was sealed shut. So I took the laptop in the bathroom. I had to get in the tub, open that window and pass it outside to that Mick guy. I could hear you all going through the paperwork. That ten minutes seemed like ten hours in there. I was leaning out the window to see what was taking Mick so damn long, when I slipped and down I went in the tub. Once I got through that bitch's interrogation of my fall, I got back to the window. Mick was still out there trying to do his computer voodoo. I could tell the time was just about up. Mick said it was gonna take longer than he thought. Said he was gonna have to take the laptop. He said he and Tony would get it back under the bed and for us not to worry. Mick said they'd get it there by tomorrow morning. So when the police show up to look, it should be there."

This update called for a big swig of Polynesian slushy. And to think, I just wanted to list and sell a house. Now I was working with Wanda the black Nancy Drew of Clinton and hoping the local mob boss would return the laptop we helped him steal. All so I would not be reported for breaking and entering on a crime scene that turned into murder scene.

36

The next day around noon I got notification that the inspection contingency for the Tilberts' house was complete. The Sally Anne and Mary Beth needed to sign off on it, agreeing to repair a few minor items. I called Sally Anne and left her a voice mail updating her. An hour later, Sally Anne called me back.

"Hi Alex, that's good news about mother's house. Fixing those few items you mentioned, should not be an issue. I have to tell you, I have had a very unsettling day. Seems the police have now got a search warrant and are searching Mary Beth's car and apartment. She left me a voice mail and said they had taken her in for questioning and released her. I feel so conflicted. I had to let the police know that I had seen the laptop that looked like Tim's at her place. I really didn't have a choice. I had to speak my conscious, you know? I don't know if the police will tell her that I told them about the laptop or not. I hope not. Anyway, I don't think I can wrap my head around this if it turns out they think my little sister killed my brother. That is just too much to take in. I think I'll have you meet me at mother's to sign the inspection response form and we can then figure out how to meet up with Mary Beth and get her signature."

With this news update, I decided a long walk with Clyde was in order. Off we went, sniffing all the neighbors' street side garbage cans, following dead end squirrel trails, and eventually checking out the rotting piers and rusty railroad tracks down by the water.

After the walk, I met Tiffany and Bart and showed them two new listings. Neither of which were suitable. We were now in the official procrastination stage where nothing would be suitable and buyer compromise was not an option. I had my doubts if these two would move thorough this stage and end up purchasing. I was contemplating firing them as clients when my cell rang. It was Wanda. She was hungry and wanted to get out of the office. I told her she could tag along with me on my trip to the Tilberts estate. She agreed and said we could stop off at this chicken take-out place on the way. I picked up Wanda and we stopped off at the Spicy Chicken Take-Out, which is a small, greasy spoon store front located on the northern edge of downtown just before the hills leading up to the Bluffs.

"Make sure they put an extra tub of that hot spice in the bag Alex and here, we gonna need some more napkins," Wanda said pulling out half of the napkins in the metal dispenser. "Damn this chicken sure is good but honey you gotta plan for the clean up."

I always thought fried chicken was a bit dubious, but Wanda usually talked me into eating it every couple of months. The spices were very hot. I always wonder what they are covering up with hot spices. Was the meat old? Was it even chicken? The urban legends of fried rats still abound. I ate one fried breast piece and was trying to stop the fire in my mouth with a Coke and drive up to the Bluffs at the same time. Wanda meanwhile, had dug into the bag of chicken and was eating and slurping from her drink straw simultaneously. She looked at my empty hand and thrust a crispy drumstick in it, "Here," she mumbled through her stuffed mouth, "eat another one honey." I did so. Wanda finished her chicken and was throwing all the used napkins in the bag when I pulled into the Tilberts' drive. Sally Anne's mint green Volvo wagon was parked off to the side. Wanda dug deep in her huge fuchsia handbag and pulled out a bottle of hand sanitizer. "Wash your hands off with this. Looks like Sally Anne is already here, I don't see psycho bitch's car. You don't need to wait for me. I gotta take care of my make-up. I'll meet you inside." Wanda pulled out a large yellow make-up bag from her purse. "That greasy chicken does some serious damage to the face." She said while yanking my rear view mirror in her direction.

"Okay Wanda, just come around the side through the kitchen door." I replied.

Wanda's eyes bugged a bit, "Ohhh, I see it's still like that up here in the Bluffs, huh? Want me to put on an apron and bring along my cleaning bucket too?" I was stunned but then Wanda let out a loud chortle, "Go on Alex, get in there—I won't be too long. Sometimes you white folks is too easily scared, coming in with a cleaning bucket, damn I got you."

I walked down the moss covered stone pavers and went up to the back door that was open. Inside the kitchen the island lights were on, even though the sun was shining in brightly through the sun room windows. I called out hello but did not see Sally Anne. I stepped down the two steps into the open sun room, the two french doors were open. Down the brick stairs I spied Sally Anne sitting by the pool. She was in a one piece lavender bathing suit, her long hair piled up underneath a white swimming cap. She looked up and waved me down.

"Nice day for the pool. Have you been swimming laps?" I called out while taking the steps down to the pool terrace.

"Yes, I have gotten in a few laps. Do you swim Alex?"

"Not so much but I can dog paddle pretty well." I replied, while setting the file folder down on a glass table. "I have the inspection contingency form here for you to sign and we'll need to get Mary Beth's signature as well. Then we should be good to move on to closing. Good thing you are enjoying your mother's pool while you can. Looks like you are doing some gardening too. What are you planting in those beds?" The flower bed near the pool was a bit dug up and an old rusty shovel was stuck in the ground.

"Oh, I thought I would put in a few flowers. You know I want the new owners to feel welcome here." She walked over to the pool's edge, "Alex, could you come over here and take a look at this? It looks like some kind of crack in the pool. I sure hope the pool does not need repairing before we close." I walked over to where she was pointing and looked down. The water looked shiny and the aquamarine pool tiles all appeared fine to me. I was about to reply when I felt thump on my head and everything went black.

Next thing I knew, a large arm was around my neck and I was deep in the water. I could see the sun sparkles on the water's surface. Then I was half way up on the pool's edge, my hips and legs still submerged. Wanda was yelling, there was a commotion, sound and my vision seemed to swirl around. A soaking wet Wanda was peering down at me, asking if I could hear her. I kept coughing up water. The sun was really bright in my eyes, and the next thing I knew there was a paramedic next to me, asking me my name, how many fingers he was holding up. I could hear Wanda's loud voice and Sally Anne

224

murmuring in the background. The paramedic said they should take me in to the ER to make sure I didn't have a fracture. They were putting me on a gurney. I heard Sally Anne telling someone that I slipped and fell in the pool, "He must have hit his head when he fell in. I turned around just for a second and the next thing I knew he was sinking. Oh thank god this woman showed up! I just froze from the shock of it all. At least she knew what to do." Wanda touched my hand as they were lifting up the gurney and told me she would be at the ER, not to worry.

37

The ride to the ER was a blur and then there was a doctor shining lights in my eyes. They told me I had knocked the back of my head and had a concussion. They decided to keep me for observation. I had an enormous headache and things were a bit blurry. I was sitting up in bed in an open observation room. They did not want me to fall asleep so a TV was tuned into some game show. Various nurses would appear from time to time to make sure I was awake and check me for signs of who knows what. Wanda appeared, dried off but sans make-up and hair help. I don't think I have ever seen Wanda without make-up so this was a bit jarring. I wanted to ask where the real Wanda was. Behind her was Detective Davies. "I brought our detective friend. Doctor says you doing okay Alex. He says you hit your head on the pool when you fell in. But I know that was not no fall. That bitch hit the back of your head with the shovel. I saw her do it, plain as day. I was just coming out of the sun room doors when she whacked you. I swear I saw it plain as day. That Sally Anne was trying to off you Alex! I got Davies here with me, so he can get it all down and arrest the bitch."

Detective Davies looked a bit confined, "I hear you have a concussion Alex and the paramedics say you fell in a pool and hit your head. Is that correct?" I told him I was not sure what happened. I remember Sally Anne asking me to check the pool and the next thing I knew, I was coughing up water. "So you did not see Sally Anne Tilberts hit you with the shovel that Ms. Billings says she saw her hit you with?"

"No. But there was a shovel there. She said she was putting some flowers in for the new owners. Why would Sally Anne hit me with the shovel?"

"Why?!" Wanda exclaimed, "I tell you why. She is the one who is offing everyone. She wants you out of the way too."

"Ms. Billings that is pure speculation. I can take a report of what you saw but Mr. Campbell cannot back up your story. Also, why would Ms. Tilberts want to harm Mr. Campbell? As far as I can see, he is just her real estate agent. He has sold her mother's house and is close to closing the deal for her. What would make her have a problem with that?"

"Humpf. You may be cute but you ain't watched enough *Cagney and Lacey* or *Unsolved Mysteries*. Need to get yourself a prime cable package and take a lesson. I am telling you that woman tried to off Alex. I bet you she is also the one who offed her mama and brother. Seem to me like she wants the Mary Beth bitch to go to jail for it all. And what is up with all this Ms. Billings, Mr. Campbell crap? We all practically family now. You talkin' like someone stuck that nightstick up your butt again Davies."

Even with my splitting headache and blurry vision, I managed to get Wanda to chill. Detective Davies said he would not write up a report now, but I should contact him if I remembered anything else.

They finally released me from the hospital and Wanda took me home. She walked Clyde and I kept touching the ugly knot that had formed on the back of my head. I had some pills the doctor wanted me to take. They said it was now okay if I slept and slept I did. For the next twelve hours I was out. When I woke up the next day, Lexi was sitting in the living area fiddling with her sound scape recorder.

"Well howdy sunshine? Does it still hurt bad? Wanda told me what went on up there. Damn, if Wanda hadn't been there, you could be dead Alex. We've been talking and I too, think Sally Anne is psycho. How it all fits together I am a bit unsure. But I don't think Mary Beth is actually the bad guy. A bitch? Yes. A former dominatrix? Yes. But the killer of her mother and brother? I'm not so sure anymore."

Wanda barged through the front door with Clyde. "We had us a walk to end all walks. I'm telling you my precious here could walk us all into the ground and still go! I see you are up Alex, how's the head?"

"No real intense pain anymore and no blurry vision." I replied while pouring myself some orange juice. "Feels like I have been asleep for decades." I went and took a shower and put on some clean clothes. When I returned, Wanda and Lexi were talking about what else? The Tilberts. Clyde was moving back and forth between them, getting in all the pets and pats he could manage.

"I see the two Nancy Drews of Clinton are hard at work on the case. So what do we do now? We have nothing for the police to use except we suspect Sally Anne might be the violent one. Whatever happened with Tony and the laptop? I guess the police questioned Mary Beth and let her go?"

Lexi shrugged, "I haven't had any word with Tony and I guess if the laptop was not back at her house, there was no reason for the police to detain Mary Beth."

"Humpf," Wanda exhaled, "that is one fucked up family if you ask me. I think we should all take a ride up to see this Sally Anne fool and do us a stake out. That's what they always do on TV, so seems like that's what we should do."

No one had a better idea, so we all piled into Wanda's huge Towncar, Clyde included. Lexi had been to Sally Anne's house/studio for an arts function a few months ago, so she navigated. Sally Anne lives in a semi incorporated part of Clinton situated to the northeast of downtown. It is the Cumberland area. Named for the furniture company that at one point had its manufacturing plant in the hills and put the goods right on the railroad cars that passed through from downtown Clinton. Cumberland consists of single family, ranch style houses on half acre wooded lots. No sidewalks and lots of road side mail boxes. Cumberland is not a shabby area and has always been home to teachers and suburban weekend artistic types. Lexi's memory was spot on and soon we spied Sally Anne's mint green Volvo wagon and also Mary Beth's red Range Rover parked in a small gravel driveway. The house was a one story, sage green, ranch style house. Wanda pulled the car down the street and we parked in the grass next to the road.

"Looks like both sisters are there" Wanda said. "Wonder what that is all about? You don't think Mary Beth is in danger do you? We gotta go and listen in, see what's what. Will Clyde be okay in the car Alex?"

I had wondered about bringing Clyde but with Wanda there is no discussion. "Sure, I think he will be okay waiting for us, just leave the door windows down half way, maybe he'll take a nap since you all went on such a long walk."

We walked back to Sally Anne's house, down the short gravel drive, around the side, to the rear of the house. We had just perched beneath what appeared to be a family room window, when there was a loud smashing sound and the shrill of Mary Beth's voice, "You are the one who did all of this! I always knew you were nuts but this is beyond---just beyond! You are insane and I---,"

Sally Anne bellowed back in a very loud, commanding voice, which was startling due to her usual soft, whispery, monotone speech pattern, "YOU, Mary Beth are going to DO exactly what I tell you. Or YOU are NOT going to LIVE!" Then there were more loud smashing sounds and a long scream.

38

All three of us immediately stood up and Wanda said, "As much as I hate to say this, we gotta get in there and help save that Mary Beth bitch." Without another word, Wanda took off to the sliding glass, patio door. Lexi and I quickly followed. We could see Mary Beth crouching by the open kitchen's wooden chopping block. In the living room, Sally Anne was standing near the fireplace with an iron poker in her hand. She was using it to smash assorted pottery items while she advanced towards Mary Beth. Wanda was tugging on the sliding glass door, "This damn thing is locked." Lexi quickly pushed Wanda aside, dropped her enormous leather bag on the ground, reached in and pulled out a medium sized stone. Wanda and I did a simultaneous double take. Lexi looked up, "What it's a stone? Ask me later. Now step aside, while I get this glass door out of the way. Do either of you have your cell phones? We should call the police."

Lexi promptly took the stone and broke the glass out of the old sliding glass door. The sound of shattering glass caused Sally Anne to stop a few feet from the crouching Mary Beth. She looked back at us with the iron poker raised in the air, "Oh TERRIFIC, we have company. I see you are letting yourselves in. You need to leave! This is a family matter and you three are next if you don't get the fuck out of my house." Sally Anne's face was bright red. She turned and smashed the iron poker down on the wooden chopping block, knocking several glasses and a knife set to the sand colored tile floor. "YOU will NOT get in my way Mary Beth. You fucking, little, spoiled bitch. GET UP!

There is NO CHOICE now but to kill you too. You HAD to go and invite these assholes here. THEY are NOT going to help you, you stupid, stupid girl. Mother ALWAYS let you have your way but I NEVER did. Mommie's little favorite, Mary FUCKING Beth!" She then advanced on Mary Beth who was trying to escape by crawling away on the kitchen floor. The iron poker smashed into the glass fronted kitchen cabinets and debris flew everywhere. "Get UP Mary Beth, it's time to DIE!" With that she brought the iron poker down on Mary Beth's head.

Everything was a blur and the next few moments seemed to move in slow motion. A moment akin to that same eerie sensation when you know your car is about to hit something. Lexi heaved the stone at Sally Anne but it fell short. Sally Anne turned away from Mary Beth, who now had blood running down her face and appeared to be knocked out, maybe dead. "You FUCKING idiots! Why did you have to get involved in this family matter? Now you have made yourselves a part of this family matter and down you are going too." She ripped open a kitchen drawer and dropped the iron poker while pulling out what appeared to be a magnum forty-five.

She fired one off one shot, then another. "STUPID PEOPLE can't mind your own fucking business. Now line up there by the fireplace, MOVE IT!" She screamed while cocking the gun again and pointing it at us. We all three slowly moved as one unit over towards the brick fronted fireplace. "Drop that DAMN bag of yours LEXI!" On the floor it went. "Put that phone down" she said pointing the gun at Wanda and taking a step closer to us. Wanda dropped her opened cell phone to the floor. "Front and CENTER of the fireplace shitheads," she screamed while stepping in closer. We were now all three lined up in front of the fireplace and Sally Anne was standing directly in front of us about five feet away.

"Damn, stupid people you are. Couldn't just sell my fucking mother's house and collect your commission Alex. You are such an idiot! You almost caught me at mother's the day you came over to list her house. With the help of Mary Shithead's Xanax, mother was finally drugged asleep. You and the police are so damn naïve. I put sleeping mother in her laundry room. Then I successfully gassed her. I was about to put little Miss Perfect Daughter's dominatrix handcuffs on her when you arrived early Alex. Dumbasses, found the cuffs too late. The police were too dumb to figure out it was a homicide. And you, tramping through the house, calling out for mother! I had to rush out of there. You almost derailed my plan Alex, but you see I'm the smart Tilberts' child! I knew how to come back and make this work, pin things on this little bitch sister of mine. I tried to warn you. To keep you away Alex, but you would not take a hint. Even when I put glass in a dog bowl, you didn't get it. Then I threw a brick through your fucking living room window. I thought the fake mob-like warnings might convince you to shut up. But NOT Mr. Boy Scout, oh no! I had it ALL worked out but Mr. FUCKING real estate agent has to show up early and almost ruin my entire plan.

But you see I am the intelligent one! Mother and Father always thought I was the less smart, artsy one. Not, ME! I am the intelligent Tilberts' child! I still recovered despite your intrusion Alex and my plan is working! I knew all about little slut Mary Beth and her

233

dominatrix work. In fact, I am the one who let my imbecile, gambling, brother know all about her little kink. Hand fed all the information to Tim, almost had to give him an instruction book, the dumbass. With his gambling debts and mob problems, I knew he'd black mail her. Then I planted the idea in his simple head to blackmail Marc as well and really get things going. I thought for sure offing Tim would get our little Mary Beth sent away for murder. But once again, YOU IDIOTS had to interfere. I had it all set. They would think Mary Beth hit Tim over the head and murdered him. The tire iron was from her damn car for god's sake! I barely got Tim taken care of when you two FUCKS showed up unannounced. Once again, mister annoying fucking real estate agent intrudes! But thanks to my quick mind, I escaped and recovered. I planted Tim's laptop at Mary Beth's dump of an apartment. Then I let the police know his laptop was missing and that I'd seen it at Mary Beth's. I was hoping they'd be smart enough to look at his emails and figure out the whole black mailing scheme and thus Mary Beth's motive for offing him."

Sally Anne shifted, pointing the gun at each of us, "Stupid Lexi, getting you two all involved with the mob. Scrap metal, shit artist thinks she can WHEEL and DEAL! I know you all stole that laptop I planted at Mary Beth's. Thought you would trip me up, didn't you? Well you won THAT round. I was plenty pissed off when I found out the police did not find the laptop at Mary Beth's. The only answer would be you fucks were somehow involved. I almost got rid of you Alex at the pool. I was going to tie your drowning death to Mary Beth, but FAT fuck here had to mess that one up! So stupid, you really think

I would plant flowers by the pool? That shovel was to be your last memory, you idiot."

I was looking out of the corner of my eyes. Wanda and Lexi on one side and on the other side there was nothing within reach, just smashed pottery shards and broken lamps. Then, "HEY" and a loud pop rang out. To the right of my ear, it felt as if a small bird had swooped by. "HEY, ALEX, pay AT-TEN-SION shit head! I am TALKING to YOU!"

Wanda turned a bit towards me and whispered, "Did she hit you?" Before I could even try to respond, there was another pop and a loud, "DAMN my designer shoe!" from Wanda. Her right shoe, a magenta, long pointy toe stiletto, had a hole in the pointy end and the attached flower ornament was blown off. I then spied Clyde! He was standing just inside the smashed patio door. He looked over at me, Wanda, and Lexi and then up at Sally Anne.

In a split second, Clyde leaped up through the air. Right into Sally Anne's side he went, his fangs chomping down on her arm that was holding the gun. The forty-five flew out of her hand and fired off into the ceiling before it hit the floor. There was a huge commotion. Clyde took Sally Anne down and was biting and tugging at her arm. Wanda lunged and landed right on top of Sally Anne. "I'll show you what's fat! Bite her Clyde, get her good honey! I'm gonna show you that FAT is WHERE it's AT, you skinny, white, hippie, killer BITCH!" Wanda spread herself out on top of Sally Anne completely burying Sally Anne's body beneath her. Lexi and I ran over. I told Lexi to get Sally Anne's legs while I dashed over to check out Mary Beth. Just then, there was a police car siren, followed by another one, and squealing tires out front in the gravel drive. Next, there was a loud banging at the front door. A police officer appeared at the smashed out patio door and shouted, "Police, FREEZE!" His gun was drawn; Clyde looked up at him and froze. The front door let out a splintering wood sound and three more cops appeared with guns drawn.

39

Life the following couple of weeks was completely surreal. Sally Anne was promptly arrested on the scene. Wanda had dialed 9-1-1 on her cell phone when we entered the house. When she dropped it to the floor, it did not hang up. The dispatch operator was able to listen in, meanwhile the neighbors had called reporting gunshots and police were dispatched. The *Clinton Observer* and the local TV stations were all over the story. Clyde had his picture taken and an article appeared in the paper about how he stopped the killer. We also were interviewed on one of the local morning TV shows. I say "we" because naturally the anchors all wanted to talk to Clyde. To be fair, it really was Clyde's moment. He was the killer stopping dog of the day. He ate up every friggin' moment of it, coyly cocking his head to the side when the cameras moved in for a close up. I have since had a phone call from an animal talent agent in LA who says he has several pet companies who might have interest in hiring Clyde as their product endorser. Go figure, me the dog stage dad. Might as well put Clyde to work and let him pay the mortgage for a while. I never have quite figured out how Clyde managed to leap through the car's half way open window but there are some things I let Clyde have for his own.

Turns out Lexi's literal bag of tricks contained her annoying sound scape recorder. It recorded the entire final Sally Anne incident. Lexi is excited to incorporate this recording in her upcoming installation project, but it remains to be seen if the police or lawyers are going to allow it, at least not until Sally Anne is sentenced. The police were thrilled to have Sally Anne's confession live and on tape no less.

She however, is still pleading not guilty. Sally Anne suffered three fractured ribs, a broken arm, and bite lacerations from Clyde, not that she did not deserve it and worse. Fortunately, Mary Beth was not killed by the blow to her head. She suffered a pretty serious head injury and is still recuperating in the hospital but expected to make a full recovery.

Last Wanda and I heard, via Detective Davies, Sally Anne is going to go to trial with two counts of murder, one count of aggravated assault with intent to kill, four counts aggravated assault with a deadly weapon, and four counts of false imprisonment.

I pulled up to Salon Wanda. I was picking up Wanda and heading out to remove the key box from Mary Beth and Marc's house. The deal was set to close the next day. I told Share that I would make sure the key box was removed and everything was okay inside the house. Wanda was tagging along because she wanted to go to lunch at this new wine bar restaurant located down the street from the Beaumont's gates. Wanda was waiting on the Salon's porch when I pulled up. "Hey baby, how you doing? I swear to you, I'm gonna have a cat fight with that Miss Liz. You know she now is trying to do those Brazilian waxes in our Salon? Said it is all the rage on Oprah, so we should be doing them. I said, that there---,"

"Ahh, Wanda," I interrupted while pulling out onto the street. "What exactly is a Brazilian wax? Is that some kind of special organic wax from the jungles of Brazil?"

Wanda did a double take, "You seriously mean to tell me that you don't know what a Brazilian wax is? Oh lord, it's worse than ever!

Here, just take this car right on over to that monastery up on Desota Street. I'll sign you in." Unfortunately, Wanda explained to me in graphic detail what a Brazilian wax is. I, for once, am in complete agreement with Wanda. Oprah or not, Salon Wanda should not be doing Brazilian waxes.

I was still getting a "how could I be so clueless" lecture from Wanda when I finally rounded the curve on Turnkey Drive and pulled up to Mary Beth and Marc's house. There was Share's black SUV with her SOLD vanity plates, a generic white van, and a smaller, beat up, red, two-door, car parked in the drive. The front door was open and when we walked into the kitchen there was all sorts of photography equipment on the counters and orange extension cords leading out of the open french doors to the pool. A photographer had lights set up and an assistant holding up a silver deflector. There was Share, perched on a lounge chair at the edge of the pool looking up at the camera. One index finger's half inch red talon was touching the edge of her blood red lips. While her other hand, held her cell phone and she appeared to be mimicking answering the phone for the camera. I called out to Share, "What are you doing here Share? I told you I was stopping by today to remove the key box and check on things."

"Ooohhh, look its Alex and his crime busting mortgage side kick! What was your name again, Winnie? Let's stop shooting for a minute." Share stood up and handed the cell phone to the photographer's assistant. She was standing tall in her spiky, black, bitch boots, their pointy stubs sticking out beneath her black slacks. She wore a mostly unbuttoned, blood red, silk blouse; which prominently displayed her inflatable friends along with a chunky gold cross nestled in the valley. Share exclaimed in her coy, mocking tone, "I simply forgot you were coming all the way out here today to get the key box Alex. Guess when you are as successful and busy as I am, these trivial details just fade away. Gosh, I could have removed the key box myself and saved you and your *little* friend there the trouble. Anyway, I'm updating my publicity shots. We are through with the indoor snaps. I think we still have a few to take by the front door. You go ahead and take down the key box. I'll make sure the place is locked when we are done."

"Share, did Marc and Mary Beth give you permission to use their house for your publicity photos?"

"Oh, you! It doesn't matter. They won't know and even if they do find out, so what? They won't be living here anymore. I need to update my publicity shots. Since I am the premier agent in the Beaumont, and all the other nice neighborhoods in Clinton, I am sure no one will care. Speaking of publicity, you two sure had enough publicity with all of your goings-on. I just don't know if that's the kind of professional publicity I would personally want. But hey, to each his own, right? You know Alex, I am not so sure Winterfrost likes your public splash. It cheapens the corporate brand and hence premier agents such as myself suffer. Only you could end up with a Bluffs' listing that involved murders and family scandal. You really should take more time to be discerning with your clients, especially when the Winterfrost name is involved Alex. You should also think about this too Wendy. But I guess mortgage people-slash-hair dressers, don't really concern themselves much with cultivating the right professional image. A little bird told me Wendy, that you run an x-rated salon? They say you have pornographic statues and employ stylists who are of uncertain gender. Stylists who also perform at, shall we say, less than desirable bar venues in Clinton."

Wanda was off. She walked over to Share while saying out loud, "Anyone else smell that stench? I could swear there is some kind of dead fruit and flowers around here. It reminds me of the stench at the viewing room over at that skanky Stadler Funeral Parlor." Wanda walked right up to Share and sniffed loudly, "Damn, if stinky ain't right here! What, you step in something honey? 'Cause your odor be lasting for blocks, long after you roll through. Humph, look like you got something crawling there on your collar. Oh my lord, it's a big roach! It must be attracted by all that stinky flower smell."

Share tittered back a few steps on her stiletto heels and screamed, "Ohh, get it off me! I hate bugs! Get the roach off me!" She was swatting around her collar with her talons and shaking her head. Wanda took another step closer, "Oh, honey it's in your hair now. Oh my lord, it's big!" With that Share started swatting her hair and then, as if in slow motion, we watched as she took one step too many backwards and down into the pool Stinky went.

Much screaming, wet theatrics, and an abruptly cancelled photo shoot later, I successfully removed the key box and secured the house. As my car approached the gate to exit the Beaumont, Wanda calmly said with a big smile on her face, "And to think, there wasn't even a roach on old Stinky."

The following are the first two chapters of the next Alex Campbell Real Estate Mystery Novel <u>No Serenity</u>.

One

"You know your dog has absolutely wonderful hip subluxion. Sort of like my little Hadley over there. See him? The Pembroke Welsh Corgi, next to that substandard poodle-- the one Barbara Moxler owns that she claims is purebred but we do have our doubts! Hadley is from the dam Montsford and sire of Pembroke, straight from the Isle of Brit pedigree. You know the line that shows at Westminster every year? Anyway, what is your adorable dog's name and isn't he an Otterhound?"

Oh god, a stuffy Capitol Heights queen on the loose at the dog park. And this one is one of the roly-poly, velvet loafer wearing, over middle age, variety. Complete with pinky signet ring and a violet cashmere sweater tied oh-so-casually over his plump shoulders. Eeeww! I knew we should not have stopped by the Capitol Heights Dog Park.

"Ahh, yes my dog over there is named Clyde. He's actually not a pure---,"

"Yes, he is just too cute! I'm Percival Emerson, Percy to my friends. No, I am not related to *the* Emerson but on my mother's side I am a direct descendant of Woodrow Wilson. Ahh, I know a purebred when I see one and your Clyde is one! Is his pedigree from a show Otterhound pairing?"

CHARLES CHAPLIN

Is there anything more nauseating than a purebred, dog park, Nazi? "Well Percival, Clyde over there is a rare Scottish Lowland Terrier. Not to be confused with the common Scottish Terrier. You may not have heard of the breed, not too many have. It's all very in-house as we say. The breed is not often shown; we don't want just *anyone* getting a Lowland. Makes the breed so *common* when they become so well known, don't you think? I mean really, look what happened with the Bichon Frise, practically on cans of Alpo." I tried to get Clyde's attention, so we could hopefully beat a hasty retreat. Clyde is actually a pure bred mutt who happens to look a lot like Benji from the late 1970s movies. I made the whole Scottish Lowland Terrier breed up. I love to use it when I encounter the Percys of the dog world. And true to form, old Percy bit.

"Oh goodness, yes! You know, I am familiar with Scottish Lowland Terriers. I think my cousin may have had one years back. The whole dog world has become so common and commercialized. Why I can remember when hardly anyone knew what a Bichon was, much less could own one! Did you say your dog's name is Clyde? Now that *is* original. And stop this Percival bit, I told you I am Percy to my friends and I can just tell we are going to be great friends! Where did you say you lived in the Heights? It is simply amazing to me how Clinton has grown. I didn't grow up here. I'm originally from Marblehead, did the whole Exeter and Crimson routine, true blue, northeastern stock. And now all these years later, I've ended up here in Clinton. It's such a cozy place to live, don't you agree? I've got my

2

investments to keep me busy and I occasionally do an interior or two. Just the stereotypical homosexual bachelor I suppose. And you?"

Oh shit. The full tilt third degree from a pretentious aging queen on the make no less. Why me? Always, me.

"Ahh, I'm Alex Campbell. I don't live in the Heights. I just stopped by to let Clyde have a quick run. I'm a real estate agent and Clyde is along with me today while I preview houses. In fact, I've got to get Clyde back on the leash; we have got to get moving. Lots of houses we still need to see on our preview list."

"Ohh, so nice to meet you Alex. Here let me give you my card. You never know when one of your listings or clients is going to need some interior design help." Percy pushed his business card in my hand, his pinky ringed, meaty little paw lingering a bit too long in my palm. Gross.

"Ahh, thank you Percy. Yes, you never know when a decorator may come in handy."

"Interior designer. Decorator sounds like someone who puts icing on cakes or a simpleton mother-in-law who thinks buying silk flowers at the local crafts store for the living room is creative. And yours, Alex? Your card? I run across all kinds of people. I would like your contact information. I think we have so much in common and need to get together, don't you?"

Not in this lifetime or the next you snobby, fruit cake. "Well, ahh, sure here is my card Percy. But you know I have to be blunt with you. I'm bisexual and currently very celibate, so I really don't think there is chance of a connection if you know what I mean?"

Percy leered, "Ohhh, one that plays hard to get! Now I do like a challenge. And you are bi to boot! That *is* so trendy these days. Well, that gives me a fifty percent chance. Anyway, we will simply have to set up a play date for my Hadley and your Clyde."

A dog play date, my ass. I managed to catch Clyde's eye and gave him a significant look. Miracle of miracles, he actually dropped the stick that was in his mouth and walked right over to me. Never, has Clyde willingly come over to be put back on his leash. He must have picked up on my desperate psychic plea to help me flee from this snotty, would-be suitor.

"Ohhh, I can see you and smoochy-pooch are going to go bye-bye. Time for you and daddy to get back to work my new doggy friend?" Percy said while leaning his face down and cupping Clyde's shaggy muzzle in his fat hands. "Tell Uncle Percy bye-bye Clyde. We'll have to set up a date for you and Hadley to play, huh?" Clyde answered by giving Percy a nice sloppy lick; right up the center of his pudgy face, from the bottom of his fat chin to the top of his poorly dyed, receding hair line. Percy leapt back, gave a sputtered gasp, while vigorously wiping his face on his pink, overly starched, shirt sleeve. When he looked up and saw us staring at him, Percy regained his composure and pretended to not be bothered by dog slobber.

"Ohh, I see our little Clyde here is a kisser! Why you little devil you." I'm sure Percy was jones-ing to whip out the bottle of hand sanitizer which he no doubt had stashed in his monogrammed leather fanny pack. "Ha, dogs, they can be just, so loving. Anyhow, Alex you *do* give me a call and we will have to set up the play date. I know

4

Hadley would just adore it!" Yeah, sure. So far, Hadley had not given Clyde a second look. Currently his snout was busy scouring the bushes at the edge of the dog park.

"Yes, well nice to meet you Percy. You and Hadley enjoy the park." With that I snapped Clyde's leash on his collar and quickly took off for the street, where my old two-door, fading blue, Volvo was parked.

Clyde and I made a hasty retreat down the hill from Capitol Heights. It was true, I had been previewing a couple of houses. Now that the real estate market was slowing in Clinton, old habits such as previewing listings appeared to be making a comeback. I have been selling real estate in Clinton going on four years now and it is always something new. Talk about a sleaze filled industry. I sometimes feel as if I am the only agent who actually just tells it like it is and let the chips fall where they may. Maybe that is not the best way to handle things in terms of my bottom line, but quite frankly I don't have the energy or interest to constantly create and work on a good "sales" public persona. At least I am no longer known at my company, Winterfrost Real Estate, as "No-List Alex." My first listing turned into a family murder saga and the drama involved was not something I relished (see Volume One). Since then I have had more sedate listings.

I was done with previewing for the day but it sounded like the perfect white lie to get us away from the clutches of the pudgy queen on the make. I had Clyde safely belted in the passenger seat and he was sitting up very straight looking out as we wound our way through the mid-size city of Clinton. The sparkling water of Warner Sound glistened below, the summer heat making it sparkle even more. As we got into the aging downtown corridor, the water disappeared and assorted office towers, older white stone 1920s office buildings, rotting piers, and railroad tracks appeared. My neighborhood lies just south of downtown and is wedged in between a greenbelt. It is the old waterfront factory section and another set of railroad tracks boxes it in. Thus far, my hood has stayed off all gentrification radars. In fact, it does not even have an official name. It falls right between two city council districts, so it is almost officially no man's land. I like it that way. It keeps it undiscovered and hey, it was affordable when I purchased my small house a couple of years ago.

There are modest bungalows which were constructed for the factory workers in the early 1900s to1920s, Clinton's boom era. My 800 square foot bungalow sits on a dead end street and was built in 1919. When I purchased, it was essentially a tear down. I tried to keep as much of the "old world charm" (as we say in the real estate agent business) but there was not too much to salvage. If in fact, there had been much "charm" when it was constructed in 1919. I gutted most of it, made it into a two room house; open living room and kitchen and then there's the bedroom and a small bath. The entire back side of the house is now glass or rather two thirds of it is comprised of two glass and steel garage door panels. Then glass floor to ceiling windows with glass paned french doors in my bedroom. My lot backs right up to a greenbelt and has a large, ancient oak tree at the back of the lot. There is also a small stream that goes through the back yard.

I put Clyde in the back yard and he promptly took off to survey the grounds, make sure no squirrels had invaded his turf. I hit the switches and the two glass garage doors went up. I like fresh air and in the summer putting the two doors up usually keeps my house fairly cool. The water front is not too far from my lot, so I do get cool water breezes (even if my part of the waterfront is rotting, undesirable piers and abandoned factories). I was pouring kibble in Clyde's food dish when my cell phone began to ring. I didn't recognize the number, so I let it go to voice mail. I do not like a lot of the technological "advances" but screening calls is one feature I am all in favor of. If I do not recognize a number, I do not answer. If it is a sales call, they will move on and if it is someone (a potential client maybe?) I need to hear from, they will leave a message. I loathe sales people of all kinds, which is ironic considering the business I am in. But I do not see myself as a sales person. What kind of ego does someone have to have to think they can "sell" a client a house? I see my role as a guide, advocate, and organizer, someone who educates my clients about the home buying or selling process. I will give my honest opinion about a property and then let the client make up their own mind if they want to buy or sell. Maybe that's why I am not a millionaire agent? But my approach keeps my life simple and my clients seem to appreciate it. I was filling Clyde's water bowl when Wanda's voice rang out.

"Hey Alex! So where's my baby at? Here honey, take this bottle and bag of fruit and give me that kibble bowl. Oh, you got them windows up and I see my little furry baby is outside protecting his turf. Here baby, come on over here to mama and get some real loving!" Wanda took the stainless bowl of kibble and let herself out on the stone patio, cackling her loud, infectious laugh while Clyde took off like a bullet for her. Clyde came crashing onto the patio; up on two legs into Wanda's arms and they immediately began their usual tango dance greeting ritual. Somewhat sickening, in my humble opinion. I do not allow Clyde to jump up on people, but over the years with Wanda and Clyde I have given up.

Wanda Billings is a mortgage loan officer with Safety Mortgage and she also owns and manages Salon Wanda. It is a well known hair salon, she founded almost twenty years ago and worked in and ran on a daily basis until she realized her skills with money could be translated into the mortgage business. She began doing loans about eleven years ago. Unlike many mortgage people, Wanda is organized and has ethics. She has not done any of the slimy subprime loans and in fact, she's saved many a buyer/seller from the far too prevalent subprime and negative amortized lenders (predators) out there. Wanda is a real force and her clothes are on the wild side, especially for the staid, buttoned downed banking/loan world. Today's summer ensemble did not disappoint. Wanda wore bright orange slacks with a swirly magenta patterned, billowing top. Her hair piece was blond-ish today and piled fairly high on her head, pushed up with an orange headband that matched her slacks. Gold, chandelier earrings fell to her broad shoulders and she was hoofing around in a pair of aqua blue mule style shoes with little spiky heels. Something I have never been able to figure out is how she (or any woman or drag queen) can walk in such shoes much less wear them all day. The feminine mystique—boy would Betty Friedan not like that spin on things. Wanda is on the latter side of forty-five and she is single, enjoys having serial boyfriends, and proud to be a woman of size, as she refers to herself.

8

"Hey, quit dawdling in there Alex and get our slushies made. It's too hot not be having us a slushy. Get that bag of fruit into that blender I gave you. The rum is on the counter too, I was guessing that you might be low, so there's a fresh bottle, no need to skimp."

I promptly pulled out the stainless steel, god knows how expensive, blender Wanda gave me as a birthday present and proceeded to start dumping in ice and pieces of fruit. Wanda has a real fetish for slushy drinks. It's as if she is stuck in 1970s Pina Colada time warp. "Slushy drink" in Wanda's world, means lots of rum. I was just finishing the last phase of blending when Wanda completed her greeting dance with Clyde and walked back into the kitchen, tapping her magenta talons on the polished concrete counter top. "Ohh, look, you got a message on your phone." Wanda said while picking up my aging flip top cell phone. "Maybe someday you gonna get with it and get yourself an up-to-date phone, start texting? Oh, the lady is asking for your message code, what is it again, your birthday?" Before I could respond, "Yep, that'll do it. Oh, honey take down them big green glasses I gave you, we need us some serious slushy with this heat." Wanda said pointing to the glasses on my open kitchen shelves. I was pouring when Wanda began to relay the phone message, "Ohh, baby this is a man, say his name is Percy. Who the hell is Percy? What kind a name is—oh never mind. Oh, he say he loved meeting you and Clyde at the park today—does this mean you finally got yourself something going on Mr. Fudge Royal? Ohh, now he saying he has a friend who needs to sell her house! Oh Alex, this could be some serious dick and money for you."

I handed Wanda her glass, grabbed my cell phone and hit nine for save. "Boundaries, Wanda. We've spoken about you listening in on my messages. Aupt---," I said putting my hand out to stop her from speaking, "Let me finish. And I do not care for the Fudge Royal reference. As you know, I am a bisexual, not an ice cream flavor." Wanda muttered something about how any sex would do me wonders these days or some such sarcastic remark. "And, if you would let me finish Wanda, this Percy is nothing to be remotely excited about. He's a snotty, pudgy, over middle aged, screaming queen who has a yippy Corgi, a decorating business and naturally he lives in Capitol Heights. He accosted Clyde and me at the dog park today. It was all I could do to get us out of there without being molested. Why is it always the ones like Percy who are hot on my case? Don't answer that! Here, let's sit on the patio, I'll light the tiki torches and see if that will keep the mosquitoes away. You can rummage around in there and whip up some chips and salsa for us. I will now listen to my message, thank you very much. Aupt, now drink your slushy and be quiet."

Damn if the assertiveness and boundaries pop-shrink book I recently read, <u>Step On My *ick And I'll Slug You</u> wasn't working wonders with Wanda. I went out to the patio table, picked up my notebook and pen and proceeded to listen to Percy's message. Wanda looked at me bug eyed, then picked her drink up and dumped some corn chips in a bowl, all the while muttering not so quietly to herself. In fact, her mutters were quite similar to the growling grumbles Clyde is so fond of giving me when he is none too pleased with one of my human decisions.

Two

Percy's message indicated that his neighbor needed a real estate agent and wanted to sell her house. After a slushy, and much prodding from Wanda, I decided to return Percy's call. Despite all my derogatory comments to the contrary, she seemed to still think that Percy and I could become an item. Bottom line was, my bottom line needed more funds. So, I dialed up Percy. Half a ring later he picked up.

"Ohhh, Alex I just *knew* that was you calling back!" Gee, I guess the phone i.d. or the fact you left me a voice message thirty minutes ago have nothing to do with your psychic powers? "Ahhh, yes Percy. I am returning your call. It sounds as if one of your neighbors would like to list their house for sale?"

"Yes, the woman to my left wants to put her place on the market. She is divorced and she and boy-toy are ready to move on. Between you and me, it is just as well because I really do not think she is Capitol Heights people if you know what I mean? Now her ex, he is already missed. God that man's chest is just something else. Not that the boy-toy is any strain on the eyes. But you know, I find more mature men to be so much more exciting and developed. Don't you, Alex?"

Oh god! "Ahh, yeah, well Percy what is your neighbor's name and contact information? I will be happy to get in touch with her and see what I can do."

"My you are a sly little fox, aren't you Alex? I am not letting you off that easy! I insist we get together for a drink tonight and I can

11

fill you in on all the pertinent details and give you her information. So where shall we meet? We could just meet at my house. I do have a very well stocked bar, if you know what I mean?"

A fucking, innuendo queen as well, barf. "Look Percy, I've already had enough to drink with my friend Wanda here and really it's almost 8:00 p.m. and I have an early day tomorrow and…"

"You know Alex, I just won't take no for an answer. After all, I have a fifty percent chance with you, now don't I? Say, if you have already had drinks, why don't we get together and have a little nosh. You haven't eaten dinner yet, have you?"

"Ahh, no Wanda and I have not eaten dinner yet but Percy---," Wanda gave me a wide eyed look and snatched the phone out of my hand.

"Hey, this is Wanda Billings from Safety Mortgage, who am I talking with?" From there, Wanda took over. So much for the "Don't Step On My Dick" book. Sure enough, in no time, she and Percy were chatting away talking about food and where to meet. I did manage to call upon the powers of my pop-shrink book and I snatched the phone away from Wanda, her magenta talons scratching me in the process.

"Percy, no it's Alex. If we are all going to have dinner then I want us to meet at a place called Mama Honey's. Do you know where it is? No, it's a Cajun place downtown."

"Ohh, Alex. Cajun is a bit spicy, don't you think? I mean spicy is something else in the *boudoir* but at the table, I really prefer something a bit more sophisticated. And downtown? Really. I don't think downtown is very safe after work hours, now do you?"

"Well, you know Percy maybe dinner isn't such a good idea. If you want to give me your neighbor's information now, we could all meet up for coffee sometime." Unfortunately, Percy did not fall for my ploy and he took down the address of Mama Honey's and said he would be there in a half hour.

We closed up the ranch, put Clyde inside, and off to Mama Honey's we went. Wanda was still under the illusion that Percy was a good potential for me and she tried, unsuccessfully, to get me to change my clothes. As if dressing up for Mama Honey's is even in the cards.

Mama Honey's sits on the edge of downtown with the Highmont neighborhood above it. It is located in a 1920s yellow brick front, former hardware store building. It is always humid inside, due to the open kitchen that sits in the middle of the restaurant. Mama Honey is the owner and she is a woman somewhere in her sixties of Creole origin. She makes the best seafood jambalaya and coconut cream pie around. The place is very popular with the lunch time crowd and has scattered regulars for dinner. Mama was happy to see Wanda and me. "It's good to see da two of ya again, Miz Wanda and Mister Alex, my dears. Where be our Mister Clyde this fine evening, at home I am supposing? I'll make sure you be takin' him a bit of my gumbo wid ya. I gots da beers on da way and your jambalaya be a coming. Let me put you two over here by da big window, it's near da conditioner for the cool." The window was fogged up and tearing, due to the humidity. The air conditioning units in the window transoms were straining to keep things semi cool inside. We let Mama know Percy was coming and to bring him what we were having. I told Wanda that

13

I picked Mama Honey's because I thought the downtown location and the ethnic aspect would keep Percy from coming.

"Well, I guess that shows you about making judgments about folks now don't it Alex? You know you really should give people more of a chan---,"

With that Percy appeared at the door and Mama Honey led him over to our table. All the while, he was busy fanning the air with his fat little hands. He had changed into a large short sleeved tropical shirt, which all pot bellied men of a certain age seem to buy. It must be the generous cut of the fabric, because in my opinion it sure isn't the predictable kitschy fabric patterns and blah colors. Percy wore his mu-mu shirt un-tucked, over stone colored chinos, pressed as rigid as a board. His shirt sported a print of olive green palm fronds on a mustard yellow fabric. The shirt too was starched and pressed within an inch of its life.

"Oh mercy, it is just so humid in here! Alex you didn't say we would be having dinner at the bath house. Not that I am opposed to bath houses Alex, but really not for dinner. That's more for dessert, if you know what I mean? Oh and lordy, you must be Miss Wanda? Nice to meet you. I feel like we are already best friends! And you are so colorful, not that I mind black people mind you. I meant your clothing, such interesting color choices and patterns. I am Percival Emerson." He said holding his pudgy pinky ringed hand out limply for Wanda to, what kiss? Meanwhile his other pudgy paw was unlocking his leather monogrammed fanny pack, which he unceremoniously plopped down on the table. "Not to be confused with *the* Emerson

14

but my mother's side does descend directly from Woodrow Wilson. Oh my, I am so hot I can hardly breathe. Have that lady bring me a glass of ice and I'd love a voddy-tonny. Oh, you two are having beer? And in the bottle I see?"

"Mama's only serves four kinds of bottled beer and one red, one white house wine Percy." I said while smiling broadly at Wanda.

"How, quaint. Well, when in Rome I always say!" Percy unzipped his man purse (fanny pack) and pulled out a blue atomizer and proceeded to spritz himself with some strong sandalwood and lilac combination. He also extracted a pale blue, monogrammed, handkerchief and blotted his sweaty brow. "Whew, I just don't know how I am ever going to eat in such heat."

Wanda was now purposely avoiding making eye contact with me. "Well Percy, no one says we have to eat you know." I said. "Oh here is your beer and we always get the jambalaya so we took the liberty of ordering it for you as well. It's what Mama Honey's is known for. So tell me about your neighbor who wants to list her house." Damn if my assertiveness book wasn't helping out yet again. No more waiting around for the information I wanted, just outright ask for it!

"Ughh, jambalaya? Doesn't that have shell fish in it? You do know that shell fish can give you hepatitis don't you? I mean we must watch ourselves you know? Oh, I see the jambalaya is here, well..."

"When in Rome! Right Percy?" I replied.

"Ohh, you are a little devil aren't you, Alex?" Percy said while pulling out his bottle of hand sanitizer and wiping down his spoon with it. Then he rinsed the spoon off in his water glass and asked Mama

15

Honey for a fresh glass of water, another glass of ice, and a chilled glass for his beer.

Wanda cut in, "So Percy, Alex tells me you got a neighbor that is divorced and wants to sell her house up in Capitol Heights?"

"Why that's right Miss Wanda, I sure do. You may even have heard of her, she's a minor celebrity of sorts." Percy demurred, while wiping his thin lips with his napkin. "You know for Clinton, she really *is* a celebrity. She's done all the local station morning spots and she keeps saying her book is going to be published soon. Now there are some things I do question about her. Her taste in décor for one, but far be it for me to judge her success. I personally think it was her success that drove her golden pec'd husband away. But that's a whole other topic now isn't it? Oh! This jambalaya is certainly spicy. I don't know how you two can eat this so quickly. It is just burning my tongue right off."

Not as fast as I am going to burn it off if you don't cut to the chase and give me the pertinent details. "So Percy, who exactly is this minor celebrity neighbor and what are the details regarding her house?" I asked.

"My, Miss Wanda, he sure is an impatient little real estate agent, now isn't he? Although, I do suppose that impatience has its place, if you know what I mean? Well, I certainly don't want to keep you two in suspense for too long. My neighbor just so happens to be the one and only Serenity! I mean can you imagine that? Living right next door to me and little Hadley? Now as I said, she sure is up and coming but the décor of that house is just simply atrocious! I tried in vain, to help her out. You know Adele Cory who owned the house before her, oh she had a front hall and living room to die for. It was yummy rose tones and chintz for miles! Anyway, as I mentioned, Serenity is divorced and she and her workout "business partner" and note my wink-wink here folks, well they are on a tear to move on to life in the big city and big time celebrity. I do hope the new owners will let me get my hands on that interior. I mean Adele would just turn over in her grave, god rest her soul, if she saw how awful her house looks now. And that dog of Serenity's is just a nuisance plain and simple. You know Adele had those adorable Pekinese? Anyhow, Serenity has the most annoying Weimaraner you have ever met. That poor dog is named Kali! Can you imagine naming your poor child or dog after some heathen god? Really! Oh, I am just going on now, aren't I?" He said while simultaneously chortling and emptying his beer glass; which he promptly held up to catch Mama Honey's eye. "Just put a drop of booze in me and off I go! So I saw Serenity after we met at the dog park this afternoon Alex and I told her I had the perfect real estate agent for her. I said I would have you give her jingle if that was okay with her. She agreed, naturally. You know most celebrities are just plain insecure underneath it all. And when you live next door to someone as well established as I am, oh I am sure she appreciates all the help I provide. We'll just leave it at that."

"Well alright then Percy." Wanda interjected. "Sounds like you da man of Cap. Heights. Got it all going on with them celebrity peeps, now don'tcha? Now I know our completely out of touch with anything Hollywood, Alex, has no idea who this Serenity is. So why don't you just fill him in, give him the real 4-1-1 on this woman."

17

Wanda took a pull on her beer bottle and quickly glanced at me. I for one was a bit perturbed, because I could tell Wanda had no clue who this Serenity was either.

"Ohh, well we all can't keep up with our *Clinton Entertainment Tonight* now can we Wanda? Serenity is only *the* number one Lifestyle Diet and Wellness Coach. Voted number one in Clinton just last month in fact. Can you beat that? I mean just because she can't figure out her house décor does not mean she is not one hot and awesome lady. She has even got me considering some of her custom protein shake diet plans. That is what Serenity specializes in; her protein meal plans. They are her own proprietary blend, powder shakes. She and that boyfriend, Javier, are just the toast of Clinton with them. You know he is the head workout coach at TOTAL. She owns that place, started it with her ex's money several years ago and she ended up with it in the settlement I suppose. You know Serenity is so much more than just a diet coach. She sees the complete picture. She offers complete wellness coaching. In fact, I think she might have even pioneered that concept. With her it is all about the total quality of life, not just a diet. And don't even say the "d" word around her unless you want a lecture! She doesn't believe in diets, just total wellness. As I said, I am thinking about signing on as one of her clients. Not that I have an issue with my weight. I just think Serenity can take me to the next level."

Oh god. What level would that be, the seventh circle of fire in purgatory Percy? I tried to look sincerely interested and said, "Ahh, yes. Serenity is a coach and her boyfriend, Javier, is a personal trainer.

I can see the connection they have. So her ex husband, what did he do and is he out of the picture now? Do you have any clue when she wants to sell and where she intends to go?"

"See there Miss Wanda, our little Johnny-on-the-spot real estate agent is asking all the right questions to get his listing! Her ex does some kind of foreign investment/consultant work. Clearly, he made quite a sum. It's just too bad they never had the sense to invest it in that house's interior. Now that may just be your listing's stumbling block Alex, that interior! Well you'll see when she shows you the house. Anyhow, her ex has been out of that house for at least the last nine months. I have not seen him in a while, not that I would mind as I may have mentioned that man is not hard on the eyes. Of course, replacement boy-toy is no strain on the eyes either. Oh dear lord, you should just see that Javier in his spandex work out shorts. He just puts online porn to shame! You know if you sign up for Serenity's total program, it includes one-on-one training with Javier. I for one, am seriously considering it. I mean if you have to be tortured at some dirty gym, might as well be some hunk like her Javier to torture you. But now mind you, I am still not too sure weight is one of my top issues. What do you think?"

What do I think? Yes you are at least sixty pounds overweight. "Ahh, well you know Percy I am not a good one to judge with health and weight issues. You'd best leave that to people like Serenity and her trainer. So any idea, when she wants to sell and where she intends to go?"

"Ohh, and a diplomat to boot! Why I am sure those diplomatic skills help out enormously in your real estate game." Percy replied while swabbing at his forehead again with his monogrammed handkerchief. "Well it is not public knowledge, so you did not hear this from me because I am not one to gossip. Serenity and Javier are planning to open a big franchise, once Serenity rolls out her protein drink nationally and her total wellness book/dvd and PR blitz. I believe they are planning to head to LA and in fact I know she's been there twice scoping things out. She told me she has an agent there who is doing some product endorsement leg work for her. I know for a fact, she wants to be out of Clinton soon. I am sure she would prefer that house be sold before she leaves. That is one of my hesitations with signing on to her lifestyle diet and wellness coach program. I mean, I want to have Javier personally helping me with those weight machines. If they relocate, I don't know how she'd find as hunky a replacement to run the gym part of things here. Oh well, we will just have to see how things all play out now won't we?"

With that said, Percy proceeded to eat two slices of Mama Honey's coconut cream pie and dinner slowly wrapped up. When the bill arrived, Percy pulled a pocket sized leather notebook out of his man purse. He scribbled a phone number down, ripping off the little sheet as he stood up, "Alex, this is Serenity's personal cell number. This is not to be given out or shared mind you. It is her personal line, not the public number. I told her you would be giving her a jingle this evening or tomorrow morning. Now, I'd love to stay and chat some more with you two, but I do have to run. I can't keep Hadley alone at home too long you know! It was divine meeting you Miss Wanda. And Alex, I expect to see you very soon, putting your sign in the neighbor's yard no less. Next time, we'll dine at a place I suggest. We won't have to suffer from such humidity while eating! Tootles, to you both, my new best friends!"

Wanda was quietly chuckling to herself as Percy bustled out the entry door. He paused briefly at the entrance to give his forehead one more quick swab with his hanky. "Well looks like you got yourself a good listing lead Alex. Now that dinner wasn't too bad, was it baby? Maybe he's not your next Romeo but he's a start, ain't he?"

I glared at Wanda and picked up the bill. "Ohh, yes Wanda. He's quite the start. Gosh, I *am* aiming high aren't I? And look, Mr. Everything there just left YOU and me with the bill for his little *nosh*!

About the Author

Charles Chaplin (no relation) lives on planet earth (for now) and works in residential real estate (for better or worse).

To receive an e-mail notification when the next Alex Campbell Real Estate Mystery Novel, is available for purchase, please e-mail charles@lifeinseattle.com and write "notify me" in the subject header.

Friend Alex at:

Facebook.com/acrealestatemystery